PRAISE FOR THE NOVELS OF

MAYA BANKS

"Definitely a recommended read . . . filled with friendship, passion and, most of all, a love that grows beyond just being friends."

—*Fallen Angel Reviews*

"Grabbed me from page one and refused to let go until I read the last word . . . When a book still affects me hours after reading it, I can't help but joyfully recommend it!"   —*JoyfullyReviewed.com*

"I guarantee I will reread this book many times over and will derive as much pleasure as I did in the first reading each and every subsequent time."   —*Novelspot*

"A compelling look at love between friends."   —*Romance Junkies*

"An excellent read that I simply did not put down . . . a fantastic adventure . . . covers all the emotional range." —*The Road to Romance*

sweet surrender

MAYA BANKS

BERKLEY BOOKS, NEW YORK

THE BERKLEY PUBLISHING GROUP
Published by the Penguin Group
Penguin Group (USA) Inc.
375 Hudson Street, New York, New York 10014, USA
Penguin Group (Canada), 90 Eglinton Avenue East, Suite 700, Toronto, Ontario M4P 2Y3, Canada
(a division of Pearson Penguin Canada Inc.) • Penguin Books Ltd, 80 Strand, London WC2R 0RL,
England • Penguin Ireland, 25 St Stephen's Green, Dublin 2, Ireland (a division of Penguin
Books Ltd) • Penguin Group (Australia), 707 Collins Street, Melbourne, Victoria 3008, Australia
(a division of Pearson Australia Group Pty Ltd) • Penguin Books India Pvt Ltd, 11 Community
Centre, Panchsheel Park, New Delhi–110 017, India • Penguin Group (NZ), 67 Apollo Drive,
Rosedale, Auckland 0632, New Zealand (a division of Pearson New Zealand Ltd) • Penguin Books,
Rosebank Office Park, 181 Jan Smuts Avenue, Parktown North 2193, South Africa • Penguin China,
B7 Jaiming Center, 27 East Third Ring Road North, Chaoyang District, Beijing 100020, China

Penguin Books Ltd., Registered Offices: 80 Strand, London WC2R 0RL, England

This book is an original publication of The Berkley Publishing Group.

This is a work of fiction. Names, characters, places, and incidents either are the product of the author's
imagination or are used fictitiously, and any resemblance to actual persons, living or dead, business
establishments, events, or locales is entirely coincidental. The publisher does not have any control over
and does not assume any responsibility for author or third-party websites or their content.

PUBLISHING HISTORY
Heat trade paperback edition / March 2008
Berkley trade paperback edition / January 2013

Berkley trade paperback ISBN: 978-0-425-26695-3

The Library of Congress has catalogued the Heat trade paperback edition of this book as follows:

Banks, Maya.
Sweet surrender / Maya Banks.—1st ed.
p.   cm.
ISBN 978-0-425-21943-0
I. Title
PS3602.A643S84   2008
813'.6—dc22
2007046898

PRINTED IN THE UNITED STATES OF AMERICA

10   9   8   7   6   5

Andrew, Jacob and Sarah Beth, you're the best helpers anyone could ever ask for.

Loo-gey, you're still the best.

Melissa and Jennifer, as always, your feedback is invaluable.

Natalie, my go-to gal, I heart you.

And Amy, my partner in whine, where would I be without you?

sweet surrender

CHAPTER 1

"*I* don't want you to go back on the job yet."

Grayson Montgomery plunked his coffee cup back on the worn diner table and stared at Mick Winslow in confusion.

"What the fuck are you talking about, Mick?"

The older man shoved a tired hand over his face, a face that was now deeply grooved with wrinkles and fatigue. He'd called Gray earlier in the morning and asked him to meet him here for coffee. Gray was due for his physical and psych evaluation in a half hour. The last obstacle in his return to work as a Dallas cop.

He'd been plagued with doubts. What sane person wouldn't be? He hadn't been completely sure he could return to a job when Alex, his partner, wouldn't. Ever. But, of course, he'd go back. Alex's killer had to be caught. Justice had to be done. All that was standing in his way was a doctor's okay on his physical condition and a shrink's assessment on the state of his noggin. He could easily bullshit his way through that one.

"You don't think I can hack it anymore?" Gray asked when Mick still didn't respond.

"That's not what I'm saying."

"Then what the hell *are* you saying?"

Mick focused grief-stained eyes on Gray. He seemed so worn down now. Not at all like the big, barrel-chested man with a booming voice and personality to match.

"Hear me out. I have a favor to ask. Son."

Gray flinched, not because Mick called him son, but because Mick's real son was gone. Lost to them both.

"I want your help bringing Alex's killer to justice."

Gray should have seen this coming. Mick was beyond frustrated at the lack of progress in Alex's murder case. Understandably so. It mirrored Gray's own burning sense of injustice. Which was why he was so eager to get back on the job. So he could find Alex's killer and make the bastard pay.

"But you don't want me back on the force."

"They dropped the ball on this investigation," Mick said harshly. "You know it, and I know it. They're all standing around with their thumbs up their asses while my boy's killer is running free. They don't even have a suspect. Alex was a good cop. Damn good cop. He didn't deserve to go down like that."

Gray's eyes narrowed at the slight. It wasn't directed personally, but still, it raised his hackles to have Mick question the departments' handling of the case. Nothing he'd seen had led him to believe anyone was taking Alex's death lightly.

"Why don't you want me to go back?" Gray prompted, trying to push Mick back to the point. He didn't want to dwell on Alex. Not now. Not when it had taken him this long to be able to think about his partner without feeling like someone torched his insides.

A waitress walked over with a coffeepot and started to refill their cups. Mick waved her away with an irritated gesture. She quickly retreated, eyebrows raised at the dark scowl on Mick's face.

"I've been doing some investigating on my own."

Gray frowned. Was this why Mick looked like death warmed over? Had he been devoting every hour of the day, forgoing sleep, in a desperate attempt to bring a killer in?

"You're retired, Mick. Leave the police work to us."

Hurt filled Mick's eyes. "I'm going to forget you said that, son."

Gray shook his head. "What have you found?"

"I think I have a solid lead on who may have killed Alex. He was at least at the scene that night, so if he didn't do it, he damn sure knows who did. But my gut is telling me he's the bastard who shot Alex in the back."

Gray's stomach churned, and all the coffee he'd consumed burned like acid. Images of Alex, facedown, like a piece of discarded trash, blood pooling on the ground.

"If you have evidence, why haven't you gone to Billings, and why are you here asking me not to go back to the job?"

"Because Billings is an obnoxious prick who has his head so far up his ass he can smell last week's dinner," Mick growled. "I went to him when I uncovered information on the guy who was there. Samuels. Eric Samuels."

"You know his name?" Gray broke in.

Mick held up his hand. "Let me finish. I know a lot more than the asshole's name."

Gray nodded and tried to relax in his seat. He glanced at his watch. He was going to be late.

"I went to Billings. Told him everything I knew. He blew me off. Told me I was a washed-up has-been who needed to leave the police work to the professionals. Told me when he needed my help, he'd damn well ask for it. It's going around the department that Alex was at fault in the shooting."

"What? What the fuck?"

"I've been hearing rumors, Gray. Seems that the prevailing belief is that Alex acted without cause, and that his death was an unfortunate consequence of his actions. The words 'blatant disregard of duty' were thrown around more than one conversation."

Gray stared at Mick in disbelief. "You can't be serious. I was there. I gave my report."

"You'd say anything to cover for your partner."

Gray curled his lip in a snarl.

Mick held up his hand. "That's what they'll say. Not me."

Gray leaned back, taking deep breaths to calm the rage boiling inside him. He took a long, hard look at Mick. Was he jacking with him? Trying to get him pissed off enough that he'd agree to whatever Mick wanted? He'd never known Mick to be anything but straight up, but losing a son had a way of bending one's conscience.

Mick propped his elbows on the table and leaned across, staring intently into Gray's eyes. "You go to your evaluation, son. You talk to Billings. If you think I'm full of shit after you've been back at headquarters for a few hours, then by all means, you go back to the job and forget we ever had this conversation. But if you find out I'm right, you give me a call this afternoon. I'll come over, and we can talk about how we're going to nail the son of a bitch who killed my son. Your partner. Your brother."

Mick slid out of the booth and threw a few wadded-up bills on the table before stalking toward the exit.

It had been hard to calmly request a leave of absence when what he wanted to do was put his fist through the wall. Gray had considered tanking the psych evaluation, but that shit went on his personnel record forever, and he didn't want that to follow him for the next twenty years.

He stood in the living room of his apartment, pacing, too agitated to sit down and wait for Mick to arrive. The old man hadn't sounded the least bit surprised when Gray had called him. Didn't even ask what the word around headquarters was.

But then he knew. He'd told Gray, but Gray hadn't believed him. Gray had gone back fully intending to ignore Mick's request. No matter what, Gray wanted to be here where he could help with the investigation, not on some wild-goose chase. But Billings had drawn a hard line in the sand. Gray wasn't allowed anywhere near the investigation. Too close and all that bullshit. Like he needed a bunch of psychobabble when his partner's killer was on the loose. When he'd point-blank asked about the rumors floating around about Alex being at fault, Billings had flatly denied it, saying the investigation was ongoing and that the department would do everything in its power to bring the murderer to justice. Gray had also asked about Samuels and his possible connection to the murder, but Billings had refused to comment.

He'd left the office frustrated, only to be met with many sympathetic stares from fellow cops. Many murmured their opinion that no way had Alex done anything wrong. But the fact that they had to say it pissed Gray off to no end. There should be no question. It had raised questions in his mind about the direction the investigation was going.

Mick walked in the door, not bothering to knock. Gray met his gaze and found raw determination simmering there.

"So now you know," Mick said quietly. "Are you going to help me?"

"I arranged for a six-month leave," Gray said shortly. "Now tell me everything you've found out so we can nail this bastard."

Mick walked over to the couch and sank down on the cushion. He eyed Gray purposefully. "I need you to go to Houston."

"What's in Houston?"

"Faith Malone."

Gray folded his arms over his chest. "What does she have to do with Eric Samuels?"

"Maybe nothing. But she's the only lead I've got right now."

"So what about her? Who is she?"

Mick scratched at the back of his neck then shifted his head. "Eric Samuels hooked up with her mother right about the time of the shooting. They both disappeared just a few days after Alex got shot. No one's seen them. I had her investigated. Pretty much a loser like Samuels. Goes through jobs like candy and has a history of drug abuse.

"Her daughter works for William Malone, the man who adopted her. He owns Malone and Sons Security. Top-notch firm. Colors outside the lines. You'd like him."

Gray waited impatiently for Mick to get to the point. It didn't much matter if he'd like Malone or not. All that mattered was whether or not his daughter could lead them to Alex's killer.

"Apparently Faith took care of the mother for most of her life until a few years ago when the mom OD'd, and Malone stepped in and took Faith back to Houston. Since then, Mom has sporadically called the daughter up, mostly wanting money from what I've gathered.

"Last time she called her was a year ago. Now, my thought is, if the mom is in the habit of calling up the daughter when she needs money, she might very well start calling her again now that Samuels has entered the picture. Samuels is desperate. He needs money now that he's on the move. Money that the mother doesn't have.

"If you get close to the daughter, do some snooping, she might very well lead us to Samuels through the mother."

Gray nodded. So far it made sense. Mom and boyfriend were on the run. Probably low on cash. She might very well contact Faith and ask for help. For all he knew, the girl might know exactly where her mother was.

"My buddy Griffin is friends with Malone, and Malone owes him a favor," Mick continued. "I've arranged for you to have a job with his security company. He knows who you are, that you're a cop and that your partner was killed."

"But nothing else, right?"

Mick shook his head. "What he knows is that you're on leave while you deal with the death of your partner and make the decision about whether or not you want to return to the job."

Gray looked sharply at Mick.

Mick shrugged. "It seemed a plausible enough explanation."

Whatever. He didn't give a damn what Malone thought his reasons for taking a leave of absence were.

"Does Malone figure into this in anyway? Does he have anything to do with Faith's mother?"

Mick shook his head. "Griffin filled me in on this much. They were briefly married ten years or so ago. Hasn't had anything to do with her since. He's a good man. His son is ex-military. He has two other guys working for him. One was in Special Forces, and the other was a cop before an injury took him out of the line of duty. They do good work."

"So it's only his daughter I need to be concerned about then." Mick nodded. "Exactly."

It sounded simple enough. Go in, get the information and get out. Hand it over to the department on a silver platter. Sounded like a cakewalk after some of the cases he'd been handed over the years. And yeah, he could use the break. Then he wouldn't have to think so much about returning to a job without his partner.

Mick stared at him for a long moment before he seemed to crumple right in front of Gray. "Thanks, son. I knew I could count on you."

"You don't have to thank me," Gray said shortly. "Alex would have done the same for me in a heartbeat."

He walked over and sat down by Mick. Neither spoke for a long moment, and then Gray reached out and put his hand on Mick's shoulder. "Alex will get the justice he deserves, Mick. I swear it."

CHAPTER 2

HOUSTON, TEXAS

Faith Malone curled into John's limp arm and tried, tried really hard not to allow the slow roll of disappointment to wash over her.

Her lover's soft, even breathing filled the room even as he gathered her closer to his chest. His hand curled into her hair, stroking the back of her neck.

She pressed her cheek further against him and tried to relax. Tried to find some measure of contentment in the aftermath of their lovemaking.

"Was that good for you?" he whispered.

"Yes," she lied. Well, it wasn't really a lie. She'd certainly had worse, and John was a considerate lover. But he was extremely passive.

She sighed and rolled over on her back and stared up at the ceiling. What was wrong with her? Why couldn't she find satisfaction? Why was she so afraid to push for more?

"Faith, I've been thinking."

She turned her head back to John. Panic hit her square in the chest. Surely nothing good ever came of a man saying he'd been thinking. Men just didn't think, and they certainly weren't prone to expressing those thoughts over pillow talk.

He shifted until he lay on his side facing her.

"I've been thinking too, John," she blurted.

He raised his eyebrow. "You first."

She rose up on her elbow and stared nervously down at him. Her mind raced to come up with a coherent way to put what she wanted to say.

"Why don't you plan our date tomorrow night? You decide what we'll do, where to eat. And maybe afterwards we could come back here, and you could . . . I don't know, tie me up, or do something kinky. Basically whatever you want to do. Your choice."

What a disaster. Could she have stated it any more awkwardly? She bit her lip as she waited for his response.

His eyes widened. Was that surprise or was it excitement?

"Uhm, I'm not sure I follow," he said uneasily.

Definitely not excitement.

"I want you to take charge," she said softly.

He sat up in bed and rubbed his head. "Faith, where on earth did this come from?"

Her cheeks burned, and she swallowed. God, she felt stupid. Nothing like sending a man running in the opposite direction.

"Are you unhappy with the way things are? Is that what you're trying to say?" he asked.

She thought about lying and backtracking. It's what she'd done in the last relationship. And the one before that. But that wasn't getting her anywhere.

"I wouldn't say unhappy. Exactly."

"Then what would you say?" he prompted.

"I'm not satisfied," she said quietly.

"You mean sexually?"

She looked up to see him staring intently at her, irritation lighting his eyes.

"No. It's not just about the sex, John. If it was, maybe I could deal with it. It's more than that. I want . . . I want a man who can take charge. Make decisions. Be . . . in control. And not just in the bedroom."

"And I'm not that man."

She twisted her fingers together, bending and squeezing. "You haven't been."

He cursed softly under his breath. "You want me to change?"

She gazed sadly at him. "No. That's not fair. To you or me. I guess . . . I guess I just hoped maybe you could be that man."

"Damn it, Faith, you make it sound like it's over between us. What is this? Some fantasy you want me to act out? I can do that. I mean if you mean role playing, but it doesn't sound like you want a temporary situation."

She shook her head. "No, I don't. I want—no, I need this. And that's the thing. There have been men who would be more than willing to spend a night playing the dominant male, but it ends there. I don't want it to end." She leaned forward, willing him to understand. "Does that make sense?"

He scrubbed a hand over his face and rubbed his eyes tiredly. "Yeah, it makes sense."

She reached out to touch him, and he flinched away from her. "I don't know what to say. Are you angry?"

A harsh sound escaped his lips as he blew his breath out in a rush. "No. Yes. Hell, I don't know. I feel like you dropped a damn anvil on my head."

He reached out and cupped her chin in his hand. He stroked his thumb over her cheek as he stared into her eyes. "I knew . . . I knew something wasn't right between us. I didn't expect this, but I knew you weren't as happy as you could be. Or should be. I want you to be happy, Faith. Hell, I want me to be happy. And I guess we just don't do it for each other."

He quirked one corner of his mouth up in a semblance of a grin, and she relaxed.

"You weren't satisfied either," she accused.

His smile turned into a rueful grin. "I guess I won't get into trouble for saying no then."

She flopped back onto the bed and let out a giggle. "Don't we make a good pair. Lying here naked after sex, breaking up."

He leaned over her, his expression serious. "You're a terrific woman, Faith. I'd hoped for more between us, and I admire the guts it took for you to tell me what you wanted."

"So you don't think I'm a perverted sicko?"

"No, but I want you to promise me you'll be careful. A lot of men out there would take advantage of the type of situation you want. They wouldn't have your pleasure or best interests at heart."

"Thanks, John," she said softly as she reached up to touch his face.

He bent and kissed her cheek before sliding out of bed to get dressed.

Faith sat behind her desk at Malone and Sons Security and nibbled absently at her pencil. The office was quiet today. Pop and the others were out on a job bid with the new guy, and she was left to ponder alone. Never a good thing.

John had left the night before instead of staying over as he usually would. But then breaking up had a way of pushing a man out of bed. She could console herself with the fact that apparently, he'd been as unsatisfied with her as she had with him, so she doubted he was suffering a broken heart.

She, on the other hand, was well on her way to major funkdom. Maybe she had been too subtle. Too afraid. Too ashamed of her needs and desires. It certainly wasn't something she'd ever discuss with her girlfriends, not that she had many. They'd probably vote to kick her out of the league of women upon hearing just what it was Faith wanted in a man.

Last night had been the first time she'd actually voiced the dark desires floating around in her head. Not that she'd gone into any great detail. Just the brief mention had made her cheeks burn with embarrassment.

But that had to end. Now.

Subtlety was not her friend. It wasn't getting her anywhere with the men she'd been involved with. Hinting and hoping wasn't the way. No, she had to be more proactive. More forceful. If she didn't make it clear what she wanted, then how could she ever expect to get it?

The ringing phone interrupted her melancholy train of thought, and she reached gratefully for it.

"Malone and Sons," she greeted.

"Hi sweetie, it's Mom."

Faith's heart plummeted. A sick curl began swelling in her stomach, and she had to physically restrain the urge to hang the phone back up. God, it had been a year since she'd heard from her mother. A year of no hysterics, no martyr acts, no lame excuses.

"Mom," she said faintly. "How are you?" Stupid question. Her mother was never all right. Always some crisis.

"I'm in trouble, Faith. I need your help."

Faith closed her eyes and bit down on her lip. Through the receiver, she heard a sound like cars passing on a highway. Was her mother at a pay phone? It wasn't likely Celia could afford a cell phone.

Don't ask, Faith. No questions. You don't want to know anyway.

"Faith, are you there?"

"I'm here," Faith whispered. If only she hadn't answered the phone.

"I need to borrow some money, baby. Just a little to tide me over until I get another job and a place to live."

Faith swallowed back the stark disappointment and closed her eyes to call back the sting of tears. As dumb as it was to hope that one day Celia Martin would get her act together, Faith clung to it nonetheless.

Why couldn't she have a mother? A real mother. Someone not so bent on screwing up everything in her path who could have a real relationship with her daughter.

"Faith, I really need it this time, honey. I'll pay you back, of course."

Of course. What a laugh. Faith's hand squeezed the receiver of the phone until a sharp pain snaked up her arm.

"Not this time, Mom," Faith said, surprising herself with her refusal.

The long, silent pause that settled over the line told Faith that her mother was just as surprised.

"But honey, I need the money to get by." Desperation edged Celia's voice. She became more forceful. "I told you I'd pay you back. I have to find a place to live, buy gas and food. As soon as I get settled and find another job, I'll be okay."

"That's what you say every time," Faith said quietly. "Only it never ends. I can't continue to bail you out. It's time you took some responsibility for yourself."

Before Celia could respond, Faith gently replaced the phone on the receiver. Her hands shook as she pushed away from the desk.

"Is everything okay?"

She jerked her head up as she heard the strange voice. Leaning on the doorframe of her office door was a man. And not just any man. He took up the entire doorway.

"C-can I help you?"

He stood upright and walked the remaining distance to her desk. He stuck out his hand to her. "Gray Montgomery. The new guy."

Her mouth rounded to an O. She slid her hand into his and instead of shaking it, he merely held on and squeezed gently.

"I'm Faith Malone."

He smiled, and his blue eyes twinkled at her. "I know."

She blew out her breath. "Of course, you know. I'm the only woman who works here, so I couldn't be anyone else."

"Am I interrupting anything?" he asked as he let go of her hand and gestured to the phone. "You seemed upset."

She shook her head and continued to stare up at him. Lordy, but he was an intimidating sort. "It was nothing. Was there something you wanted?"

The phone rang, and she jumped about a foot. The sick feeling in her stomach returned with a vengeance. It was probably her mother. She continued to stare at the phone, unwilling to pick it up, not wanting to deal with an overwrought mother who manipulated her at every turn.

A large hand covered the receiver and yanked it up.

"Malone's," Gray bit out. There was a long pause, and he looked up at Faith with that searing gaze. "I'm sorry, but she stepped out for a moment. Can I take a message?"

Please, please don't leave a message. She couldn't take some hysterical spiel from her mother. Not to a complete stranger.

Gray put the phone back down.

"Thank you," she said quietly.

"No problem. Are you okay? I got the impression you definitely didn't want to talk to whoever was on the phone before."

She shivered as he continued to stare at her with those intense blue eyes. "I'm fine. Really. Now, was there something you wanted?" she asked again.

The corners of his mouth quirked up in an amused smile. "You trying to get rid of me?"

She flushed. "Sorry, of course not. I'm very glad to meet you. I've heard a lot about you from Pop and Connor. Are you settling in well? I haven't seen you around the office."

Shut up, Faith. She wanted to drop her head on her desk. She sounded like a complete airhead.

He cleared his throat. "I'm glad to meet you as well. I've also heard a lot about you from Pop and Connor. I'm moved into the apartment just fine, and this is my first time in to the office."

His eyes twinkled as he continued to regard her with a smile. Beautiful eyes too. Deep, rich blue. He wore his hair short, spiked slightly on top. Probably didn't have to do much more than rub a towel over it, wave a comb in the general direction and go.

"I was hoping you could direct me to my office?"

She blinked and yanked herself from her slow perusal of his attributes. She stood up, knocking her knee against the desk. Pain shot up her thigh, and she grimaced.

He raised a brow but didn't comment. She opened her top desk drawer and rummaged around a few seconds before pulling out a set of keys.

"These are the keys to your office and to the building. I'm sure Pop has given you all the security codes, but if not, I'll write them down for you."

She thrust them toward him, and his hand closed around hers once more. A warm tingle skittered across her skin as his thumb brushed across her knuckles. She yanked her hand back and walked around the desk toward the door. When she reached the hallway, she turned back to see him still watching her. She was pretty sure he'd been eyeballing her ass, but as soon as she'd turned around, his gaze shot upward.

"If you'll follow me, I'll show you your office."

He pushed off from where he'd leaned his butt on her desk and started toward her. She swiveled back around and walked three doors down to the vacant office that had been assigned to him.

She opened the door but didn't go in. She gestured inside with her hand. "Here you are. If you need anything, let me know."

"I'll do that," he said in a low voice as he walked by her.

Gray felt her gaze, knew she was watching him as he moved inside the doorway. They'd both done their share of looking. When Mick had given him details on Faith Malone, Gray hadn't expected her to be so beautiful. Or so innocent looking.

"I, uhm, I'll get back to my office now. I'll see you around. If you need anything, just holler."

He turned to see her back from his office and hightail it down the hall. He shook his head and smiled to himself. He made her nervous. She'd been on edge ever since he walked into her office.

Once he was sure she was gone, he backtracked to shut the door then pulled out his cell phone to call Mick.

"I finally met Faith Malone," he said as soon as Mick answered.

"And?"

"Not what I expected," Gray confessed.

"What do you mean?"

Gray paused and once again conjured up the image of her sitting in her office, her face a mask of upset. Her distress bothered him more than he wanted to admit.

"She's young. Pretty. Seems nice. Very wholesome looking. According to Pop she's extremely intelligent and as good-hearted as they come."

He heard Mick's sigh of impatience. "Have you gotten anywhere with the phone taps? Do you know if her mother's called?"

"I only just got access to the office today. I'll tap her phone here and at her apartment as soon as I can get in to do it. And I think her mother may have called today."

Mick's breathing ratcheted up, echoing over the phone line. "Are you sure? What was said?"

"I have no idea. I came in when she was on the phone, and she said very little. But she was visibly upset. She hung up at one point, and when the phone rang again, she refused to answer it. I picked it up, and a woman asked for her by name but refused to leave a message when I told her Faith wasn't available."

"Why the hell didn't you put Faith on?" Mick asked in exasperation.

"Because she wouldn't have done it," Gray replied. "Be patient,

Mick. I'll get to the bottom of this. I promise. Give me a few days to get the taps in place. These guys aren't slouches. I'm going to have to be careful."

"Let me know when you find out something," Mick said.

"I will."

They rang off, and Gray shoved the phone back into his pocket. He stood there for a moment, pondering all that he needed to do. To his surprise, a sense of guilt nagged at him. Chewed on his ass like a pit bull.

He liked Pop. Liked the job, even if it was gained under false pretenses. He fit in well with Pop's team. Connor, Micah and Nathan were all his age, and they all had a lot in common. For the first time, he wondered if going back to the police force was really what he wanted. It wouldn't be the same without Alex.

Alex.

The one word that filtered across his mind brought a surge of pain, one he'd tried to block ever since the funeral, but lately he'd been unsuccessful.

Gray closed his eyes. The idea of Alex's killer out there. Free. Escaping from justice. Gray had seen enough of the bad guys winning in the sorry-ass neighborhood he'd grown up in. He wasn't going to let it happen again. This time it was personal.

"Uh, Gray?"

He looked up to see Faith standing in the doorway of his office. His gaze flickered down her long legs sheathed in tight-fitting jeans. The thin turtleneck she wore clung to her curves in all the right places.

He shifted uncomfortably in his chair, and he chased images of her body from his mind.

"What's up?" he asked, hoping he sounded casual enough.

"Pop called. He and Connor, Nathan and Micah are going to eat and want you to meet them for lunch at Cattleman's."

Gray shoved his hand in his pocket, reaching for his keys. "Thanks. I'll head over now. Want me to bring you something back?"

She shook her head and looked away, her cheeks stained pink. God, she looked so soft and feminine. He was half-tempted to reach out and touch a strand of her long blond hair. See if it was as silky as it looked. As silky as her skin must be.

He forced himself to look away, but then he heard her walk out of his office, and he glanced up to watch her shapely ass bob down the hallway.

He was attracted to her. Hell, what red-blooded man wouldn't be? But she was wrong in so many different ways he couldn't even stop to count. She sure as hell wasn't a girl a man played with. No, she had *keeper* written all over her, and he wasn't in a position to walk into that kind of situation. He'd scare her silly anyway.

With a shake of his head, he tossed his keys from one hand to the other and headed out to his truck. He'd need to find a time later when everyone was out of the office so he could tap the main line. If it had been Faith's mother calling today, she obviously hadn't gotten whatever it was she wanted. Which meant she'd call back.

CHAPTER 3

Gray leaned against the brick of the apartment complex and watched as Faith struggled to heave two large grocery bags out of her backseat then nudge the door shut with her hip.

He started forward, reaching for the bags when he was close enough. Wide, startled green eyes flashed up at him as she took in his presence.

"Here, let me help you with that," he said.

She relinquished them, still staring at him in surprise. Though they both lived here—Pop owned the apartment complex and Connor, Nathan and Micah also lived here—he and Faith hadn't yet crossed paths since he'd moved in.

He made his way to her door and turned back, waiting for her to unlock it. She cocked her head to the side.

"How did you know which apartment was mine?"

"Your brother told me," he said with a shrug.

She frowned. "Connor's usually so tight-lipped. I'm amazed he'd tell you for fear you'd break in and murder me in my sleep."

Gray chuckled. "Is that your way of saying he's a little protective of you?"

"No, he's just cautious," she said as she slid the key into the lock. "And private. Very, very private. It's not like him to offer personal information." She opened the door and gestured for him to go inside.

"Does it bother you that he told me your apartment number?" he asked as he shouldered by her. "I merely offered to keep an eye out since my unit is so close by."

She followed him in and shut the door. "No, it doesn't bother me."

"Well, then, now that we've settled that, where do you want the groceries?"

She pointed toward the kitchen. "On the bar, please. I'll put them away later."

He took his time walking across the living room, glancing around at the interior of her apartment. From the impression he'd formed of her, he'd expected pink, maybe yellow, lighter pastels. Girly colors and decor. Frilly shit draped from one end to the other. He couldn't have been more mistaken.

The apartment was decorated in rich, dark earth tones. There was a decidedly masculine feel to the furnishings. Burgundies, dark blue, greens. The couch and love seat were dark brown leather, and they actually looked comfortable, like they were sat in and not used solely for decoration. She was an interesting contradiction. One that intrigued him greatly.

He set the groceries down and glanced over at the telephone. Looked like a standard land line. Easy enough to tap, only he'd have to get into her apartment when she wasn't around and make damn sure she never found out about it.

He'd gleaned enough information from Micah and Nathan to know that she was fairly routine in her comings and goings. Most weeknights she stayed home. Friday and Saturday nights she spent out with the guy she was currently dating, and Sundays she usually went over to Pop's. She occasionally spent time over at her brother's or at Nathan's or Micah's place, but for the most part, she appeared to be a loner.

When he turned back around to face her, he found her studying him, her eyes hooded and wary. There was a subtle curiosity in her gaze, despite her reserve. Like she couldn't quite figure him out. *Join the club, babe.* He hadn't exactly been able to figure her out either in the short time they'd been acquainted.

Her arms were crossed, folded protectively over her midsection. They inadvertently plumped her breasts, pushing them upward until they strained against her shirt. He could just see the outline of her nipples, pressing gently outward.

"Would you like something to drink?" she asked politely, though her body language told a different story. She wasn't comfortable with him here. In her space.

He smiled. "Thanks, but I have to go. I'm meeting Micah for drinks."

She pulled a face. "I know what that means."

He arched his brow. "Oh?"

She laughed huskily. "If it's Micah, it'll involve lots of gorgeous women, usually brainless gorgeous women, okay, make that half-dressed, brainless, gorgeous women."

"Sounds like my kind of guy," he drawled.

She flushed again. "I didn't take you for the brainless type."

The corner of his mouth went up. So she'd been analyzing him. Very interesting. And she didn't take him for the brainless type. Good observation, though it could have been a lucky guess. Frankly, he'd rather suffer a case of blue balls before getting his dick wet in a chick with more dead space than a black hole.

"I like the half-dressed part," he said with a grin.

Faith rolled her eyes. "I guess I'll see you tomorrow then."

Ah, dismissed. He retreated. No sense spazzing her out. He'd meet Micah, throw back a few, then he'd head over to the office to tap her phone. He'd wait until she was at work to get into her apartment.

As he walked toward the door, her soft voice brushed over his ears.

"Thanks for the help."

He turned his head. "Anytime."

Faith watched him go with an odd hitch in her breath. She hadn't expected to see him again so soon after their first encounter, but then she imagined they'd be bumping into each other a lot, given they worked together and lived in the same apartment complex.

She knew from Connor that Gray was a Dallas cop on leave after his partner had been killed in the line of duty. According to Nathan, Gray wasn't much of a talker. He and Connor should get along famously then, because Connor was as tight-lipped as they came.

Micah and Nathan on the other hand . . . they more than made up for Connor's seriousness with their antics. Fun loving. Not a serious bone in their body.

Faith grinned. Just where Gray would fit into the eclectic mix was anyone's guess.

She turned to put away all the groceries, and when she was

done, she poured herself a tall glass of tea before heading to her computer.

Setting her drink to the side, she slid into the chair and moved the mouse to bring up the screen. She opened her browser and typed in the address for Google.

Now, what to search. She sat there a long moment, staring at the empty search field. What was she looking for? Did it have a name, this nebulous craving twisting inside her?

Maybe she should be Googling what to do when you lost your ever-loving mind. Finally she opted to type in a variety of words. Maybe by narrowing her choices a bit, she wouldn't be inundated with superfluous information, and if she were really lucky, she'd actually get one or two sites that weren't porn.

Dominance. Control. Hmmm. What else? Oh wait, back up. *Male Dominance. Control. Submission?* No, that just sounded wrong. Okay, so she'd just go with *Male Dominance* and *Control* for now.

Oh, geez. Research statistics. Was this actually a research topic? Maybe she could find a hunky professor willing to bend her over and . . . ohhh the possibilities. She started scrolling faster, trying to outrun the erotic images swimming in her head.

Spanking. Tied hand and foot. A man having complete power over her. Bending her, making her submit.

Taking care of her.

And there was the biggest attractant of all.

She sighed as she clicked through countless useless pages. Impatient, she typed in another series of search words.

Dominance. Control. Bondage.

At least these looked more promising. She scanned the topics and clicked on a few of the offerings. Her brow furrowed as she began reading about female submission.

Honestly, she'd never considered herself a submissive person. Yeah, she wanted a strong man. Someone who didn't have to ask. Who was confidant enough to act. But did that make her submissive?

She wrinkled her nose. Well, it wouldn't hurt to read up on it. At least then she'd have a better idea of how to find this elusive creature: the dominant male.

God, she made it sound like an endangered species. But in today's world, she supposed they were. A dying breed. Emasculated by a politically correct society.

Great. Now that she'd figured out what she wanted in a man, she was going to discover there was no such animal.

She clicked until her finger was numb. Read well into the night, her eyes glued to both the fascinating and the downright bizarre. Honestly, she had no idea there were so many people out there who shared her desires, and certainly not so many women. But strangely, it didn't make her feel any less isolated.

She heaved a sigh as her tired eyes perused yet another listing. Just as she was ready to give it up for the night, an ad on one of the pages caught her eyes.

She leaned closer. Houston. The address was Houston. For an exclusive, *private*, members-only club. "Specializing in themes of dominance, bondage and a variety of fetishes guaranteed to satisfy even the most discerning palate."

One of her eyebrows went higher. Thought highly of themselves, apparently.

Intrigued, she clicked on the ad and was transferred to a surprisingly sophisticated website. Not your average trashy porn site high on shock value.

It was discreet, a website that could host a variety of different businesses. Subdued colors. Easy on the eyes. No pop-ups or flashing little boxes screaming that you just won an iPod.

Her pulse fluttered as she read on. Membership was exclusive and only open to a limited number each year. Security was a high priority, and the "club" wasn't a flashy, neon-sign-bearing business in the heart of Houston's downtown. Instead, it was a stately home in the northern outskirts of the city. Big wrought-iron gates. High security fences. No sign advertising what went on behind closed doors. Basically a meeting place for like-minded individuals.

She shivered. Could it be that easy? Somehow she doubted it. But where else was she going to start her search? Her cursor hovered over the telephone number listed on the site. She reached for the cordless phone she kept by the computer and punched the On button.

For several long seconds, she listened to the dial tone. When it started its obnoxious loud beeping to let her know it was still on and she wasn't dialing, she turned it off and stared at the computer monitor.

Then she turned the phone back on. And off. And on. Cripes. What could possibly be so bad about calling the place? It wasn't like they could reach through the phone, snatch her bald and leave her tied up and naked on the floor. Though, if the guy were hot enough, she might be up for it.

She touched the phone to her forehead and closed her eyes. *Just do it, Faith. You just want information. They don't even have to know your name.*

Taking a deep breath, she punched the On button and quickly dialed the series of numbers. She put the phone to her ear and squeezed her eyes shut in dread. Maybe they wouldn't answer.

Her stomach gave a painful lurch when a smooth male voice offered a greeting.

"Hello?" he said again when she didn't respond right away.

"Uh, hello," she offered, barely able to squeeze the words from her lips. "I was calling for some information. I mean, I saw your club, er uh, your establishment on the internet."

"What's your name?" the man asked cheerfully.

Damn. She guessed they would know her name after all.

"It's Faith," she said, not volunteering her last.

"Hi, Faith. My name is Damon, and I'll be happy to answer whatever questions you may have."

She relaxed a teeny bit. "Well, the thing is, you see, I'm not sure what questions to ask."

"Ah. Okay then let me ask *you* a question."

"Oh. Okay. I guess."

"What is it you hope to find at our establishment?"

"Not much of a loaded question," she muttered.

Damon chuckled. "Don't be shy, Faith. There isn't anything you could possibly say that would shock me. Or make me judge you. I can't help you if you aren't honest with me."

Her mouth went dry. Moment of truth. How to tell a complete stranger what it was she was looking for when she wasn't completely sure herself?

"I want . . ." She sucked in another deep breath and started over. "I want a man to take control. Take. Not ask. In all aspects. Not just sexually." She broke off, but still Damon waited, as if sensing she wasn't yet done. "I want to be taken care of," she finished softly.

"You want to be dominated."

The word still made her uncomfortable, but in essence, that was precisely what she wanted. So she muttered a low agreement.

"There's no reason to feel shame for your desires," Damon said gently. "A woman who knows who she is and what she wants is the most beautiful of creatures."

The compliment brought a delighted smile to her face until she realized she was giddy over a phone call with a stranger who, for all she knew, could be getting his rocks off while listening to her fantasies.

She cringed at *that* mental image.

"Membership is very exclusive here and offered sparingly. If you like, you can set up an appointment time to come and tour our facility. Once you've seen what we have to offer, then you can make a decision as to whether you'd like to pursue membership within our confines."

She swallowed the knot growing in her throat. "I'd like that."

"Fair warning. If you come, you should know what you're getting into. This won't be a trip through the halls of the manor where you'll look at empty rooms and unused furniture. You'll come at our busiest time. And you'll see all."

Her eyes widened, and she wondered just what *all* she would see. Her heart did a strange pitter-patter, and she realized she was excited. Looking forward to the tour.

"When can we set it up?" she asked.

"I can show you around Friday starting at 11 P.M. Things tend to get started late around here. If you give me your e-mail address, I'll send you detailed directions and the address."

Faith supplied him her e-mail, and they confirmed her

appointment time. She thanked him for the information, and they rang off. She dropped the phone on the desk and leaned back, puffing her cheeks out and blowing a long, hard breath.

Friday. Eleven o'clock. She let out a small groan. She had all week to do nothing but wonder about what she'd see.

She licked her lips nervously then smoothed a hand over her bubbling stomach. What the hell had she gotten herself into? And worse, she couldn't wait to find out.

CHAPTER 4

"Hey, baby doll," Micah Hudson said as he rounded the corner into Faith's office.

She smiled as she put down the phone. "Hey, yourself."

He flopped into the chair across from her desk, his long legs sprawling in front of him. Arching his hips up, he fished in his pocket before pulling out a crumpled pack of cigarettes. Seconds later, he shoved one end of the cigarette in his mouth and flicked his lighter.

She emitted a sigh just as he inhaled like a man drawing his last breath.

"Micah, what have I told you about smoking in my office?"

He flashed her a sexy grin and exhaled a long plume of smoke. "Come on, Faith. You know I'm trying to quit. Down to just a couple a day. Pop gives me hell, so I can't smoke around him anymore. You're my only safe haven."

She rolled her eyes. "So because I'm a softy, I get to die from secondhand smoke inhalation." She rummaged in her drawer for

one of the old plastic ashtrays she kept on hand and shoved it
across the desk at him. "At least use this so you don't get ashes
everywhere."

He grinned at her and blew her a kiss as he reached for the
ashtray. She shook her head. It should be a sin for any one man to
be so damn sexy. Micah was a man clearly unused to being told
no over anything, and with good reason. What woman could
possibly stand her ground against his wicked charm?

"You're the best."

He tapped his cigarette against the ashtray then looked back
up at her, his warm brown eyes questioning. Still holding his cigarette between his fingers, he reached up and tucked his unruly
hair behind his ear. His diamond stud earring glittered as it was
exposed to her view.

A lock of hair, upset by his impatient shove, fell forward over
his brow. He thrust his free hand through his hair above his forehead, pulling it tight against his head in a backward motion.
When he let it go, the loose curls flopped over his head once
more. She grinned at the disheveled image he presented. Somehow he just made it work. Messy was sexy on him.

"What you got going on today? Have you met Gray Montgomery yet?"

She cursed the rush of heat that flooded her cheeks and
hoped like hell her fair skin, so prone to blushing, hadn't just
given her away.

"Yeah, I met him yesterday. Showed him to his office."

"And?"

"And what?" she asked, arching a brow at him.

"What did you think?"

"Uh, I didn't think anything. He seems nice. Quiet. Maybe a

little brooding. He should fit in well around here. He and Connor could be best friends forever."

Micah burst out laughing. "Just what we need. One more brooding bastard."

"Well, someone has to even things out. You and Nathan give poor Connor so much shit."

"Well hell, someone has to. Nobody should be that serious."

Faith cracked a small smile. Finally she started giggling and raised a hand to cover her mouth. "Okay, so he's a little uptight."

Micah snuffed his cigarette. "A little? You could bounce a quarter off his ass."

"Whose ass are we talking about?" Nathan asked as he sauntered in.

"Uh, well, Micah seems to have developed a fetish over Connor's ass," Faith said innocently.

Micah flipped her the bird.

"Jesus, man, you been smoking again?" Nathan asked as he wrinkled his nose. "It smells like a damn bar in here."

Faith heaved a sigh of exasperation and reached into her drawer for the air freshener. Both men coughed as she sprayed a cloud of the floral-scented spray.

"I wish you guys would get off my ass," Micah grumbled. "I'm doing my best."

"Yes, you are," Faith said loyally. "But in the future, I wish you'd do your best outside my office."

Nathan chuckled and shoved his hands into his pockets. His shaggy, light brown hair curled outward over his ears and flipped rebelliously at his neck. A goatee framed his mouth and chin. It was in need of a good trim. Green eyes, full of mirth, rested underneath a set of ridiculously long lashes. Lashes that Faith would kill to have. It was so not fair that eyes that gorgeous were wasted on a man.

"When are you going to get a haircut?" she asked.

Micah snickered.

Nathan ran a hand through his hair and looked at her in surprise. "What's wrong with my hair? You don't bug Micah about getting a haircut, and his is longer than mine."

"Because he looks good with long hair. You don't."

"Ouch," he grumbled, shooting Micah a resentful glare.

She shook her head. "I swear you both need a woman to keep you in line. And I wish you'd hurry up and find one so I can stop babysitting your asses."

"Or you could just volunteer for the job full time," Micah said, shooting her another sexy look. Damn the man.

"I don't think John would appreciate you propositioning his woman," Nathan said dryly.

Faith tensed for a minute and sat back in her chair. "Uh, about John."

Two sets of curious gazes focused intently on her.

"Is something wrong, Faith?" Micah asked. All the teasing had dropped from his voice, and now he sat forward, his face drawn into complete and utter seriousness.

She'd forgotten how protective they could be. That was usually Connor's job. As much as Micah and Nathan liked to tease, they still watched over her like a hawk.

"No, nothing's wrong," she said, injecting the right amount of lightness into her voice. "It's just that John and I won't be seeing each other anymore."

Nathan raised his brow in silent question.

"Relax. It was my decision," she said. "It just wasn't working. And don't you go interrogating him."

Another blush worked its way up her neck. The last thing she wanted was John to share the reasons for their breakup with Micah and Nathan.

"And for God's sake don't tell Connor," she muttered.

They both hooted with laughter.

"I'll make you a deal," Micah said, an evil gleam in his eye. "I won't rat you out if you don't rat me out for smoking."

She blew out her breath in annoyance. "You're such a manipulator."

He grinned. "But you love me."

She smiled. She couldn't help it. "Yes, I love you. Now get out of my office. I've got work to do. And so do you two clowns." She checked her watch. "Pop's going to have a coronary if he finds out you're both here and not out on the job."

The phone rang, and her stomach fell. She reached over to pick up the receiver but hesitated, willing the sick nervousness to abate. When she noticed Micah and Nathan looking suspiciously at her, she swallowed and yanked up the phone.

"Malone's."

Pop's gravelly voice barreled through the line. "Faith, tell those two lug nuts to get their asses out of your office and out to the job they're supposed to be doing."

She burst out laughing, her relief nearly overwhelming. "Good morning to you too."

He chuckled in her ear. "Good morning. Things going okay at the office?"

"Sure thing. You going to be around for lunch?"

He sighed regretfully. "No, Connor, Gray and I will get something out. This security system is acting all wonky, so I think we'll be here awhile."

"Okay, Pop, I'll see you when I see you then."

They rang off, and she replaced the receiver, still chuckling.

"Yeah, yeah," Micah grumbled as he shoved himself out of his seat. "I could hear Pop all the way over here. I swear he has this place bugged."

Nathan laughed. "I wouldn't put it past the old fart."

They waved at Faith then trudged out of her office. Quiet descended over the building. She leaned way back in her chair and stared at the ceiling.

Three years. For three years she'd lived an idyllic life. At times it was hard to remember the years before Pop and Connor had come for her. Then Pop had adopted her. Yeah, sure, she was an adult. A woman full grown, but she'd burst into tears when he'd told her of his desire to adopt her and legally make her his daughter. It was the first true sense of belonging she'd experienced.

And now her circle had grown to Nathan and Micah. It was an atmosphere she was comfortable in. Finally at home. Now if only her mother would fall off the face of the earth.

She eyed the phone, willing it to stay silent.

With a sound of disgust, she whirled around in her chair and stood. She would not allow her mother to ruin her day, week, month . . . okay year.

She stalked out of her office and made her rounds to the other offices to collect outgoing mail. When she had a sizable pile, she lumped it onto her desk to wait for the mail carrier. Then she busied herself going over the new job contracts, flagging the ones that needed Pop's signature.

At noon, she pulled out the lunch she'd brought from home and ate it while fielding phone calls from potential clients. Micah called to say he and Nathan wouldn't be back into the office and would be working late. Then Pop called to tell her to go home early and that he'd lock up when he came through later in the afternoon.

She smiled as she hung up. Pop always seemed to know when she wasn't her best. He never asked intrusive questions, but he worried over her just the same. That kind of unconditional love was comforting.

The phone rang again, and she picked it up, expecting to hear Pop again. He usually got sidetracked when he called and would forget what he'd called for in the first place. Which precipitated an immediate call back ninety percent of the time.

"Malone's," she said cheerfully, prepared to tease Pop.

"Faith, baby, we need to talk."

Faith closed her eyes, and her lunch burned a hole in her stomach.

"Faith, are you there? I need to talk to you."

"I'm here," Faith said faintly.

"I need some money," her mother said, forgoing her usual cajoling. "I'm in a bind, baby."

"I can't help you this time," Faith gritted out. "I'd appreciate it if you would quit calling."

A shocked silence fell between them. "Faith, you don't mean that. I'm your mother. You can't just cut me out of your life. I need your help. You can't turn away from me. After all I've done for you."

Rage curdled Faith's system. Her vision blurred as the anger built. "All you've done for me? You've got a hell of a lot of nerve,

Celia. What have you ever done for me? I'm happy now. I have a nice life. Without you. I can't help you. I *won't* help you. Not this time. Not ever again. Please don't call me again."

She slammed the phone down, her breath coming in ragged spurts. Her hands trembled, and she felt dangerously close to vomiting. She closed her mouth and sucked in deep breaths through her nose, willing the nausea to pass.

When her stomach settled, she surged up from her chair, making a grab for her keys and purse. She needed some air. Needed to get away before she succumbed to the urge to start throwing things.

CHAPTER 5

*G*ray stepped into Cattleman's Bar and Grill and headed for the bar area, intent on throwing back a cold beer. Connor had introduced him to the local pub, a place he and the other guys gathered at after work several days a week.

When he walked around the divider that separated the bar from the eating area, he was surprised to see Faith sitting on the far side, her legs dangling off the high barstool. One elbow rested on the bar top, and her other hand stirred a drink with the straw.

He walked forward, but she never looked up. She seemed lost in her own world, not a happy one either. He slid onto the stool next to hers and motioned for the bartender.

She glanced up at him in surprise as he ordered his beer.

"You and I seemed to have developed a habit of bumping into each other," she murmured.

He smiled. "I'm not following you, if that's what you're implying. I've been here every day after work. First time I've seen you here."

She flushed, and he watched in fascination as pink spread into her cheeks. "I didn't mean to imply anything of the sort. I know Connor and the others come here a lot. But I thought you were all working late today."

He shrugged. "We finished up. Pop headed to the office to lock up, and Connor headed home." He cocked his head and looked probingly at her. "What brings you here?"

Distress flickered in her eyes, and she quickly looked away. "Just didn't feel like going home yet," she said vaguely.

Gray cursed himself. He'd lay odds her mother had called again, and he hadn't yet been able to get into the office to do the tap.

"Have you eaten anything?" he asked.

She shook her head. "Don't really feel like eating."

"Care if I eat then?"

She looked back at him, and a small smile tugged at the corner of her mouth. He watched in fascination as her tongue swept over her top lip, catching a droplet of her drink.

"Suit yourself. Far be it for me to get between a man and his meal."

"Spoken like a woman who is well acquainted with a man's needs," he said, letting her make what she wanted of that statement.

To his delight she blushed again and ducked her head. She really was too cute with her rampant blushing. He'd begun to harbor the most vivid fantasies of seeing just how far down her body she flushed. Would she be timid in bed? Would her lover have to coax each piece of clothing from her body?

His entire body tightened. He was as willing as the next guy to have a firebrand in bed, a woman who took charge and rocked his world, but the idea of calling the shots, of maintaining every moment of Faith's seduction sent a thunderclap of desire shooting straight through his groin.

Seduction? Jesus. He wasn't here to seduce her, though God knew he'd enjoy each and every moment. He was here to pump her for information. To use her, by any means necessary, to catch his partner's killer.

He motioned for a passing waitress and asked for a burger and fries before turning his attention back to Faith.

"So how was your day at the office? You look . . . stressed."

She twitched uncomfortably on the stool and took another sip of her drink. Then she forwent the straw and drained the glass in one long swallow.

"Office was fine. Just tired. Didn't sleep well last night." She swiveled on her stool and flashed him a bright smile. "So how are you liking the job so far?"

Classic change of subject. She was definitely hiding something. A complete moron could figure that out. But he didn't exactly have the kind of personal relationship with her where she would confide in him, and he damn sure didn't have time to cultivate one.

"I like it. It's going well."

"Connor said . . . Connor said that your partner was recently killed."

He tried like hell to keep his brow from creasing at the pain her question caused. He didn't say anything for a long moment.

"I'm sorry. I shouldn't have pried."

Her gaze softly caressed his face, her eyes flashing with sympathy. Lord, but she was sweet. And he'd bet money she felt every bit as soft and delicate as she looked.

"You aren't prying," he said quietly. "It's not a secret. Yes, my partner—Alex—was killed in the line of duty."

Her face scrunched with dismay. "Did they catch the person who did it?"

"No. Not yet."

Her long blond hair fell forward over her shoulder as she turned completely to face him. He wanted to touch it, imagine what it would feel like to wrap his fingers in the strands while he slid his cock into her pussy.

A tortured groan welled in his chest and stuck there. Okay, granted, he hadn't gotten laid in longer than he could remember, but he couldn't blame his reaction to Faith on that. There was something about her that just did it for him. Pushed all the right buttons.

She elicited all his protective instincts. He wasn't thinking of hot sex—okay, well, maybe a little. What he was fantasizing about was hot, slow, lovemaking. The kind where a man worshipped at the altar of woman. Where every taste and touch was enjoyed and savored.

Then they could progress to the hot, sweaty fucking.

Got this all figured out, eh, Montgomery?

He downed the last of his beer and wondered where the fucking air-conditioning was.

"How long are you on leave?" she asked. "I mean when do you go back?"

She leaned forward, giving him just a glimpse of the pale mounds of her breasts, plumped up by the lacy bra she wore.

"I, uh, I'm not sure yet. I'm just taking it easy. Deciding what to do next."

She smiled then, and his eyes were drawn to her face. He

couldn't look away. He'd never wanted to kiss a woman so bad in his life.

"I'm glad you're here," she said sweetly. "Pop is a great man to work for. He views his employees as family. Sometimes . . . sometimes you just need to get away from everything, you know? Maybe that's just what you need. Time away."

"What kind of things do you need to get away from, Faith?" he asked softly.

Her expression froze, and he could see her mentally retreating. Damn it all to hell.

The waitress returned and plunked the plate of food down in front of him, and the bartender slid another beer across the bar to him.

Gray reached for the ketchup and opened the cap, prepared to douse the burger and fries. He paused then looked back over at Faith. "Sure you don't want some of this?"

She smiled and reached for a fry. "Typical guy. Have to drown everything in ketchup."

"I'll refrain just for you." He pushed his plate over so it straddled the space between them. Then he proceeded to dump ketchup in a confined space on the plate.

As he watched her nibble on one of the fries, a sudden thought occurred to him.

"Are you meeting someone here? Am I keeping you?"

She gave him a puzzled look and shook her head.

He dunked a fry in the ketchup and raised it to his mouth. "Not hooking up with the boyfriend?"

Again a delicate pink blush bloomed on her cheeks.

"There's no longer a boyfriend," she said lightly.

Could this be the reason for her melancholy? But no, she had a wariness about her that signaled more stress than sadness. He was still betting on the mother. He just wished he knew how involved Faith was at this point.

"He's an idiot," Gray muttered.

She laughed, and he pulled his head up, transfixed by the sound.

"I guess I'm the idiot. I was the one who ended things."

"He's still an idiot."

Smiling, she motioned to the bartender for another drink. "You sound just like one of the guys."

He raised a brow. "Which guys?"

"Connor, Micah and Nathan."

"Well, I definitely don't see you as my damn sister."

Her eyes widened. "What do you see me as?"

Now that was a provocative damn question. Maybe she wasn't as shy as he thought. She stared back at him, unblinking.

"Beautiful."

He chuckled as she blushed yet again.

"What? What's so funny?"

"You're adorable when you blush, and you do it so easily."

Her brow furrowed, and her lips turned down into a frown. "Adorable? I much prefer beautiful to adorable."

He reached over and touched her arm. "What if I find you both?"

A warm tingle spread up Faith's arm as Gray's fingers brushed across her skin. She swallowed the knot in her throat. She wasn't some inexperienced virgin, but here, sitting in such close proximity to a man telling her she was beautiful—and adorable—had her completely flustered.

She loved the subtle complexities of attraction. Loved the

feeling and challenge of meeting someone new and exploring those first awkward moments as they felt around, both being subtle yet forward.

"I can live with that," she said huskily.

He withdrew his hand and resumed eating. She wanted him to touch her again. A simple caress, him looking at her just so, his masculine scent . . . her stomach curled into a nervous knot of anticipation.

She studied him as he ate, watched his movements. He was strong and confident. She liked that. But would it extend to the bedroom? Would it extend to his relationships? She shook her head a bit. No more was she leaving it all to chance. How many more men would she have to go through before she found what she wanted? Would she ever find what she wanted—no, needed?

Friday seemed a light-year away. She was nervous as hell at the idea of waltzing into some fetish club by herself, but another part of her was proud of the fact that she'd ventured so far out of her comfort zone.

Strong. Confident. If she *wanted* those qualities in a man, then maybe it was time she started exhibiting them herself. Like attracted like, didn't it?

"I'd give up beer for a week to know what's going on inside your head right now."

She blinked and refocused and saw that Gray was staring at her. "Oh, sorry. Was just thinking."

He chuckled. "Like I said, I'd love to know about what."

She wouldn't blush. Would. Not. Blush. She could feel herself losing the battle as the wave of heat crept up her neck. Damn it.

He hooted with laughter and picked up a napkin to wipe his mouth. "That blush just gave you away, darlin'."

She groaned. "It's not polite to keep pointing out my faults."

He leaned forward and tipped her chin up with his finger. "Not a fault at all. I find it sexy as hell."

Goose bumps trickled down her spine, back up again and over her shoulders. Her nipples tightened, and the muscles in her pussy constricted.

A dot of ketchup rested in the corner of his mouth, and it gave her an excuse to touch him. God, she wanted to touch him. She raised a finger and gently wiped the ketchup away. When she would have withdrawn her hand to wipe it on a napkin, he captured her finger then raised it to his mouth.

His lips closed hot over the tip, then his tongue swirled over the skin, licking away the ketchup. The action sent a shock wave through her system. She sat, stunned at her reaction.

Slowly he pulled her hand away, sliding his tongue along her finger until it left his mouth. When he released her, she let her hand fall to her lap, trying to disguise the shaking.

"I should go," she said, saying the first thing that popped into her mind. That was a lie. She didn't want to go but didn't know what to say or how to react to the blatant sensuality between them.

"Why don't I follow you back?" he offered. "I'm headed home too. I'll see you to your door."

"O-okay." She sucked in several steadying breaths so her voice didn't waver so damn much. After collecting her purse, she dug for her cash and started to flip a few bills onto the countertop.

Gray held out a hand and shoved her money back to her. "I got it."

She slowly pulled the money back and stuck it back in her purse. "Thanks."

She waited as he paid their tabs, and then he turned around to face her. "Shall we?" he asked, gesturing toward the exit.

Why did this feel like a freaking date? And why was she so damn nervous? She was never this insecure, this jittery. She'd never felt anything but comfortable with her dates. Was that the problem? Had they all been nothing more than buddies? Nice boys whom she had nice sex with?

Nice sex. Ugh. She wanted the dirty kind. The hot, sweaty, make-you-scream sex.

She walked ahead of him, but he caught up to her and put his hand to the small of her back as they walked into the parking lot. It was a protective gesture, one that made her feel cherished. And she liked that feeling. Liked it a lot.

He opened her car door and ushered her inside, closing the door behind her. She sat there and watched him return to his truck. Watched his determined stride, the way his jeans hugged his ass.

When he slid into the driver's seat, she started her car and backed out of her space. Fifteen minutes later, she pulled into her assigned parking spot outside her apartment and cut the engine.

She got out and walked around to the front of the car, waiting as Gray approached from three spaces down. There was an awkward pause as he waited for her to start ahead once more. Then, as before, he put his hand to her back, sliding his fingers seductively down her spine to rest in the hollow.

She barely controlled the tremble that threatened to take over her body. When they reached her door, she couldn't help the pang of disappointment that their interlude was over.

Withdrawing her key, she unlocked the door then looked up at him. His eyes burned into her and seemed to concentrate on her lips. Was he thinking of kissing her?

Her lips parted, and she sucked in a catchy breath. "I guess I'll see you tomorrow."

He leaned in closer and trailed a finger down her cheek. "I'm counting on it."

His mouth hovered temptingly over hers. Her gaze flickered over his face. She could see the pulse in his neck. He swallowed once then twice and slowly pulled away as if he'd just undergone an epic battle with himself.

A surge of disappointment knifed through her. He wasn't going to kiss her. She smiled shakily. "See you then." She turned and walked into her apartment, turning only to give him a small wave.

He stood, unmoving, watching her until finally she shut the door. Once fully inside, she sagged against the door and closed her eyes.

You are such a chickenshit.

She could have just kissed him. No law said she had to wait on him. And he'd wanted to; she could tell that much. She mentally replayed the sensation of his tongue sliding over her finger. She could easily imagine his mouth on her body, moving delicately across her rib cage, to the underswell of her breast and then finally to her nipples.

A groan escaped her as her breasts ached, a tingle knotting the tips into taut beads. Hard to believe that just the other night she'd enjoyed mediocre sex with John. Now in light of what she felt Gray could give her, her past experiences paled in comparison. And she hadn't even gone to bed with him yet.

Yet. A giddy smile curved her lips as she shuffled toward her bathroom. *Yet* implied intent.

CHAPTER 6

*G*ray yawned and stretched tired muscles as he let himself into his apartment. He'd only get a couple of hours' sleep. If he was lucky. But the phone tap on Faith's office phone was in place, and all that remained was for him to get into her apartment to bug her personal line.

A twinge of guilt nipped at his gut as he palmed the key he'd lifted from Pop's office. Pop kept spares of all the apartment keys there, and so Gray had taken the one for Faith's apartment.

He needed to get in today as soon as she left for work and return the key before it was missed.

As he shed his shirt and tossed it on the couch, he saw his answering machine light blinking. Knowing it could only be from Mick or one of the guys from work, he shuffled over and hit the Play button.

"Gray, it's Mick. Call me no matter what time you get in."

Short and sweet. There was an urgency to Mick's voice that woke Gray from his lethargy. Glancing at the clock, he shrugged and picked up the phone. Mick had said no matter what time it was.

A few seconds later, Mick's disgruntled voice fed over the phone line.

"I didn't send you down there to party. Where the hell have you been?"

Gray sighed in irritation. "I was getting the phone tap in place. Can't exactly do that in broad daylight. Now what is so all-fired important?"

"Samuels was spotted in Huntsville earlier today. Woman was with him."

"You think he's on his way here?" Gray asked.

"I think it's a damn good possibility. Stay close to the girl. I bet anything Samuels and the mother are headed straight for her. They probably set up the meeting when the mom called the other day."

Gray frowned. Was that what had Faith so edgy? And did she have any idea what her mother was involved in, or was she just acting the dutiful daughter?

"I'll keep my eyes and ears open, Mick. You know that."

"Just wanted you to know," Mick said gruffly. "Let me know if the tap turns anything up."

Gray hung up the phone, not liking the implications of what Mick had reported. Was Faith involved, or was she just being used by her manipulative mother?

He scrubbed a hand over his hair and then rubbed his palm down his face. Maybe he'd call in sick tomorrow. That would give him time to slip into Faith's apartment after she left for work, then he could return home to get some sleep.

He trudged into the bedroom and set his alarm for six. Two

hours. He'd sleep for two hours then get up and wait for Faith to leave.

When the alarm went off, Gray groaned and slapped his hand over to stanch the annoying cacophony. After several long minutes, in which he argued the need to get up at all, he finally swung his legs over the side of the bed and sat there, face buried in his hands.

Knowing that Faith would leave at seven sharp, as she did every morning, he got up and headed for the shower.

At six forty-five, he called Pop's cell phone and told him he was home sick for the day. After enduring a gruff lecture to get plenty of rest, Gray hung up and nursed his cup of coffee.

At six fifty-five, he moved to the living room window that overlooked the parking lot and nudged the curtain aside so he could see Faith's car. As expected, at seven, she hurried out of her apartment and got into her vehicle.

One down, three to go.

He kept vigil by the window until one by one, Connor, Nathan and Micah also got into their trucks and headed off. Knowing he needed to be quick, he retrieved Faith's key from the kitchen table and slipped out of his apartment.

He didn't waste any time looking around. He didn't want to arouse suspicion. When he reached her door, he slid the key into the lock and went inside.

As he scanned the living room, he grinned. Weren't most women supposed to be neat freaks? Clutter abounded, and it looked as though she performed a striptease on the way to her bedroom. Pieces of clothing lay tossed aside, forming a path from the door toward the hallway.

His gaze focused in on her computer several feet away. It sat atop a wooden desk, piles of paper and books scattered across the surface. Her screen saver hadn't come up yet, and what was pictured on the monitor gave him serious pause.

Porn? She'd been looking at porn? Despite the urgency of the task at hand, he simply couldn't walk away. The idea that she'd be surfing pornographic websites seemed incongruous with the image she projected.

He walked over and leaned in closer. Hmm, not a porn site, at least not in the typical fashion. The website was actually an informational on bondage and submission. Couples in a variety of poses dotted the page, and Gray couldn't help but picture Faith in the woman's stead.

Did she harbor dark fantasies? Sweet, easily blushing Faith with a penchant for kink? The dichotomy turned him on and intrigued the hell out of him.

Then he frowned. Was she just another woman all too willing to give up control in the bedroom, live for the fantasy then forget the whole thing the next morning? It wasn't as if he hadn't had his fill of those women.

Oh, they were more than willing to play a role, one that only extended to the bedroom, but when it was over with, they became a completely different woman.

He wasn't into pretend shit. He wasn't some damn puppet to have his strings pulled then be put back on the shelf until it was time to play again.

He shook his head and smiled ruefully. He was getting worked up over nothing. And letting past experiences color his perception of something he had no idea about. Who knew what Faith was up to or why she was looking at submission sites. It wasn't any of his damn business.

Remembering the fact that he had a job to do, one that didn't include figuring out a dozen ways to fuck Faith, he hurried into the kitchen. After arranging the tap, he headed for her bedroom, sure he'd find another phone there, but after a quick search of the house, he only discovered the one in the kitchen.

Quickly surveying the living room and kitchen to make sure he hadn't disturbed anything, he strode to the door, opened it a tiny crack and peered out. Not seeing anyone, he let himself out, locking it behind him. Then he hightailed it back to his apartment and the promise of a nice long nap.

Faith raised her hand to knock on Gray's door but hesitated at the last minute.

"Don't be such a ninny," she muttered. "Just because you can't be around him two seconds without blushing doesn't mean you're a spineless wimp."

Shifting the sack she held in her arm, she pressed her lips together and knocked. She waited several seconds then knocked again, louder this time.

Finally the door opened, and she blinked as Gray, a shirtless Gray, stood in the doorway. He leaned against the frame for a minute, and she let her gaze wander down his body. He wore only a pair of jeans, and his bare feet stuck out from the pants legs.

As she glanced back up his body, she stopped at his chest. He folded his arms over his rib cage, and she couldn't help but admire the bulging muscles of both his arms and his upper chest.

He only had a smattering of hair in the hollow and then a fine line leading downward to his navel. She felt the dreaded heat of a blush as her eyes settled on the fly of his jeans.

Finally she jerked her gaze back up. He was eyeing her lazily, his blue eyes studying her much as she'd been studying him.

"I, uh, sorry to bother you. Pop said you weren't feeling well." She thrust the bag toward him. "I brought you some homemade chicken and dumplings."

He smiled as he took the bag. Then he stepped back. "Come in, please."

She hesitated for a minute then followed him inside.

"This was sweet of you. You shouldn't have come all the way over here. I'm feeling much better now."

He set the bag down on the bar separating the small kitchen from the living room then looked back at her again. "Just let me grab a shirt, and I'll be right back."

She fidgeted as he walked down the hallway to his bedroom, and when he disappeared she let out a long breath. She turned her attention to the bag on the bar and removed the plastic container holding the chicken and dumplings.

Not wanting to stand there like an idiot, she walked around the bar into the kitchen and set about looking for a bowl. When she found one, she hastily transferred the contents of the plastic container to it and thrust it into the microwave.

She set it for two minutes then rummaged around for a spoon. Just as the timer went off on the microwave, Gray sauntered back in, this time wearing a T-shirt. It was all she could do not to sigh in disappointment.

"You didn't have to do this," he protested as she gestured for him to sit down.

"Sit," she directed. "It's all done anyway."

She removed the bowl and stirred the dumplings before plopping the bowl in front of him. "Do you want something to drink?"

He put his hand on her arm. "Faith, sit down. You don't have to wait on me."

"I should probably be going," she hedged.

"Do I make you nervous?" he asked as he stared intently at her.

"W-why would you ask that?"

"Because you're making a habit out of running away from me," he said.

She sank onto the barstool across from him like a deflated balloon. "Oh, no, I mean, well, yes, you make me nervous."

Her hand came up to her mouth in mortification. Had she just said that?

He chuckled. "At least you're honest."

"I've made a pact with myself to start being more direct," she explained. *God, Faith, shut up!*

His eyes twinkled, and he grinned. "Then maybe you'll tell me why I make you nervous."

"Not that direct," she muttered.

He laughed and picked up his spoon. "Mmm, this is really good. Not only are you beautiful—and adorable—but you're an excellent cook as well. I'm dying to know why you're still single."

She glared at the mischief in his eyes. He was totally yanking her chain.

"Maybe I haven't found a man worthy of my beauty or culinary skills," she said airily.

He raised his spoon in salute. "Touché."

"I really should be going. My lunch hour is almost over, and I have a lot of paperwork to do this afternoon."

"Have you eaten anything?" he asked.

"I'll get something when I get back to the office. I just wanted to see how you were feeling."

His gaze caressed her face, his expression intense. "I appreciate it."

She stood awkwardly, smoothing down nonexistent wrinkles in her jeans. She reached into her pocket for her keys and headed around the bar. As she passed him, he reached for her wrist.

A surge of warmth raced up her arm as his fingers pressed into her skin.

"Thank you," he said huskily.

For a minute, she thought he'd kiss her, just as she'd thought he would last night. But again, she was disappointed as he let his fingers slide off her wrist.

"I'll see you later," she said as she started for the door once more.

CHAPTER 7

$\mathcal{F}$aith got out of her car and headed back into the office building. When she rounded the corner into her office, she was surprised to see Connor and Pop sitting in chairs eating pizza.

"Hey," she said in delight. "I thought you guys were eating out today."

"Well, we came by to eat with you," Connor said. "But you weren't exactly here."

Her cheeks prickled, and she fought to maintain a neutral expression. "I took some chicken and dumplings over to Gray. I wanted to see if he was feeling any better."

"That was nice," Pop said with an approving nod. "How was he?"

Faith walked over to the open pizza box and took out a slice. She picked up a napkin and took her chair behind the desk. "He seemed to be feeling better. I think he must have been in bed when I knocked because he looked like he'd been asleep."

"Have things been okay with you, Faith?" Connor asked bluntly.

She blinked in surprise, the pizza stopping its rise halfway to her mouth. She set the slice back down and looked over at her brother.

"Things are fine. Why on earth do you ask?"

"Pop and I have been worried," Connor said. "You just seem distant lately."

A momentary rush of panic swelled in her throat. Had her mom called when she wasn't in the office? Did they already know that Celia was in dire straits again?

She hated these situations. She never wanted Pop or Connor to regret inviting her into their lives. No way would she burden them with issues involving her deadbeat mother. They'd done more than their fair share of dealing with Celia.

"Faith?" Pop's gravelly voice interrupted her dire thoughts. "Is everything okay?"

"Yes, everything's fine. You two worry too much." She smiled reassuringly at them both.

Connor grunted. "Worrying is what we do best."

Faith concentrated on her piece of pizza, chewing and swallowing mechanically. What would she do if her mom called when Faith was out of the office? What if Pop or Connor answered? Would her mom hang up or lay out her sob story regardless of who was on the other end?

Embarrassment, hot and raw, crawled up her spine and wrapped around her neck like a vise grip. Why now? Why after all this time did her mother have to worm her way—or try to worm her way—back into Faith's life? Because if Faith had her way, Celia would stay the hell away.

"What do you think of Gray?" Pop spoke up.

Faith looked up in surprise. "Huh?"

"Seems like a good fellow," Pop continued. "Too bad about his partner. I bet Gray made a damn fine cop."

"Is he quitting?" Faith asked curiously. Had Gray decided to take a permanent position with Pop?

Pop shook his head. "No, not that I know of. Far as I know, he's just taking a break."

"Ah, you made it sound like he wasn't going back or something."

Connor swallowed his last bite of pizza. "I don't see him as the quitting type."

On that he and Faith agreed.

Pop shrugged. "Sometimes a man just needs a change. That's all I'm saying."

The phone rang, and Faith dropped her pizza. Pop looked quizzically at her as Connor reached for the phone. Faith lunged for it and slipped the receiver from underneath Connor's grasp.

"Malone's," she said as cheerfully as her frayed nerves would allow.

Her shoulders sagged in relief when she heard the person identify himself and ask to speak to Pop.

She held the phone out to her father. "It's for you. Raymond Jarrell."

Pop wiped his hands on a napkin and reached for the phone. As he took it, Faith's gaze flickered over to see Connor staring at her, his brow furrowed as if he was trying to see right into her head.

She looked away then gathered up the empty pizza box and escaped the office with it, heading to the larger trash can in the back. As she stuffed it into the large plastic can, Connor's hand closed over her wrist.

She turned, and his concerned gaze met her head-on.

"What's going on, Faith?"

When her gaze drifted downward, his other hand cupped her chin and directed her eyes upward to meet his.

"You know you can come to me with anything, right?"

She smiled, feeling the sting of tears at his loving concern. "Yes, I know, big brother. Everything is okay. Really."

He looked doubtfully at her but let his hand fall. "I'm here when you're ready to talk about whatever's bugging you. Just remember that."

He bumped her nose with his knuckle then turned and walked back toward the front.

Faith sighed and closed her eyes. She hated lying to them, but she also hated the idea of them knowing her mother was calling again. She knew Pop would take over, shield her from the calls, even going as far as to change the business number or screen all the calls, but she couldn't allow that. It was time for her to take a proactive stance, one that didn't allow for her mother's manipulation.

Was it horrible to admit that she simply felt better when her mother was out of sight and out of mind? When she didn't have to think about her or wonder what mess she'd gotten herself into.

Again the prick of tears stung her eyelids, and she gritted her teeth in irritation. *Don't let her do this to you. Not again. She's caused you enough emotional angst for a lifetime.*

Faith took several steadying breaths as she tried to gain control of the surge of emotion and grief she felt. No matter how hard she tried to steel herself against the emotional fallout her mother caused, it always hit her square in the chest. There was

too much sadness and regret buried behind the protective barrier
Faith had built to keep her mother out.

"It wasn't your doing," she whispered. "It wasn't your fault."

She forced herself forward, down the hallway back to her office. She was careful to adapt a serene expression, hopefully
something that didn't belie her inner turmoil. As she headed toward her desk, Pop looked up.

"We're heading out, Faith. You going to come over for dinner
tonight? I'm cooking your favorite."

She grinned. "Would I miss corn dogs and Tater Tots?"

"Smart-ass. I'm making lasagna and garlic bread. Connor's
coming, so you two could ride together if you wanted."

She glanced over at Connor, who raised his eyebrow in question.

"Sure, that sounds great, Pop. I'll look forward to it."

Pop put a hand on her shoulder and dropped a kiss on top of
her head. "You take care and be sure and leave here at a decent
hour. We'll be out for the afternoon, so if you need us, just holler."

On impulse, she reached out and hugged him, burying her
face against his chest. He seemed surprised at first then folded his
arms around her, squeezing her tight.

"I'll see you tonight," he said gruffly.

CHAPTER 8

*G*ray increased his pace as his feet pounded the padded indoor track. He still wasn't one hundred percent after taking a bullet in the leg the night Alex had been killed, and his body didn't mind letting him know it.

Sweat rolled down his neck and soaked into the muscle shirt that clung to him like a second skin. Thoughts of Faith crowded his mind, and it pissed him off.

Since arriving in Houston, he'd thought of everything but what he should be thinking about: catching Alex's killer.

Guilt weighed heavy on him. Fact was, ever since he'd left Dallas, he'd felt lighter, like a great burden had been lifted. In Dallas, he'd woken up every single day to the reality of Alex's murder. He'd eaten, drunk, and slept with the memories of that night ricocheting through his head like a Ping-Pong ball.

But here . . . Here he felt freer. A little lighter. When he was with Faith, he forgot about Alex, Mick and that Faith was his only viable link to Samuels.

His body screamed, and he realized he'd pressed to a full run. The muscles in his injured leg quivered and rolled. He forced himself to slow, and then he came to a stop, his chest burning like he'd just sucked on a blowtorch.

He put his hands on his knees and bent over, drawing deep mouthfuls of air into his aching lungs. Punishing himself wouldn't help. It might make him feel a little better, because in his mind, he deserved it, but it still wouldn't change anything.

He picked up the towel he'd discarded earlier and draped it around his neck. With one of the ends, he mopped his sweaty brow as he walked toward the locker room.

After a quick shower, he changed into jeans and a T-shirt then slid his cell phone into his pocket. He hadn't even gotten to the door when his pocket pulsed and vibrated against his leg. He sighed in exasperation and dug it out again.

He flipped it open and put it to his ear. "Montgomery here."

"Hi, Gray. It's Faith."

Her soft voice whispered through his veins, and his shoulders relaxed as the tension uncoiled and loosened.

"Hey," he said, irritated at the catch in his voice.

"I just wanted to check in and see how you were feeling."

Gray felt a twinge of guilt. He was supposed to be at home sick, and instead, he was working out in a gym in plain sight. Not entirely smart.

He shielded the mouthpiece of the phone as he stepped out of the club and into the parking lot. He hurried over to his truck and got in so Faith wouldn't hear the noise of the city around him.

"I'm good, thanks to your cooking," he said.

She laughed softly, the sound sending a little spasm of pleasure through his chest. "I thought I'd stop by a little later and bring you some supper."

He paused and shook his head at the giddy rush he got over the idea of seeing her again. He was acting like a lovesick fool.

"Unless you're resting," she added in a rush. "I don't want to disturb you."

"No, not at all," he hurried to say. "I've been up and around all afternoon."

"Okay then, I'll come by around five thirty if you're sure I won't be a bother."

"I'll look forward to it," Gray said truthfully.

He hung up the phone and checked his watch. Plenty of time to get back to the apartment before Faith and the others got home from work.

It was becoming a habit of hers, standing on Gray's doorstep, nervous about going in. Which was ridiculous when she thought about it. He was just a man. Okay, well maybe not *just* anything. But still, she could do without the quivery knees every time she came into contact with him.

She knocked and waited, determined to be confident and composed. When he opened the door, she donned her brightest smile and held out the casserole dish to him.

"Sausage and potato casserole. Guaranteed to cure what ails you. It's great comfort food."

He smiled and took the still-warm container from her. "Come in, please."

Their fingers brushed as she relinquished the casserole to him, and she acknowledged the latent pull between them. It was there even when it wasn't. If that made any sense.

He set the dish down on his bar and walked around to the fridge. "I just made some fresh tea. You want some?"

She nodded and took a seat on a nearby barstool, watching as he collected ice in glasses. He poured the tea, and the ice crackled and popped, clinking against the glass as it moved around.

When he set her glass in front of her, she took a long sip, savoring the sweet flavor on her tongue.

"Any good?" he asked, nodding his head at her glass.

"Mmmm delicious," she said as she ran her tongue over her lips to collect the droplets.

He grinned. "It's my grandma's recipe. Sun tea. When I was a kid, she'd brew a whole gallon on a post in her garden. She'd let it sit out the entire day in the sun. Always swore there wasn't anything better."

"I think I agree," Faith said as she savored another long swallow.

After draining the glass, she set it back down on the bar and let her gaze wander lazily over Gray. "You look like you feel much better," she observed.

"Yes, much. Thanks to your TLC."

She blushed and ducked her head, and he chuckled as if he knew it was how she'd respond.

"Will you be back at work tomorrow?" she asked as she peeked back up at him from underneath her lashes.

"Count on it," he said.

She put her hand down on the bar and pushed herself up off the stool. "Then I'll see you in the morning."

He looked vaguely chagrined, as if he had no desire for her to go. His next words confirmed it. "Do you have to go so soon?"

She smiled. "Yeah, I promised Pop I'd be over to eat with him and Connor. It's lasagna night."

He circled around the bar and stopped mere inches from her. He was so close his body heat enveloped her. His scent flitted across her nostrils. Clean. He smelled of soap and a fresh shower.

"One of these days, you're going to quit running every time we get close," he murmured. "You're harder to catch and hold onto than a greased pig."

"Pig?" Her mouth fell open. "Did you just compare me to a pig?"

He laughed, his eyes twinkling as he raked a hand through his short-cropped hair. "Hell, that didn't come out well. My point is that one of these days, I want you to actually stick around for more than two minutes. You have a habit of hightailing it every time we get together. I might start taking it personally if it doesn't stop."

Heat bloomed in her cheeks, and a tendril of pleasure wrapped around her chest and snaked up her spine.

"I'll keep that in mind," she murmured.

He seemed to be closer than he was a few minutes ago. She nervously wet her lips and knew that if she didn't leave, he was going to kiss her. Did she want him to?

Part of her did. Very much. But another part of her loved the anticipation. The subtle cat and mouse game they played. The attraction between them was building, and she knew it was only a matter of time before things erupted between them.

He hovered even closer. She closed her eyes and leaned forward, but instead of kissing her lips, he cupped the back of her neck with his hand and pressed his mouth to her forehead.

Her eyes flew open as he pulled away. She almost grinned. So . . . he was giving her a dose of her own medicine, was he? She reached up on tiptoe and brushed her lips briefly across his, certainly not hard enough to constitute a full-blown kiss.

Then she smiled as his eyes sparked and his pupils dilated. She settled back on her heels and sashayed toward the door. When she reached it, she turned around and stared at him.

"I guess I'll see you tomorrow then."

CHAPTER 9

$\mathcal{F}$aith shoved the coffeepot under the spout just as the first drops of hot liquid seeped through the filter.

Once a week, Pop held a morning meeting to discuss jobs and divide up duties. Mondays would have been logical, but then Pop tended to be rather illogical about the little things. Meetings such as this were called at random and usually precipitated by a 5:30 A.M. phone call from Pop asking everyone to come into the office before seven.

Faith always rushed in ahead of the guys so she could pick up donuts on her way in and make a fresh pot of coffee.

Not surprisingly, Gray was the first to arrive. He glanced appreciatively at the donut box when he walked into her office and took a seat on the other side of her desk.

"Mornin'," she said cheerfully. "Feeling any better today?"

He grunted in return but reached eagerly for a donut when she shoved the box across the desk at him.

"There's fresh coffee made," she said.

"You're a goddess," he said as he rose and made for the pot.

He tugged one of the mugs from the neat row she'd arranged them in and poured a steaming cup of the potent brew.

"Want some?" he asked after he'd taken a sip.

She shook her heard. "I don't drink it."

He sauntered back over and slouched in the chair. "Not drink it? I'm pretty sure that's listed as a cardinal sin somewhere in the Bible."

She wrinkled her nose. "Never could stand the stuff. Once I drove all night from Louisiana to Kansas. Kept drinking coffee to stay awake. By the time I got to where I was going, I puked my guts up. Just the smell of it now makes me queasy."

"Yet you still make it for us," he observed.

"I'm a regular saint," she said with a saucy wink.

His gaze drifted lazily up and down her, and her cheeks warmed under his scrutiny. She positively loved the way he looked at her, like he wanted to undress her, touch her, explore every inch of her.

"I'd give an entire paycheck to know what you're thinking right now," he drawled.

She blinked out of her reverie to see him watching her, his blue eyes flickering with undisguised interest. She managed to control her blush—barely.

"A woman has to keep a few secrets," she said.

He chuckled and took another gulp of his coffee.

Faith's gaze averted to the door as Micah strolled in, followed closely by Connor.

Micah did a quick survey of the room. "Nathan not make it in yet?"

"Obviously not," she said dryly.

Micah grinned. She recognized that gleeful gleam for what it was.

"I don't even want to know what you two have been up to now," she said with an exasperated sigh.

"Mornin'," Connor said as he leaned against her desk, coffee mug in hand.

"Morning," she intoned sweetly.

Connor took a long swallow of his coffee then closed his eyes and sighed. "I swear you make the best coffee, Faith."

"That ain't no lie," Micah said. His back was to them as he poured himself a cup.

"It is damn good," Gray agreed. "What kind is it? I'd like to get some for the apartment."

Connor grinned, and Micah let out a hoot of laughter. Gray looked at them both in confusion.

"We've asked her to tell us for the last two years," Connor explained. "She won't. All we know is that she orders the shit from somewhere."

Faith chuckled. "If I told you guys, you'd all buy your own coffee, and then you'd never come to my office to get any, which means I'd never see you."

Micah snorted as he walked over to join the others. "Not see us? Hell, you run this place. Most of the time it's you telling us when to jump and how high."

She glared over at him. "You were supposed to say that you couldn't possibly go a day without seeing me."

Connor reached over to tousle her hair. "Well, that goes without saying, kiddo."

A tiny spark of irritation ricocheted up her spine. It wasn't the first time Connor had ever called her kiddo, but now, in front of

Gray, she didn't want to draw attention to the disparity in their ages. Not that it was huge or anything, but the last thing she wanted him to see her as was a kid. Or even worse, a kid *sister*.

She glared her annoyance at Connor.

A shuffle at the door directed their attention in that direction, and Faith's eyebrows lifted as she watched Nathan walk in wearing an Astros baseball cap. Not that the cap was an oddity, he was a big fan after all, but there was no hair sticking out from under it. None!

She let out a gasp at the same time Micah snickered and Connor muttered, "What the hell?" She stood and hurried around her desk, not stopping until she stood directly in front of Nathan. She reached up on tiptoe and yanked the cap off.

She stood there stunned and let the hat fall from her fingertips. It landed with a soft thunk on the floor about the time her mouth did the same.

"What the hell have you done?" she demanded.

Nathan sighed then ran his hand over his head, his very *bald* head. Micah escalated from snickering to outright howls of laughter. He was soon joined by Connor and finally Gray.

Nathan bent down to retrieve his hat and slapped it back on his head. "Well, hell, Faith, you said I needed a haircut."

Micah started howling all over again.

"I didn't mean for you to shave it all off," she squeaked.

Connor walked up behind Faith and slid a hand over her shoulder. "He's dicking with you, Faith."

"Yeah, tell her why you really shaved your head," Micah said gleefully.

Faith yanked Nathan's cap off again and took a step back to study him. Now that the initial shock had worn off, she had to admit he didn't look bad at all. His goatee was freshly trimmed and neatly groomed. Without all the shaggy hair flopping over his ears, he looked damned sexy.

"Shut the hell up, Micah," Nathan muttered.

Faith whirled around and eyed Micah. "If you know so much, then spill it."

Micah grinned like a loon. "Oh no. I wouldn't miss hearing this from Nathan himself for anything."

She turned back to Nathan, who wore a resigned expression. Gray still sat slouched in his chair, an amused grin on his face.

"Yes, do tell," Connor said.

"I lost a bet," Nathan said tightly.

Faith's mouth sagged opened. "A bet?" Then she rounded on Micah, her finger up and wagging. "Why on earth would you make him shave his head because of a lost bet?"

Micah's eyes widened innocently. "What makes you think I had anything to do with it?"

She put her hand on her hip and narrowed her eyes. "Oh please. You can't tell me this isn't payback for the time he made you go out with the governor's daughter."

Connor and Nathan both dissolved into laughter. Connor had to put his cup down on Faith's desk as he wheezed and his eyes watered. Micah scowled, and Gray's eyebrows went up in question.

"Governor's daughter?" Gray asked. "I didn't know she could get a date. Last I heard, her daddy was pulling some serious strings to get her an escort."

Nathan laughed harder. "She can't. Well, except Micah there. He tripped all over himself to go out with her."

Micah glowered at Nathan. "Shut the fuck up, bald boy."

"Now this I gotta hear," Gray said.

Faith cleared her throat. "Not that I don't enjoy seeing Micah squirm, but we already know about the governor's daughter." She looked apologetically at Gray as she spoke. "I'm sure Nathan will be more than happy to fill you in later. What I want to know is why Nathan had to shave off all his hair."

"Because he bet me the Astros wouldn't lose yesterday afternoon," Micah said smugly.

Connor regarded Nathan with an incredulous expression. "Dude, you bet they'd win with their best batter out with a torn rotator cuff?"

"I didn't know that when we placed the bet," Nathan said tightly.

"Oh, but I bet Micah did," Faith said.

"How would he know?" Nathan asked.

Micah slid an arm around Faith and squeezed her shoulders. "How indeed. Just a lucky thing, I guess."

"You know something we don't, Sis?" Connor asked.

"Just that Micah happens to be very good friends with the team doctor. Micah was the one who replaced his security system last year."

"You son of a bitch!" Nathan exclaimed. He launched himself at Micah, who ducked and backed away just as Nathan flew past Faith to grab Micah's head in a lock. "You knew. You knew the whole time. That's why you made the bet with me."

Micah laughed even as Nathan flipped him to the floor. "The stunt you pulled with the governor's daughter was far worse, so don't give me that shit."

"He's got you there," Connor said with a laugh. "I'd rather shave myself bald than have to endure what Micah did."

"You guys really have me curious," Gray grumbled.

Micah picked himself up off the floor, and Nathan clapped Gray on the back. "I'll tell you all about it over lunch today."

"Asshole," Micah muttered.

"Well, if it's any consolation, I think you look hot," Faith spoke up.

Nathan looked at her in surprise. "Really?"

She laughed. "Yeah, I like it. I'd definitely do you."

"Well, hot damn, let's blow this joint and go back to my place."

Connor scowled at Nathan. "Not funny, man. Not funny at all."

"All you need is an earring," Faith said.

He gave her a horrified look. "An earring? Are you serious? So I can look like sissy boy over there?" he said with a flip of his head in Micah's direction.

Faith shrugged. "I think his earring is hot. You'd look great with one. Shaved head, goatee, a diamond stud or even a gold hoop, a small one. Mmm, I get all quivery just thinking about it."

Nathan massaged his earlobe between his fingers. "Are you shitting me? You really think I'd look good with an earring?"

Faith nodded. "Yeah, and all you'd need is a little sun on that lily-white skin of your scalp, and you'll be a regular lady killer."

"Give it to me straight, Faith. Speaking as a woman. Quit trying to make me feel better. You honestly think the bald look is hot?" Nathan asked doubtfully.

"Vain bastard," Connor teased.

"Well shit, if Faith'll do Nathan because he's bald, I think I'm gonna go make an appointment with the barber," Gray said with a sly grin.

Connor and Micah both turned around, frowns on their faces. Even Nathan eyed Gray through narrowed lids.

Faith cleared her throat again. "Yes, Nathan," she began, pretending she hadn't heard Gray's provocative statement. "Bald looks very good on you. I never did like the shaggy look. I wouldn't have thought I'd like a bald guy, but you look seriously hot."

Nathan grinned and gripped her by the shoulders before planting a sloppy kiss on her face. "You're a sweetheart."

"Get your damn hands off my daughter," Pop grumbled as he walked through the door.

"Mornin', Pop," Faith said as Nathan dropped his hands off her shoulders.

Pop laid a hand on her shoulder as he walked by her en route to the coffeepot.

The others voiced their greetings, and Pop nodded his acknowledgment as he poured his coffee. Cupping the mug in his hands, he looked over at Faith. "You got that schedule printed out for me?"

She walked around the back of her desk and reached inside her drawer to pull out the pages she'd printed off earlier. She handed them over to Pop.

"We have a couple new jobs," Pop said. "Nothing that should be too much trouble. But we have a couple queries that could be a bigger deal. Nathan, I want you and Connor to take the first. It's an entertainment gig. Some bigwig performer is coming to town in a couple of months. They want to line out security well beforehand so that everything goes off without a hitch. I want you to listen to what they want then come up with a proposal to throw at them."

Connor nodded. "No problem, Pop."

Pop eyed Micah and Gray. "I want you two to take the other two queries, meet up with the prospective clients and do what it takes to land the deal. Then I want you to tackle jobs A and B on the list. I'll take C and D and Nathan and Connor can take the remaining one. That should keep us all busy for the next week or so."

He paused and looked over at Faith with a soft smile. "And you'll keep us in line as always." He glanced around at everyone else. "Be sure and keep in contact with Faith. Update her regularly so she can stay apprised of our progress. If there are any problems, let her know immediately so she can relay them to me."

Then as if just noticing, he stared at Nathan and shook his head. "What the hell happened to you, son? Get into a fight with a lawnmower?"

CHAPTER 10

*F*aith drove by Cattleman's after work, looking to see if Micah and Gray were there. She knew Nathan and Connor were still out on jobs, so they wouldn't be around. She'd talked to Micah earlier, and he made it sound like he had a date after work. Which meant that Gray might be here alone. Or he could have just gone home to his apartment.

Still, she pulled into the parking lot and scanned the area for Gray's silver Chevrolet pickup. When she spotted it, her stomach lurched, and she whipped into an empty parking space.

She got out, ran a hand through her long hair, tucking the strands behind her ears as she headed for the entrance. A nervous thrill tickled down her neck when she saw Gray sitting at the bar, his back to her. For a moment, she simply stared, trying to work up the courage to walk over and pretend this was yet another chance meeting.

But then why should she pretend? Direct. She was supposed

to have a pact with herself to be more direct. That didn't mean playing stupid games reminiscent of high school girly ploys.

Finally she started forward, and when she got to the bar, she slid onto the stool next to Gray and smiled when he looked up at her.

"Hey," he said, a genuine-looking smile lighting his face. "Fancy seeing you here again."

She'd had more practice trying to control her mad blushing since meeting him than she ever had before.

"I wanted to see you," she said simply, mentally applauding how cool and casual she sounded. And direct. No pussyfooting around for her.

One of his eyebrows lifted, and he cocked his head to the side. "Is that so?" he said softly.

She hid her hands in her lap to control the trembling of her fingers. When the bartender stopped in front of her, she ordered a Coke.

"So how was your day?" she asked as she turned once more to face him.

"It just got a lot better."

This time she did blush, and he grinned. His fingers reached out and touched her cheek. "I love that you blush so easily. It's very feminine."

His finger trailed to the corner of her mouth, and her lips parted the barest of centimeters in response. He rubbed his index finger over her bottom lip before slowly pulling it away.

"I've been wondering all day what you taste like," he murmured.

She swallowed then licked her lips. What to say to that? Invite him to see? Damn, but why did they have to be in a public place and double damn, why did she have to be at a hair appointment in an hour?

"Maybe I could arrange a sample sometime," she said lightly.

"I'd like that. I'd like that a lot."

The bartender shoved her Coke across the bar at her, and she took it, grateful to have something to cool her rising temperature.

"So what's the deal with Micah and the governor's daughter?" Gray asked in a swift change of subject.

Faith grinned and chuckled lightly. "Nathan didn't get around to telling you?"

"Nah, not yet."

She shook her head. "Those two, I swear. Ever since Micah came to work with us, he and Nathan have been pulling prank after prank on one another. Micah moved here from out of state, so he had no idea who the governor's daughter was. Pop had the job of providing security for the governor's ball he held here in Houston. Only his daughter needed a date after hers stood her up. It came down to Connor, Micah or Nathan. Connor, of course, was over the entire security so he couldn't, not that he would have anyway. Nathan immediately started in on how gorgeous the governor's daughter was and how the only fair thing was for them to flip a coin, but he sure hoped he'd win because he'd heard that in addition to being drop-dead gorgeous, she was also a complete nymphomaniac. Now knowing what you know about Micah, you can imagine he was chomping at the bit. He wheedled and cajoled until finally Nathan gave in graciously and allowed Micah the honor of escorting the daughter for the evening."

"Ah shit," Gray said as he dissolved into laughter. "I would have loved to have been a fly on the wall."

"It was pretty funny," Faith admitted. "She was velcroed to Micah the entire evening. They spent most of it on the dance floor with her hands glued to his ass and her lips wherever she could plant them. I thought Micah was going to kill Nathan the next morning."

Gray chuckled and shook his head. "Those two are pretty funny."

"Yeah, they're great."

"So you think bald is sexy, huh."

She raised her head in surprise. "Uh, well, on him it looks good."

His eyes twinkled. "Do I need to shave my head so you'll drool over me that way?"

To her never-ending irritation, she blushed again. "So uh . . ." She scrambled to direct the focus from her bemusement. "We've talked enough about me. What about you?"

"What about me?" he asked.

"Got a girlfriend? Someone back in Dallas you see?"

He shook his head. "Nope."

She frowned. "I find that hard to believe."

"Oh? Why is that?"

"You're too damn good-looking not to have at least one woman in the wings," she muttered.

He grinned. "Well, I'm glad you think so, but there's no woman. Scout's honor. Truth is, I haven't really gotten around to looking for a woman yet."

"And what are you going to be looking for when you do?" Faith asked softly.

He looked surprised by her forward approach. He shifted forward in his chair and rested his elbow on the bar. Then he turned to look at her, his expression pensive, as if deciding whether or not he wanted to tell her.

"Soft and feminine. Not *too* soft, but not harsh." His lips curled upward in a rueful smile. "Someone who doesn't feel her femininity is a strike against her."

She cupped her cheek in her palm and leaned her elbow on the bar as she stared at him. "Given this a lot of thought, haven't you?"

He shrugged. "Not really. I just know what I want."

That makes two of us. She wanted someone strong, unyielding, someone who could take care of her, someone not afraid to make decisions. Could he be that person?

She looked down at the napkin under her drink and played with the ends. Natural power radiated from Gray. Like a second skin he was comfortable wearing.

"Want to hear my other deep, dark secret?" he asked.

She grinned. "Of course."

"I want a woman willing to let me call the shots."

She stared at him in shock, unable to formulate a response. The seconds ticked by as silence settled between them.

Gray cleared his throat. "I've shocked you. It's hard to make a statement like that and not come across as a knuckles-dragging-the-ground Neanderthal." He shrugged again. "I don't see a lot of women lining up for a guy like me."

"That depends." Her fingers gripped her drink, pressing into the damp glass until her fingertips were white.

"On what?"

"On what you're willing to give a woman in return."

Their gazes locked. She could see the flickers of interest in his eyes. If she gave him any sort of encouragement, they'd no doubt go back to her apartment and have sex. She licked her lips again.

"And what do you think a woman would want in return?" he asked silkily.

"More women wouldn't mind a man being the proverbial man of the house if he didn't abdicate his responsibility. If he took that responsibility seriously," she said and immediately cringed at how preachy she sounded.

He nodded slowly. "That makes sense."

Unable to stop herself, she continued on. "When a man isn't willing to accept responsibility, a woman has no choice but to step up to the plate. Many times she has children to think about. Herself. Her family. As a result, women have figured out that they are not only capable, but oftentimes more adept at running the household than a man."

"You make it sound like men as a species have dropped the ball entirely," Gray said dryly.

"Women have done their fair share of fucking up," Faith muttered.

God, she needed to just shut up before Gray tucked tail and ran as fast and as far away as he could. She sounded like a starchy man hater. Nothing could be further from the truth. But she was only just now sorting out her feelings when it came to relationships. She was on the cusp of a strange new world where she was trying to reach out and grab what she wanted. She felt edgy and impatient, and worse, she felt doomed to failure.

"I'm making a mess of this," she muttered. "I should have just kept my mouth shut. I sound like a preachy, man-hating piranha, when in fact what I really want—" She broke off, mortified that she'd almost blurted out just what it was she did want.

He gave her a probing look. "What *do* you want, Faith?"

"Hey, you two!"

Both Faith and Gray whirled around to see Micah heading

across the bar toward them. She couldn't be sure, but she thought she heard Gray utter a curse under his breath.

Micah dropped a kiss on Faith's cheek then stood between her and Gray as he motioned to the bartender for a drink.

"What are you doing here?" Faith asked. "I thought you had a hot date."

Micah grinned. "I do. Later, though. We're meeting somewhere."

"Sounds positively mysterious," Faith said.

Gray cleared his throat. "I was just about to ask Faith if she wanted something to eat. You want to join us, or are you eating later?"

Faith checked her watch and grimaced. "Sorry, but I have a hair appointment I have to get to." She'd leave off the fact that she was getting waxed and pampered for her Friday appointment. "I should be going if I want to to make it on time."

Gray caught her hand as she stood. She looked over at him and was surprised to see something that looked like regret simmering in his eyes.

"I'd like a rain check on this conversation," he said.

She blushed and caught Micah's curious stare out of the corner of her eye.

"Sure. Some other time maybe."

She reluctantly pulled her hand from his then flashed a smile in Micah's direction before shoving past him to walk out of the bar.

CHAPTER 11

"*G*ot those surveillance cameras set up?" Pop asked from behind Gray.

Gray stood from his crouched position and turned to face the other man. "Yeah, just got the last one operational. I'll give Connor a call right quick and make sure they're all online."

Pop nodded and put his own cell phone to his ear to make a call.

Gray punched in Connor's number. "Everything's set up on my end," he said when Connor answered. "See if you get a visual from each one."

Connor was upstairs in the surveillance room where the computerized system for monitoring all the cameras had been installed. He was the computer expert. A real geek when it came to technology. Gray was more of a grunt worker. He understood enough to install cameras and bugs, but the more sophisticated measures he left to those who understood all that shit.

"Yeah, looks like I've got a clear bead from all corners. Though it looks like camera B needs to be angled up maybe an inch. If you did that, I'd not only get a clear shot of the hallway, but I'd be able to monitor the doorway at the end."

"Will do," Gray said.

"Tell Pop I'm going to be a while up here, so I'll catch up to y'all later," Connor said.

Gray agreed and rang off. Shoving the phone back into his pocket, he strode out of the room and across the building to where camera B was installed. After adjusting the angle, he gave Connor another call back to confirm the position. Then he went in search of Pop.

"I'm all done," he said as he walked back to where Pop stood. "Connor said he'd be a while with the computer system and not to wait on him."

Pop nodded. "Let's grab some lunch then."

Twenty minutes later, the two sat in a small diner drinking coffee while they waited for their food. Gray wanted to ask about Faith and her relationship with her mom, but he didn't know how to lead into such an unlikely topic without arousing Pop's suspicions.

Pop may be outgoing and generous but Connor didn't get his closemouthed ways by chance. Still, Gray needed to find out as much about Celia Martin and any potential connection to Faith as he could.

"Do you like the job so far?" Pop asked, breaking the silence.

Gray nodded. "I do." He did. Far more than he'd expected. "I was doubtful when Mick suggested the change of scenery, but in retrospect, getting away from Dallas has been a relief."

"Mick's your partner's father, right?"

Again Gray nodded, swallowing around the sudden lump in his throat.

Pop made a sound of sympathy. "I know it has to be hard losing a partner. I was a cop myself a lifetime ago. Losing one of your own . . . Well, it's like losing a brother."

"He *was* my brother," Gray said bleakly. "In every sense except actual blood."

Flashes of his childhood raced through his mind. Alex laughing. Them racing down the street. Throwing a baseball. Nights over at Alex's house and his mother's home cooking. Wrestling matches with Mick in the backyard. All the things Gray never had with his own family. Alex and Mick were his family. His only family.

Pop nodded his understanding. "Sometimes blood's not all it's cracked up to be. Faith couldn't be more of a daughter to me if she was my own flesh like Connor. I love them both just as deeply."

Gray searched his memory for whether anyone had told him that Pop had adopted Faith. He'd learned it from Mick's investigation, but it wasn't knowledge he'd be expected to have.

Pop must have taken his silence for confusion, because he went on to explain.

"I adopted Faith. Three years ago."

Gray raised a brow. "But she was an adult."

"True. But I wanted her to have my name. I wanted her to have that love and acceptance she'd missed in her life."

"It doesn't sound like she had a great childhood," Gray said in a low voice. One thing they seemed to have in common.

"I was married to her mother years ago." Pop waved his hand in a dismissive gesture as if wiping away that part of his life.

"What happened to her mom?" Gray asked casually. "No one mentions her. I assumed she was dead."

Pop's face darkened, and a scowl pinched his eyebrows together. "Her mother is a leech plain and simple. She uses people, including her own daughter, and when she's gotten what she wants, she's on to someone else."

"So Faith has nothing to do with her?" Gray asked.

"No, and that's a damn good thing in my book. Faith is too kindhearted for her own good. She spent a lot of years taking care of Celia. Years she should have spent being a normal kid with a parent who looked after her, not the other way around."

Anger boiled from Pop's voice. He swallowed and took a long drink of his coffee.

"I married Celia when Faith was fourteen. She was such a sweet kid. Quiet. It took her a while to warm up to me. Connor had just gotten out of the service. It was obvious it wasn't going to work out between me and Celia, but I wouldn't end things because I was concerned for Faith. I wanted her to have a good home. But then her mother up and left in the middle of the night and took Faith with her. I went crazy trying to find her. It wasn't until five years later that I got a call in the middle of the night. Celia had overdosed. Connor and I went to collect Faith. She'd spent the last years working her tail off to support herself as well as Celia. I brought her back home with me, and she's been here ever since."

"That's tough," Gray murmured.

"Yeah," Pop muttered. He took a deep breath and ran a hand through his graying hair. "I shouldn't be boring you with all this. It's just that I've been worried about Faith lately. I want her to be happy."

"Would she tell you if something was bothering her?" Gray asked carefully.

Pop narrowed his eyes. "Of course she would. She tells me everything. It took a while to gain that little girl's trust when Connor and I first brought her home, but she's come a long way since then."

"So her mom just disappeared after that and never contacted her? That seems pretty low."

Gray found himself holding his breath. He hoped Faith had confided in Pop. Then it wouldn't look so much like she was trying to hide something.

"Last time her mother called was over a year ago." Pop leaned forward, fixing Gray with a hard stare. "Faith doesn't know this, so don't go telling her."

It was on the tip of Gray's tongue to ask why he was telling Gray, a veritable stranger, if he didn't want Faith to know. But Pop seemed upset, and maybe it made him feel better to get it off his chest.

"When I learned Celia was calling Faith and bugging her for money, I tracked her down and paid her off. Told her not to come anywhere near Faith again." Pop rubbed a hand wearily over his face. "Not my proudest moment, I'll grant you, but I wasn't about to let her step in and ruin Faith's life after Faith finally started living for herself."

"So she took the money and agreed to back off?"

Pop nodded. "Hell of a note when you view your only daughter as a meal ticket and nothing else."

Gray grimaced. If Mom had gotten money from Pop before, no way she'd back off now. Which could be good for him and Mick, because with Samuels pulling Celia's strings, her desperation would only increase with each passing day. Desperation made people sloppy.

Mick's report of Samuels being seen in Huntsville came back. In all likelihood they were on their way to Houston. If Celia had been successful in getting money through Faith's connection to Pop, then she'd be quick to exploit that angle. There was also a possibility she'd forgo Faith and go straight to Pop.

"I don't want her hurt," Pop continued. "She's had enough hurt in her young life." His voice took on a more purposeful tone, and he leaned back, surveying Gray with keen eyes. "You seem interested in Faith."

Ah, here it came, and now Gray understood that the long spiel was all a lead-up to the "warning." Don't fuck with his daughter. Gray didn't rise to the bait. He merely sat and waited for Pop to say his piece.

"You'll go back to your job at the end of your leave. I've seen guys like you. I admire you. You make a damn fine cop. I have no doubt about that. But I don't want you messing around with my daughter or using her as a diversion then leaving town to go back to Dallas."

Pop's way of putting it irked Gray. "You make her sound like a damn toy. I like Faith. She's a sweet girl."

Pop nodded. "That she is. She'll make some man a damned fine wife. Have a passel of kids. A nice home and security." His emphasis on security drove home to Gray what Pop wanted for his daughter. And to his credit, it was what most fathers wanted for their daughters.

"I understand," Gray said calmly.

Pop's expression softened. "I like you, son. I like you a damn lot. I don't want you to take it the wrong way. Faith could certainly do a lot worse than a man like you. I just don't see your pathways paralleling each other. That's all."

"Not a problem," Gray said, not wanting to point out that he'd never expressed the desire for a relationship with Faith. No sense pissing the old guy off.

Chapter 12

*F*aith bopped around the office with ill-contained excitement. She was nervous, excited and petrified, all rolled into one, about her appointment tonight. Sex on the brain made for some interesting daydreams, and she could only be grateful it had been a slow day in the office.

The sexual tension between her and Gray simmered like a cauldron, and it made her even more determined and anxious to explore her most secret desires. He brought out every lustful fantasy she'd ever thought of, and even some she hadn't.

She wanted him. That was certainly *not* one of her most secret desires. There was nothing secret about it. And he'd have to be awfully thick not to realize she wanted to have sex with him. But. There was always a *but*.

She wanted a strong, masterful man. From all outward appearances, Gray was that man. He talked the talk, but then she'd had a few talkers in the past. They'd promptly fizzled in bed and out.

Which is why you're going tonight. To identify, to own, to take what you want. She sensed this was the first big step, and once she embraced this change, this desire to be her own person, there would be no looking back.

She emitted a tiny sigh as she arranged a pile of contracts on her desk. Then she logged onto the internet and opened an e-mail from Damon, the man who'd set up her appointment at The House.

They'd actually exchanged several e-mails since her phone call a few nights ago. He had put her at ease with his friendly, open attitude. He'd encouraged her to ask questions and in return had given her a wealth of information about what went on at The House and also what she could expect from her tour.

In one of her sillier moments, and after spending five hours poring over internet pictures of leather-clad Klingon look-alikes, she'd e-mailed Damon to ask what she should wear. Because if she was expected to don a black rubber suit with no ass and a hole where her tits were supposed to go, they could kiss her ass. Her bare ass.

She skimmed over the e-mail, smiling at the reminder that the environment she was entering tonight would be raw and explicit. She felt an excited tingle all the way down to her toes.

She was reasonably prepared for her visit to The House. Or so she imagined. She'd scoured countless sites on the internet, researched all the links that Damon had sent her, and she'd even worked up the nerve to sneak into Micah's apartment and raid his porn collection. She'd certainly gotten an eyeful. Apparently soft porn wasn't in Micah's vocabulary.

She grinned as she mentally went over the list she'd compiled of scenarios and positions she wanted to try. All she needed now was a willing partner, and maybe a better understanding of the need driving her. Which she hoped Damon and company could shed some light on.

She spun around in her seat, feeling just a little giddy and more than a little ridiculous. She slapped her hand down on the desk to stop her motion when the phone rang.

Stifling a giggle, she reached for the phone. "Malone's," she said breathily.

"Faith, we need to talk." Her mother's strident voice scratched over Faith's ear like a tree branch on a tin roof. "I need money. I need you to help me. You have to help me."

Gone was the wheedling and cajoling she was so used to hearing in her mother's calls.

Forgoing any attempt to soften her rejection, Faith gripped the phone tighter. "I asked you not to call me again."

She started to peel the phone away from her ear when a distant sound raised her hackles. She pressed the phone back to her ear again and strained to hear.

". . . tell the bitch to get the money, or you'll both be sorry."

"Mom, who was that?" Faith demanded.

"No one," Celia said in a faltering voice. "It's nothing you need to concern yourself with."

Familiar sadness settled over Faith, crowding her mind with a lifetime of regrets. Celia would never change. Faith had to accept that. She *had* accepted it, but it didn't make it any easier to acknowledge.

"Let me say this so we're perfectly clear," Faith began in a halting voice. "Don't call me." Her voice got stronger and steadier as she allowed the force of her anger to spill out. "I have nothing to say to you. I can't help you. I won't help you. I can't be any clearer than that."

Her words came out shaky in the end as she expelled unsteady breaths. "I love you, Mom." Her voice cracked, and she swiped at her eyes with the back of her hand. "But I hate what you've become—what you've always been. I don't want any part of my old life back. My life with *you*. I'm happy now. I'm sorry, but I don't have any desire to reconnect with you, to allow you to use me anymore."

Faith heard a sob and honestly didn't know whether it was her or her mother. She hung up the phone with shaky hands then buried her face in her arms on the desk.

Her shoulders shook, and she felt tears slide over her arms. When the phone rang again, she reached over, yanked the cord from the wall and flung it across the room. She lowered her head again and wept. Noisy, raw sobs racked her body. So much grief, anger and betrayal coiled in her chest like an angry snake ready to strike.

Why did she hand over so much power to her mother? Why did she give Celia the capability to hurt her so easily?

A firm hand gripped her shoulder, and she stiffened.

"Faith, what's wrong?" Gray's urgent entreaty cut through the red haze circling her mind.

Slowly, she pulled her head up, suddenly feeling foolish for her undisciplined emotional outburst. What if Pop or Connor had been the one to walk in? She'd have a devil of a time explaining why she was sobbing her eyes out at her desk.

She scrubbed impatiently at her eyes and looked away, determined for him not to see her tears. Her chair moved slightly, and she glanced over out of the corner of her eye to see him kneel beside her.

Gentle fingers curled around her chin and tugged, forcing her to look directly at him.

"Are you okay?" he asked quietly.

Another quiet sob whispered from her mouth, and she clamped her lips shut to prevent any more from escaping.

"No, you're not all right. That's obvious." He stroked the back of his knuckles over her cheek then tucked her hair behind her ear. "What's wrong?" he asked again.

"It's nothing," she said shakily. "Really. I feel like such an idiot. I just got upset and overreacted."

"It's obviously not *nothing*. You're not the type to overreact. What upset you so badly, Faith?"

No, he wasn't stupid, and she was insulting his intelligence by denying her upset.

"All right, it wasn't nothing, but it's not something I want to discuss. Can you understand that?" She silently pleaded with him not to push any further.

He stared at her for a long moment. "Yeah. I can."

He thumbed a tear from the corner of her eye. Their gazes met and hung, suspended in a timeless echo.

"I shouldn't do this," he whispered, his voice hoarse and edgy.

"Do what?" she murmured back.

"Kiss you."

"Are you?"

Instead of responding, he edged closer to her, his lips hovering precariously close to hers. Her sudden intake of breath was all she had time for before their mouths met.

His hands framed her face as he pressed hot and hard against her. Their tongues met and tangled. She gasped for air but wouldn't pull away. It consumed her. *He* consumed her.

His mouth inched upward until his teeth nipped and caught at her upper lip. He pulled outward then sucked it farther into his mouth. His tongue licked and laved before he released her lip and moved to the corner of her mouth.

Forgotten were her tears, her anguish. All that existed in this moment was the man in front of her. His touch, his kiss, his very essence wound around her, filling her until everything else vanished.

She reached for him, sliding her hands over his broad shoulders. Her fingers inched toward his neck until one hand cupped the nape of his neck, pulling him closer. She nibbled back at his lips. Kiss for kiss, bite for bite, lick for lick.

A moan built deep in her chest, welled in her throat, until it escaped in a sound of sweet agony. The tension between them that had, over the last few days, built into an enormous entity, exploded in a rush of molten lava.

She moved her hands in front, down his chest until she tugged at his shirt. She wanted to feel his bare flesh. Impatiently, she yanked until it came free from his jeans. Then she slid her fingers under the hem and pressed her hands to his stomach.

He flinched, his mouth stilling over hers. Her hands worked higher, gliding over the muscles of his chest, shoving his shirt upward.

His fingers dug into her head, and his thumbs brushed over her cheeks. There was strength in his touch. A strength she craved, needed, wanted so badly she ached.

She whimpered against his lips when they didn't resume the passionate kiss but instead remained still. His body tensed underneath her fingers, the muscles rippling across his chest.

"Gray," she whispered.

He pulled away and closed his eyes. A harsh expletive danced in the air between them, souring the moment. His hands fell away from her, and he pushed himself upward, tension rolling off of him like sand pouring from a bucket.

His palm crept to the back of his neck, and he rubbed up and down in agitation. "God, Faith, I'm sorry. That should have never happened."

She looked at him in confusion. "Sorry? I wanted it to happen. You wanted it to happen. I don't see what you have to be sorry about."

He stalked around the desk, pausing in the middle of the floor, his movements jerky and indecisive. Then he turned to look at her. His eyes blazed with a multitude of emotions. Desire still flamed brightly, so she knew it wasn't a matter of him not wanting what had happened. But there was also regret, and—self-loathing?

"This shouldn't have happened," he said with a shake of his head. "I took advantage of you in a weak moment. What kind of asshole does that make me?"

She rose from her seat. Her knees trembled, and she placed her palms down on the desk to steady herself. "We've been working up to this point for the last several days. You know it, and I know it. It was as inevitable as breathing. Don't tell me it shouldn't have happened when I know damn well you wanted it as much as I did."

"Wanted it?" He gave a short, barking laugh. "Hell, Faith, I want you so bad, I ache. But it shouldn't have happened. I never should have let it."

With that, he turned and stalked out of her office, leaving her to ponder the sheer oddity of his statement.

She sagged back into her chair, her emotions a rioting mess. Her gaze flickered over to the telephone cord, and she heaved a sigh. Pushing herself upward, she went over to retrieve the cord she'd yanked in her fit of rage. No telling how many calls she'd missed while she was trading heavy breathing with Gray.

After fumbling with the cord for a few seconds, she replaced it in the wall socket then glanced uneasily back at the phone, hoping to hell it didn't ring. When the silence remained unbroken, her shoulders folded in relief.

This had to end. This constant stress over her mother's calls had to stop. Would Celia finally get the message and stop trying to contact Faith? She doubted it, but then she'd never stood up to her mother in the past. This had to be as shocking to Celia as it was to Faith.

You have a life. You owe her nothing. You're finally crawling out of your shell and embracing your wants and needs. Don't screw it all up now.

As pep talks went, it wasn't the best, but there wasn't an untruthful word in it. She did have a life. One she was content with. She was finally spreading her wings and stepping out of the shadows of her past. Finally reaching for what she wanted. Finally unafraid to confront a side of herself that she'd long denied existed.

Maybe Gray wasn't what she needed. Maybe what she wanted was out there, just out of reach, but close. Maybe she'd find it tonight. She wouldn't know until she took the leap.

Feeling moderately calmer after her earlier fit of rage, she squared her shoulders and made a silent vow to herself. She wasn't going to let her mother pull her down again.

CHAPTER 13

*G*ray parked his truck outside the office and cut the engine. It was late. Ten o'clock on a Friday night. Everyone likely had plans that didn't involve being anywhere near the business office. Which was why he was back.

He slid out of the truck and looked warily right and left. He hadn't bothered to park around back, because if he was seen, he didn't want to appear as though he had anything to hide. If Pop or one of the others happened by, he could always say he'd forgotten something.

Welcome, cool air hit him square in the face as he stepped inside the dark building. He disabled the security system before he took a step forward, and then, not bothering to turn on the lights, he headed down the hallway toward his office.

Waiting had been aggravating, but he couldn't listen to the playback of Faith's conversation until he was damn sure no one was around, and he wouldn't risk discovery. He walked to his desk and inserted the key into the lock he'd changed so only he'd have access.

He sat down and pulled out the small digital recording device. He skipped through several routine phone calls before he finally came to the one he wanted. As Faith's mother's voice aired through the recording, he leaned forward, intent on deciphering every sound, every word.

When he got to the part where Faith asked her mother, "Who was that?" he stopped and backtracked to listen again. On the third attempt he could make out the male voice in the background and the threat he'd issued. Samuels. It had to be.

He listened on and flinched at the raw emotion in Faith's voice, her low sobs as they filtered into the quiet night air around him. He now knew without a doubt that there was no way Faith was a willing participant in any plan Celia Martin and Samuels had hatched.

It was telling how relieved he was, but it also made him uneasy that he was deceiving an innocent woman. She was being used by her mother, and she was being used by him.

Fuck.

He stuffed the recorder into his desk and locked it. Then he leaned forward, resting his elbows on the polished wooden surface. He ran both hands through his hair and closed his eyes in frustration.

Was her mother on her way here? Would she exploit the fact that Pop had paid her off in the past? And would she even bother involving Faith, or would she use Pop's desire to protect Faith against him?

Hell of a mess. So many lives involved. And justice was at the heart of the whole cluster fuck. Alex was dead. His killer had to pay.

The end justified the means. If Alex's killer was put away, all of this would be worth it. Even Faith's anger.

If he was truly convinced of this, why then did guilt weigh so heavy on him? Why did he picture Faith's sweet smile, remember the feel of her skin against his, her lips on his? And why did he want more?

It was stupid and foolhardy to initiate any sort of romantic entanglement with her. He snorted. Romantic? Who said anything about romantic? Last he checked, wanting to fuck a woman's brains out wasn't construed as romance.

He had a lot of thinking to do. He needed to call Mick so together they could come up with the best plan of action. Gray still wasn't convinced that he and Mick were handling this just right, but with Billings brushing them off and not devoting the resources necessary to bring Alex's killer to justice, Gray didn't see that they had a lot of choice in the matter.

He shoved back from his desk, stood, then headed for the door. As he passed Faith's office, he halted and backtracked. He may as well make sure the tap was still securely in place in case the mother called again.

Moving swiftly, he walked around her desk in the darkness and turned on the small desk light so he could see. He examined her phone and made sure everything was to his satisfaction. Then he made sure everything on her desk was as he'd found it. His gaze flickered across her open day planner as he reached for the button on the light.

His hand stilled, and he pulled it away as he read the entry circled in red. *The House. 11:00 P.M. Friday night.* It was written on today's date, and below was an address in north Houston.

The name was familiar to him, and he searched his memory

for why. He could swear it was the name of the kink club Micah had gone on about one day over lunch. But why on earth would Faith be making plans to visit if they were one and the same?

He opened her drawer and yanked out a pen and a piece of paper from a notepad. He scribbled the address down then closed the drawer again. After turning the light off, he hurried back to his own office where he turned his computer on.

He drummed his fingers impatiently as he waited for it to boot. As soon as the screen lit up with his desktop icons, he clicked on the browser and went to a search engine page.

There, he typed in the name and address he'd lifted from Faith's planner and waited for the results. When he clicked on the first link, he bit out a curse. Faith's *house* and Micah's were one and the same. Somehow Gray knew that Faith wasn't a regular member, because surely that wouldn't have escaped Micah's notice.

What the fuck was she doing making an appointment at a freaking kink club? Did she not have a clue what went on there? Hell, he'd never set foot in the place, but the things Micah had talked about were more than enough to paint a vivid picture in Gray's mind of what happened behind those big wrought-iron gates.

Which could only mean she had no idea what she was getting into. And the idea of another man putting his hands on her made him feel slightly murderous. He didn't even want to get into the whys and wherefores of that particular quirk.

"Jesus, Mary and Joseph," Gray muttered. "Get a grip."

He ought to call Pop and let him or Connor deal with it. But as quickly as that thought popped into his head, he tossed it aside. He wasn't a kid busting a gut to run and tattle, for God's sake. Faith was a grown woman. Maybe she was doing a little experimenting.

No need to embarrass her by having her brother haul her out of the place.

Which left him. No way he could let her walk into that kind of situation. She was sweet. Far too innocent for the likes of what a place like The House offered its patrons. Shit, knowing his luck, she'd end up as someone's damn sex slave for the night.

That thought propelled him to his feet. He was out the door in a few seconds. He fumbled with the security codes on his way out before he strode out to the parking lot and his truck.

He flipped open his cell phone and punched in Micah's number. The damn club was exclusive, and he couldn't get in without Micah's help. Hell, he might not get in anyway. But he'd damn sure see if could.

He tried Micah's home number and his cell without any luck. Growling in frustration, he stepped on the accelerator and headed toward the apartment complex.

When he whipped into the parking lot a few minutes later, he saw Micah's truck parked outside his unit. Faith was already gone.

He hopped out of the truck and hurried up to Micah's door. He knocked loudly and waited. When Micah didn't immediately come to the door, he pounded harder.

A few seconds later, the door jerked open, and Micah stood in the doorway holding a towel around his waist. He glared at Gray. "This better be damn good, Montgomery."

Before Gray could respond, he heard a female voice in the background ask Micah who it was. Micah turned and held out a placating hand. "Give me just one minute, babe."

Gray sighed. Interrupting Micah during sex couldn't be all that uncommon, considering the guy had a girl over every other day. He didn't have time for this shit.

Micah turned around to stare at him again, his scowl ferocious. "Now what the fuck do you want?" he demanded.

"I need you to get me into The House or whatever the fuck it is you call it."

Micah blinked several times. His mouth popped open, and a look of incredulity spread over his features. "You came over here at eleven damn o'clock at night because you've got an itch you want to scratch?"

"Not me, dumb-ass. Apparently Faith has an appointment there. As we speak."

Micah's expression rapidly changed from annoyance to sharp interest. He held up his hand. "Whoa. Wait a minute. Faith is going to The House?"

"That's what I've been trying to tell you," Gray said impatiently. "Is there any way you can get me in? Pull some strings or something?"

Micah ignored Gray's question and shook his head in confusion. "What the fuck is she doing going there? That's no place for a girl like her."

Gray threw up his hands and growled in frustration.

"Okay, okay, look," Micah said, holding both hands up in appeasement. "Let me get dressed. I'll head over there to see what the fuck is going on."

"No."

Micah looked up in surprise.

"I'll go. You just get me in there," Gray said emphatically. "Besides, you've got company to entertain. I'll take care of Faith."

Micah gave him a long, assessing look. His eyes narrowed, and he frowned. "What the hell is going on between you and Faith?"

Gray sighed. They were wasting a hell of a lot of time. "Nothing is going on between me and Faith. I was just concerned when I learned where she was going. I don't think she has a clue what she's getting into. I don't want to see her get hurt."

"On that we agree," Micah said. "You head over there. Do you know where it is?"

Gray nodded.

"Okay, you go. I'll call over and arrange for you to get in. I'm good friends with the guy who owns it."

Gray turned without responding and hurried back out to his truck. He felt a little foolish making such a big deal out of this, and he'd risked looking an even bigger fool by coming over to Micah's like this, but he couldn't shake the feeling that Faith was in way over her head.

CHAPTER 14

$\mathcal{F}$aith pulled up to the gate guarding the driveway to the large house looming up the hill. When she drew abreast of the small security box, she rolled down her window and leaned out to push the button.

"Can I help you?" a polite voice inquired.

She breathed in nervously. "I have an appointment. My name is Faith Malone."

"Please proceed, Miss Malone."

The gate slowly swung open, and she started forward, accelerating up the winding lane. When she pulled up to the house, she saw a secluded parking lot, not visible from the entrance. A large brick wall covered with ivy separated the lot from the sprawling front lawn.

She drove around the partition and eased into a parking spot beside a sleek Mercedes. As she got out and surveyed the array of very expensive cars, she glanced self-consciously back at her Honda Accord.

What kind of people gathered here? Were they all rich, bored types looking for cheap thrills?

"Nothing like making sweeping generalizations," she muttered as she headed for the double wooden doors ahead.

Before she could raise the heavy knocker, the door swung open, and she found herself staring at a good-looking, well-dressed man. Okay, not just good-looking, but *very* good-looking.

He smiled broadly at her. "You must be Faith." He held his hand out to her. "I'm Damon."

She took his hand, shook it and smiled in return. She felt some of her nervousness dissipate. "I'm so glad to meet you. I feel as though I know you with all the e-mails we've exchanged in the last week."

He chuckled then gestured for her to enter. "Please, come in."

She walked in ahead of him and paused, waiting for him to go in front of her. The foyer was elegantly decorated, the lighting dim enough to make the interior look warm and inviting but not so dark as to give off a sinister aura.

Damon walked up beside her and placed a hand to her back. "If you'll come this way, our first stop will be the sitting room where you can relax for a moment and have a drink."

He ushered her into a smaller room just beyond the foyer. The inside was classy yet comfortable. A large Oriental rug stretched across highly polished wood floors, ending just in front of a dark brown leather couch. To the right sat two overstuffed casual chairs, the kind that would swallow you up whole as soon as you sat down.

"Why don't you have a seat. Would you care for a glass of wine?"

Faith nodded and started toward one of those comfy-looking chairs.

"By the way, I like what you decided to wear very much."

She turned around, her cheeks heating as she saw his gaze slide up and down her bare legs. Damon's lips lifted in a half smile before he walked over to the wall and pressed a button on what looked to be an intercom system.

She glanced down at the form-fitting skirt that clipped her legs about two inches above her knee. The shoes, well, she had to admit, they were purely for show. In a moment of pure weakness, she'd spent a hell of a lot of money on the sex-on-a-sole shoes.

But they made her feel sexy, vibrant and a little bad. Okay, a whole lot bad. With a tiny grin, she sank into the soft leather chair and forced herself to relax.

Damon joined her a few seconds later. Moments after he sat down on the couch across from her chair, the door opened, and a man who looked every bit the butler out of some stodgy English movie walked in carrying a serving tray.

He bent and offered her one of the crystal flutes. Her eyes widened, and she smiled at the oh-so-proper man. She was only a little disappointed that he didn't have a British accent.

She took a glass and lifted it to her nose to inhale the aroma of the wine. The butler offered Damon a glass next then inclined his head toward Faith and retreated from the room.

"I'm guessing most of your clients are higher end," Faith said before sipping the wine.

Damon chuckled. "It's all about appearances. If you want to attract the right clientele, you have to establish yourself on their level."

"You certainly dress the part," she said dryly, her gaze moving up and down his expensive silk shirt and designer slacks.

He smiled lazily at her. "Are you comfortable here?"

She blinked at his sudden change of topic. After a moment's thought, she realized she wasn't nearly as nervous as she had been. But then this was probably part of the game plan. Ply the potential member with booze until they were too soused to worry about what they were getting into.

A giggle escaped her at that thought.

Damon looked at her in amusement. "You truly are as delightful in person as you came across on the phone and in your e-mails. I was prepared to be disappointed. I'm glad I wasn't."

Faith blushed, her cheeks warming under his scrutiny.

He leaned forward and set his glass on the mahogany coffee table. "The House is divided into two levels. The lower level is where all the socializing occurs. We invite a very relaxed, laid-back atmosphere. Rooms are set up for patrons to mingle, talk, get to know each other. We have strict guidelines for what occurs on the main level."

She pressed the rim of the glass to her lips and took a long swallow of the wine. Flutters abounded in her stomach as she listened. It was real. She was really here about to dive headfirst into . . . what? She wasn't even sure.

"The second level is where the action is, so to speak. There are a variety of rooms. Some private. Some open to the public. There is a main room, quite large, where the space is divided into different sections. This is the common area, where you'll find a variety of activities concentrated in one place. Some of our patrons enjoy the public aspect of it while others prefer and demand strict privacy. We accommodate both."

She leaned forward, her interest alive, her curiosity insatiable. "And what happens in these public areas?"

Damon smiled. "Anything and everything. You must prepare yourself for any possibility. The House is a place to let your inhibitions fly away. When you step through our doors, you are free to become someone else entirely, or, as I suspect in your case, embrace who you really are. No one is judged here. We are very open and accepting of all lifestyles."

"And the membership qualifications," Faith began. "You said they were stringent. I assume this means that members are screened and that the 'activities' here are monitored for safety?"

"Excellent question," Damon said, his eyes flaring with approval. "Our members do go through a strenuous screening process. We require extensive background checks. No one with any criminal record, regardless of charge, is allowed membership.

"All rooms are monitored by our staff. For those congregating in the public areas, staff members maintain a presence at all times. For the members who prefer private accommodations, well, even then they aren't afforded complete privacy because we have surveillance cameras installed in each room, and a staff member closely monitors them at all times.

"Not only are we dedicated to providing an environment where members may play out their fantasies and lifestyle choices, but we absolutely guarantee the safety of each and every participant."

Her eyes widened. "That seems a lot to guarantee."

Damon nodded. "Yes, but we are one hundred percent committed to keeping that promise. We do not hesitate to step in if we feel the situation is unsafe for one or more members."

Faith was impressed by his confidence and his air of authority. In fact, he managed to make her feel not so much like a weird freak sneaking around some seedy sex club looking for cheap thrills.

"Are you ready for your tour?" he asked.

She swallowed and set her glass down on the coffee table. "Yes. Yes, I think I am."

CHAPTER 15

*H*e stood and offered his hand to her. She took his hand and let him help her rise. Her legs trembled, and she hoped she could keep her knees from knocking together. She found she wasn't so much nervous as she was excited. Intrigued. And more than a little turned on.

"I'll be with you every step of the way. If you have any questions, any concerns, I'll be happy to address them."

Faith smiled. "Okay then. I'm ready."

He tucked her hand under his arm and escorted her out the door of the sitting room. "We'll tour the social rooms on the lower level first. It will give you an idea of how relaxed things are here. No one will expect you to interact or to greet them unless that is your wish. Everyone here is well used to circumspection."

She squeezed his arm with her fingers. He turned and looked questioningly at her.

"I really appreciate all you've done to make me feel at ease. If you do this with all your members, I can understand why your establishment is so successful."

He smiled and laid his hand over hers. "I just hope you find what it is you're looking for."

So do I.

They entered a larger room where several people stood and sat around talking. It was a party environment, but not the loud, raucous variety. This was more like an upscale gathering where the talk was hushed. Soothing piano music played in the background, and a waiter walked among those gathered, distributing glasses of wine and hors d'oeuvres.

A few turned and smiled at Damon, but none approached him.

"This is the main meeting room. Usually the first stop for anyone coming into The House. From here, people split off or go on upstairs to other pursuits. It's not always about sex or wanting to play. Many of our members just come here to meet with like-minded people and spend the evening talking and visiting."

They spent a few moments circling the room, and Faith tried hard not to study the other members. They'd certainly afforded her the courtesy of not staring. But still, she couldn't resist quick glances from the corners of her eyes.

There was an interesting mix of people. Some were dressed to the nines while others had adopted a much more casual look. Jeans, T-shirts, tennis shoes. She was glad she'd opted for a compromise between übercasual and very dressy.

Absent, much to her relief, were the leather Klingon costumes she was embarrassed to admit she'd thought she'd see. To her further surprise, the people gathered all looked like normal, average, everyday people.

Maybe she'd expected replicas of the oddities she'd found

while scouring the internet, but clearly, those weren't to be found here.

Damon touched her arm, and she looked up at him.

"Are you ready to move on?" he asked.

She nodded, and he led her out of the room and down the hall to a smaller, more intimate gathering. Here, most people were seated in tight-knit groups. Two men sat on a love seat, and a woman perched on one of their laps conversing with both guys. The second man smoothed his hand up and down her leg while the other man's hands clasped loosely around her hips.

Faith's cheeks grew warm again. It was obvious the woman held the attention of both males. A satisfied smile curved the beautiful woman's lips.

Faith's gaze was riveted to the scene before her so intently that she had to force herself to drag her stare away to take in the other occupants of the room.

Several feet away, a large man turned around, and when he saw Damon, a wide smile split his face. He waved and motioned them over. Faith panicked a moment as Damon started forward.

Damon looked down at her and smiled reassuringly. "It's okay," he murmured.

They walked up to the man, who studied Faith with undis-guised interest. He was older. Not *old* but older than Faith. She put him in his upper thirties.

"Damon, it's good to see you," the man said, extending his hand.

Damon smiled broadly and shook his hand. "Tony, good to see you." He looked back at Faith. "Faith, I want you to meet Tony. Tony, this is Faith. She's my special guest tonight."

Faith shivered as Tony's intent gaze flickered over her. He slowly held his hand out to her. "Very glad to meet you, Faith."

When she slid her hand into his, instead of shaking it, he pulled it upward to kiss the back of her hand. She blushed madly.

Tony gave a delighted chuckle as he released her hand. "I love a woman who blushes."

"We won't keep you," Damon said to Tony. "I have a tour to give."

"It was very nice to meet you, Faith. I do hope to see you again," Tony said in a low voice.

The blatant invitation sent goose bumps over her skin. Her stomach churned with nervous anxiety, and she was grateful that Damon was even now pulling her away.

Her fingers curled just a little tighter around Damon's arm as he led her toward the stairs. On the way, they passed two other side rooms where people had broken off into smaller groups to talk and socialize.

"Ready?" he asked as they reached the bottom of the stairs.

She took a deep breath and tried to settle all the butterflies doing somersaults in her stomach. "Ready."

He smiled and started up the stairs. When they reached the top, she was surprised by the closed door. Damon reached for the knob. "The walls up here are soundproof. It's to keep distractions to a minimum."

When he opened the door, the murmur of voices reached her ears. She strained to hear more as they eased down the hallway. They passed several closed doors, and Damon made no move to open those. They must be the private accommodations he'd mentioned. What she wouldn't give to know what was going on behind those doors.

As they ventured farther down the long hallway, other sounds tickled her ears. Curious sounds. Moans, a few gasps, a slapping sound, like the smack of skin on skin. They grew louder until she and Damon paused inside the doorway to a large common room.

Though there was no actual divider, the room was arranged into several sections merely by the arrangement of various furniture. The decor was also different for the segments.

Women, men, some nude, some not, some indulging in passionate embraces, some in positions she couldn't quite discern the purpose for, dotted the room.

Damon seemed to realize she needed the time to sort through the barrage of images coming too hard and fast for her to digest right away.

"Let's start to the right," he murmured to her. "We'll make the circle."

Damon drew up short when someone touched him on the arm and leaned in to whisper in his ear. It looked to be one of the people who worked for him, though she couldn't be sure.

Damon frowned then put a hand to her back. "There's a phone call I must take. I won't be but a moment. Joseph will stay here with you until I return."

He squeezed her hand with his other one before turning away and retreating down the hallway.

Joseph stood attentively by her side as her gaze again wandered over the room. There was so much to take in that she had a hard time processing it all.

To her immediate right, where Damon had intended for them to begin, two men were entangled in a passionate embrace on a pallet that reminded her of something you might find in a Japanese bedroom.

Though their kisses were wild, rushed, heated, they set about removing their clothes in a slow, measured manner. When she realized how hard she was staring, she looked away, embarrassed and ashamed to have ogled them.

"It's okay," Joseph whispered close to her ear. "No one in the public areas minds being watched. Many of our regulars routinely observe such displays. Voyeurism is a very legitimate sexual pleasure."

Her gaze shot to his face, and heat crawled all the way up her neck and burned her ears. Just the word *voyeur* sounded ugly and more than a little icky.

Joseph smiled patiently at her as if understanding her discomfort.

But even though she was embarrassed by her close scrutiny of the two men, her gaze drifted back. The sight of two men locked in such an erotic embrace fascinated her.

Her eyes widened more when one of the men pulled at the other man's pants, freeing his turgid erection. Her lips parted, a little in shock, a little because her breaths were coming in short, rapid spurts.

When the first man gently moved his lips over the other man's cock, Faith's pulse began racing. The sight should repulse her. Something told her it should, but just as quickly she discounted that absurd notion.

The man's eyes cut over in her direction, and for a moment their gazes locked. She should look away, but she found herself unable to do so. A soft, secret smile curved the man's lips as he worked his mouth up and down his lover's cock. Then he winked saucily at Faith. She grinned and winked back then promptly scolded herself for being so brazen.

She jumped when Damon put his hand on her arm. She hadn't even realized he'd returned. He smiled at her. "My apologies. I had to take a call from one of our members. Are you ready to continue?"

Her gaze returned to the two men making love on the silk-covered pallet before she nodded.

The next area featured two couples, one on a couch and the other on the floor, pillows surrounding them. The woman on the couch leaned back against the back, her legs splayed out in front of the man kneeling in front of her. His head lowered to her pussy, and her hand threaded through his hair, urging him on.

The woman on the floor was positioned on her hands and knees as the man behind her thrust eagerly into her body.

"Partner swapping," Damon said in a low voice.

Faith's eyes widened. "Oh, you mean like swinging?"

Damon smiled. "I suppose you could put it that way."

He cupped her elbow in his hand and pointed with his other hand to an area in the corner. "I think the next few might interest you."

When she looked up and saw what he was gesturing at, her mouth went dry. A woman was tied to a bed, her arms pulled above her head and secured to the bedposts.

She was blindfolded and gagged. A man held her legs apart and draped her ankles over his shoulders as he thrust into her repeatedly. Despite the gag, Faith could hear her moans of pleasure. Mixed with the heavy slap of the man's thighs against the back of her legs, it sounded incredibly erotic.

A tingle began in Faith's stomach and worked its way downward until her clit tightened and strained between her legs. Her nipples beaded and formed taut points. She crossed her arms self-consciously over her chest, not wanting anyone to see her visible reaction to the scene playing out before her.

Her eyes were riveted, and she was unable to tear herself away from sight and sounds of the couple. She blinked in surprise when another man sauntered to the bed, one hand wrapped around his jutting cock.

The first man pulled away from the woman while the second settled between her legs and immediately began rocking against her. The first man moved up the bed and began toying with the woman's nipples, plucking them between his fingers. Then he bent and began sucking and nipping at them while the second man seemed intent on fucking her silly.

All the while, the woman writhed beneath them, her arms straining against her bonds. Faith's eyes were glued to the ropes around the woman's wrists, and a peculiar ache settled in her chest as she imagined herself in the woman's place.

"You like this," Damon said quietly.

Faith nodded, unwilling to voice her agreement.

"Then come. There's more," he said simply.

She followed, though she was reluctant to leave the triad. She wanted to see it played out until the end. Until the men relented and gave the woman her release.

They moved to the back of the room, directly across from the doorway they'd entered. Faith cocked her head in curiosity as she watched a man push a woman to her knees in front of him. He reached for the zipper of his pants and a few seconds later pulled out his cock.

With his free hand, he cupped the woman's chin and tilted her head up so her mouth brushed against his erection.

"Open," he commanded.

She dutifully complied.

He arched his hips forward, sliding his cock deep into her

mouth. His hand still cupped her jaw, and his thumb pressed into her cheek to keep her mouth open. He slid his other hand to the back of her head, his fingers tangling in her hair as he fucked her harder.

For several long seconds, the only sound was the wet sucking noise as his hips met her cheeks. The image did more for her than the action. Here was a man who obviously exerted control over the woman. He wasn't loud or obnoxious, in fact, he very quietly uttered his commands, but there was a thread of authority in his voice that sent shivers skirting down Faith's spine.

The man suddenly pulled back. "Rise," he ordered the woman.

The woman rose on shaky legs, her naked breasts bobbing as she caught her breath. The man reached for a wooden paddle resting on a nearby table then motioned the woman over with his hand. Faith's gaze followed the woman as she moved to an oddly shaped object that was a strange mixture of metal and leather padding.

The center had a scooped-out spot that reminded Faith of an inverted saddle. Its use was made clear when the woman bent over it, the notch cradling her abdomen.

Her legs rested against the inverted V that sprouted from the cradle until her body maintained the exact line of the apparatus.

Her head fell over the other side, and her arms dangled, then her hands grasped at the base to steady herself.

Faith's gaze flitted back to the man, who circled behind the woman, his steps slow and measured. His fingers curled around the paddle that resembled some old-school discipline stick.

His hand cupped and caressed the woman's bare ass. Then he pulled the paddle back and connected with her ass cheek. Faith jumped as the smacking sound filled the air.

The woman also jumped then let out a small moan as she settled back into position.

"You are to make no sound," the man commanded. He struck her again, this time on the other cheek.

Blood rushed to Faith's head, and her pulse pounded hard against her temples. Her fingers shook, and she curled them into balls at her side.

The man continued his show of dominance, and Faith had little time to ponder her extreme reaction to this particular scene.

She was too busy absorbing it, experiencing the confusing thrill.

"Tell me, would you like to try it?" Damon asked.

CHAPTER 16

$\mathcal{F}$aith jerked her gaze from the couple and stared at Damon in surprise. "I don't understand."

"Would you like to take her place?" he asked, gesturing to the woman being spanked. "Of all the scenes, you seem to be the most keenly attuned to this one. You're here to explore your desires. What better way than to experience it firsthand?"

"You allow that?" she asked incredulously.

He smiled patiently. "We don't make choices for our members or prospective members. You're here to make a decision about whether this is something you want. I merely want to aid you in that decision. Think of it as test-driving a car before purchasing it."

She laughed. She couldn't help it. The idea of comparing getting naked in front of strangers to test-driving a car seemed ludicrous. But then as she gazed around at the people milling about the room, no one seemed to put much stock in nudity. She was the only one gaping like a kid in a candy store.

"What do I do?" she whispered. God, could she do this? She wanted to. No doubt about that. But the thought of doing it nearly made her sick with nervousness.

Damon touched her cheek and rubbed a finger down her jawline in a soothing manner. "I'll be here the entire time. I'll help you undress, and I'll stay beside you. You can do as much or as little as you'd like. I'm just here to monitor, to make sure you aren't hurt and that no one makes you do something you don't want. Those are the only rules. Everything else goes."

She swallowed, closed her eyes then opened them again to see him staring at her. Then she nodded. "Okay. Yes. I want to very much."

He smiled then. "Good. See, you're already taking control of your desires."

Again her gaze flitted around the room. To her relief, no one seemed to be paying her any attention. She had this embarrassing image of everyone stopping what they were doing to stare at her.

Damon gestured at the man, who paused and nodded. Then the man touched the woman's shoulder and helped her into an upright position. To Faith's surprise, he bent to kiss her before motioning her away.

"I'm not intruding on a relationship am I?" Faith asked hesitantly.

Damon shook his head then put both hands on her shoulders. "I'm going to undress you now. Are you sure you want to go through with this?"

Oh hell, please, please don't puke. She inhaled deeply through her nose and nodded.

Damon let his hands trail from her shoulders to the waistband of her skirt. "Turn around," he ordered softly.

She did as he asked, shivering at the firm tone of his voice. Did he know how much the air of authority turned her on? He must. He'd pretty much been her sole confidant in this venture, which was odd, considering they were virtual strangers. Or maybe they were virtual friends since they'd only talked through the internet. A nervous giggle quivered in her throat, and she swallowed it back.

His fingers fumbled with the button and zipper of her skirt. He undid both and let the material fall in a pool at her feet. She didn't look down. She wouldn't look down. She had no desire to see herself standing in heels, underwear and her shirt.

"Back around," he ordered.

Slowly, she rotated, her gaze cast to the floor.

Gathering the material of her silky camisole in his fingers, he tugged upward. "Arms over your head," he said.

She complied, and he pulled the shirt free of her body. She closed her eyes and crossed her arms over as much bare skin as she could.

"Arms down."

Again, his voice sent shivers quaking over her body. Slowly, she let her arms fall until she stood in front of him, clad in only her panties and bra.

"Open your eyes. Look at me," Damon said.

She pried one eye open then the other. Behind Damon, the man with the paddle stood looking at her, interest darkening his brown eyes.

"You're a beautiful woman, Faith. Embrace it. Don't be ashamed of it."

He tugged at her bra straps until they tumbled down her shoulders. He stepped close to her and reached around to undo the clasp. All too soon, the bra fell away, and her immediate reaction was to cover herself with her hands. But Damon grabbed her wrists with his hands.

"No."

The one word shot over her, and she stood, knees quaking, waiting for the rest.

"Slip out of your shoes," he said calmly.

She kicked them off and nudged them away with her toe.

His hands glided down her sides to her hips, where his fingers dug into the lacy band of her panties. Slowly and methodically, he inched them down until they too fell to the floor.

Oh God, she was naked. Was it possible to endure a full body blush? Because she felt red-hot from head to toe, and she bet her skin had to be flushed.

Damon's hands returned to her hips. His fingers brushed her skin lightly as they climbed higher to her breasts. He palmed the fleshy mounds and rubbed his thumb over the nipples until they hardened to puckered buttons.

Liquid heat pooled between her legs, and more than anything she wanted to slide her fingers down to her clit so she could alleviate the burning ache.

He reached down for her hand then turned to the man standing behind him. "She's all yours, Brent."

Faith gulped and waited for the man's command. Brent's eyes narrowed as he studied her. She felt his gaze on parts of her body that already tingled and pulsed.

"Come to me," he said.

She moved forward with halting steps. He pointed to the same apparatus the last woman had lain across.

"Stomach down, arms over the other side, legs spread and lined up with the legs of the stool."

She bit her lip but complied, moving forward to fit her stomach to the warm leather pad. She leaned forward then felt Damon's hands on her back as he helped her into position.

"If at any time you want to stop, just say so," Damon said close to her ear. "I'll be right here."

Another hand, one more unfamiliar, caressed her ass. The sheer forbidden quality of a stranger touching her so intimately should be more exciting. Though her legs trembled and felt jelly-like, Brent's touch failed to fire her senses.

Without warning, the paddle met the flesh of her ass in a loud smack. She jumped. It startled her. Then she frowned. While she hadn't envisioned some stinging, lashing blow, the light pat on her ass had been just that. A pat.

The paddle fell again, this time on the other cheek as he had done with the other woman. Her brow furrowed. Was this all there was to it?

Her nerve endings were on fire with anticipation. She wanted—no she needed—something, though she wasn't sure what. More of a push, more of an edge. Not this light pat on the butt she was getting.

Another blow fell, and tears of disappointment pricked her eyes. She raised her head, prepared to tell Damon to make Brent stop when her gaze locked on the entrance across the room.

A gasp escaped her that had nothing to do with the blow that landed on her backside. Standing in the entrance, his gaze solidly locked on her, was Gray.

CHAPTER 17

*G*ray stood in the doorway, arms crossed, a fierce expression on his face. What on earth was he doing here? Mortification gripped Faith as he continued to stare at her, tension rolling off him in waves.

But then she shook her head. No, she had nothing to be ashamed of. She didn't know what the hell he was doing here, and she didn't care. She gazed defiantly at him, determined not to back down in shame.

Her head slowly lowered, and she shut her eyes tight in disappointment as another tap landed on her behind. It wasn't real. None of it was real. A tear dripped down and hit the floor beneath her.

Clearly this was all for show, a spectacle more for the observer than the participant. Or maybe it just didn't do it for her. She felt so close. On the cusp of something.

Her skin crawled with need. She felt edgy, restless, and she'd had enough.

Once again, she raised her head and opened her mouth to halt the entire process. Her mouth continued to gape open when she saw Gray standing just a foot away, his eyes blazing with promise. Promise of what?

Brent stepped back, then moved toward Gray. Out of the corner of her eye, she saw the two men size each other up. Then Gray turned his head to Damon. "May I?" he asked as he gestured toward the paddle in Brent's hand.

Damon shook his head resolutely. "Absolutely not."

"Ask her," Gray said in a steely voice. "Ask her if she wants it." His blue eyes caressed her face, challenging her, baiting her.

God, he wanted to spank her? Her body prickled to life, and her blood roared like a raging river in her veins. She gulped, trying to breathe around her heavy tongue.

Damon looked between her and Gray, his expression questioning. "Faith? Is this something you want? He isn't a member here. He'll be escorted out. All you have to do is say the word."

She licked dry lips, trying desperately to work up the nerve to go where she dared. Slowly she nodded.

"No, Faith, I have to hear you. You tell me what you want," Damon insisted.

"Yes," she whispered. "Yes," she said in a louder voice. "Please." Her voice cracked, and she relaxed her neck for a moment, the strain of holding her head up uncomfortable.

She was crazy. This cemented it. But Brent wasn't doing it for her. In fact, for as turned on as she was by the visuals she'd experienced, as soon as Brent had touched her, she'd gone as flat as day-old Coke.

The idea of Gray touching her, of him being the one to

dominate her . . . She shuddered and felt a surge of moisture between her legs.

A firm hand cupped her chin and directed her gaze up. She met Gray's eyes and blinked as he stared piercingly at her.

"Can you take it, Faith?"

He'd thrown down the challenge now. Her eyes narrowed.

"Don't play games," he said softly. "I'll take you where you want to go, but you have to be willing to get there."

He stared at her for another long second before letting her chin slide from his hand. She cocked her head to the side to watch him as he turned to Damon.

"Tie her hands," he directed.

She swallowed in surprise and started to protest, but she bit her tongue. No, this was what she wanted. And she knew Damon would call a halt if she so much as squeaked.

Damon bent and tied one wrist to the leg of the stool with a leather thong. Then he secured her other one.

"And her ankles," Gray said.

She closed her eyes, anticipation nearly undoing her as both ankles were tied to the wooden legs. Lord, but she felt vulnerable. Tied hand and foot, ass in the air, pussy exposed for the world to see.

And it stirred her as nothing ever had before.

She heard his footsteps as he moved around behind her. One finger trailed down the seam of her ass and paused just above her pussy entrance.

Touch me. Oh please touch me.

But he didn't.

He pulled his hand away, and then the paddle met her flesh in a stinging smack. Her body lurched forward, and her eyes flew open in shock.

"Wait for it," he murmured from behind her.

The burn radiated from her buttocks and was soon replaced by a hazy glow that bled into her body. Before she had time to fully process the sensation, he delivered another stinging blow.

Her eyes closed, and she relaxed her head. A moan escaped her as the heat simmered over her skin. Again, the paddle connected. One side. Then the other. Soon her body was awash in what she could only describe as an edgy, euphoric shimmer.

He placed the swats strategically, never hitting the same spot twice. She strained against her bonds, nearly weeping with her need to achieve her release. She wanted more, craved more, and yet she wasn't sure she could handle more.

What was happening to her?

Ten? A dozen? She lost count. Then nothing. Silence fell. Cool air washed over her burning bottom. She let out a low wail.

"Please," she whispered.

He leaned over her. She could feel his shirt against her shoulders. "What do you want, Faith?" he whispered in her ear. "Tell me what you want."

"I want to come," she gasped out.

His fingers found her pussy. As soon as he touched her clit, she went off like a firecracker. Her head arched, and she cried out as the explosion rocked her to her core.

He continued to massage and manipulate her clit until she cried out for him to stop. She collapsed her tense muscles, lying over the stool like a limp, overcooked noodle.

Gentle hands untied her wrists, and she pried open her eyes to see Damon in front of her, his gaze questioning.

"Are you all right?" he asked.

She nodded, unable to do more than that.

Gray put his hands around her shoulders and pulled her up to stand beside him. When she got enough nerve to look him in the eye, she saw a mixture of confusion, desire and anger in his eyes.

"Get dressed," he muttered.

Damon handed her clothes to her, and she yanked on her skirt and blouse, not bothering with the underwear.

"She's going home," Gray threw out in Damon's direction.

Damon lifted a brow as he looked at Faith for confirmation. She bit back a smile. Then she leaned over and kissed him on the cheek.

"Thank you," she whispered. "I think I found exactly what I wanted."

CHAPTER 18

Gray all but hauled her from the room and into the darkened hallway. As soon as they were away from prying eyes, he shoved her against the wall, forcing her hands over her head. His lips met hers in a frenzied rush.

Her body, still shaky from her explosive orgasm, nearly folded. He lowered her arms then moved his hands to her waist, then up her body to her breasts.

"I wanted to touch them," he said hoarsely. "I wanted to touch you everywhere."

He shoved her camisole up until his hands found her breasts. He cupped them, brushed his thumbs across the sensitive peaks. Then he bent his head and sucked one of the nipples into his mouth.

Her knees buckled. She made a grab for his shoulders, wrapped her hands around his neck and clutched him to her. The air coalesced around her. Bright, shimmery sparkles seem to suspend in midair.

Every nerve ending was still supercharged from her earlier release, and his mouth on her nipples sent a raging inferno through her system.

His hand slid down her body to the hem of her skirt, and he yanked it up, baring her thighs then her pussy. He suckled her nipple then moved his head to her other one, working his mouth rhythmically.

He parted her thighs with his hand then slid his fingers into her wet folds. She groaned at the dual sensation of his fingers in her pussy and his mouth on her breast.

He let go of her nipple and stared her in the eye as he slid two fingers deep into her opening. His thumb found her clit, and he stroked.

"Come for me," he growled. "Give me one more."

As his fingers worked deep, an uncontrollable shudder rolled over her body. It started deep in her groin and radiated outward. It tightened until she felt near to bursting. And then she did.

As she cried out, he dropped his head to her neck, kissing and biting at the skin under her ear. He held her up with his free arm while his other hand slid in and out of her pussy.

She closed her eyes against the sudden burst of pleasure. It was too much and not enough all at the same time. "Oh, God," she panted.

She clung desperately to him as she rode the fierce storm of her release. He kissed her, passionately, savagely, taking everything she had and offering in return one of the most intoxicating sexual experiences of her life.

As her shudders diminished, and he withdrew his hand from between her legs, she whimpered softly. Slowly, he eased her down until her feet were solidly planted on the floor. Her gaze flickered down to his groin.

In the shadows of the hallway, she couldn't make out the bulge covered in the dark denim, but she'd felt it a moment ago. She lowered her hands and cupped him.

He went rigid against her.

"Show me how to please you," she said softly.

He hesitated and then put a hand on her shoulder. He pushed her down to her knees while reaching for his fly with the other hand.

He fumbled with the button and the zipper. As the fly parted, he reached in and pulled out his cock. Another liquid surge of desire blazed through her veins.

His hand tangled in her hair as he cupped the back of her neck. With his other hand, he guided his cock to her mouth.

"Take it deep," he rasped.

She opened her mouth and let him slide between her lips.

"Oh yeah, like that," he said with a groan.

He inched forward, pushing her head against the wall. His hand left her head, and he placed both hands above her, leaning into her.

She tasted him, curiously, wanting to absorb his flavor, his essence, everything that made him the powerful male. She enjoyed the rougher texture of his cock and the smoother, velvety softness of the head as it rubbed against her tongue over and over.

There in the hallway, for anyone to see as they passed, he fucked her mouth against the wall. She was on a high she might never come down from. It was heady, exhilarating in a way she'd never experienced.

He plunged deeper, and she forced her throat to relax around him. His hips worked back and forth, and she slid her hands around to cup his firmly muscled ass.

Again he reached down, tangling his fingers in her hair, holding her as he fucked in long strokes. Then he took her head in both hands.

"Swallow it," he said. "Take it all."

She closed her eyes as he swelled larger in her mouth. His thrusts became more urgent, shorter and faster. Then he slid deep and held himself against her, his legs and buttocks straining underneath her hands.

The first warm pulse hit the back of her throat, and she swallowed quickly to keep from choking. He eased back then thrust forward again as her mouth filled with his musk.

His hands relaxed against her head, but he continued stroking her hair as he rocked back and forth in her mouth. There was such strength in his movements, yet they echoed such gentleness. It was an addicting combination.

With seeming reluctance, he pulled away from her, his semierect cock falling from her mouth. He tucked it back into his pants and fastened them up.

She knelt there, too stunned, too out of sorts to get to her feet. She wasn't sure she had the strength anyway.

He reached down, curled his hands underneath her arms and pulled her to her feet.

"It's time to get out of here," he said gruffly.

He wrapped an arm around her waist and started to lead her to the stairs. As she glanced back down the hallway, she saw Damon standing in the doorway to the great room. How long had he stood there? Had he watched the entire interlude?

Strangely she felt no panic over the thought.

Gray hustled her down the stairs, past the social rooms and out the door leading into the small parking lot. A blast of humid air hit her in the face, sucking the breath right out of her lungs. Not that she had much to spare.

When they stepped onto the pavement, she realized she hadn't gotten her shoes. She halted and stifled a giggle.

Gray stopped and shot her a sideways look. "Something wrong?"

She looked curiously at him. He seemed so . . . pissed. So out of sorts.

"My shoes," she said. "I left them. I need to go back."

"You're not going back in there," he ground out.

She opened her mouth to protest, but he silenced her with a look.

"I'll buy you another pair. You're not going back."

Some part of her wanted to tell him to fuck off, but another part, the cautious, *smart* part of her warned her not to push right now.

He urged her forward again, his hand at her elbow. He guided her between her car and his truck, but instead of opening her door, he opened the passenger side of his truck.

"Get in," he directed.

"But my car!"

"I'll get it for you later," he said. "Get in. I'll take you home."

She stared at him for a long moment before sighing. With a resigned huff, she climbed in, and he closed the door behind her. She sat in the dark, staring straight ahead until he walked around and opened the driver's side. He slid in beside her and thrust the key into the ignition.

She watched from her periphery but he never looked her way. He backed out of the lot and headed down the long driveway, his gaze locked in front of him.

"Want to tell me what all that was about?" she asked when they turned onto the highway.

She heard something that sounded like a grunt. Unwilling to let the silence continue, she turned in her seat to face him.

"It was nothing," he muttered.

Her face twisted with incredulity. "Nothing?" She stared at him in shock. "I can still feel the marks on my ass, feel your fingers in my pussy. I can still taste you in my mouth."

He gaped at her, his eyes wide with surprise. "Don't be crude, Faith. It doesn't suit you."

"Why did you show up here, Gray? How did you know I'd be here? Because I don't believe in coincidences."

He stared out the windshield, his jaw clenched.

"Gray?"

"I saw your day planner," he mumbled.

"That doesn't explain why you showed up, why you stepped in, why you—"

"Okay, Faith, I get the point. Really, I do. Can we just drop it?"

She sucked her cheeks in until her lips pursed. Then with a shake of her head, she turned her back to him and stared out her window.

The traffic passed in a blur. The distant glow of the Houston skyline reflected off her window and bathed the night with an iridescent shine.

Had she imagined the whole damn thing? Because right now it all seemed the product of one too many vivid dreams. Good dreams, mind you. Really, *really* good dreams.

Unfortunately for her, the man behind those dreams was treating her like his worst nightmare.

What the hell had happened back there? And what the hell was Gray's problem? He acted jealous, but she wasn't anything to him. One stolen kiss didn't grant a license to spank her ass. Even if she loved every minute of it.

"You need help," she muttered. The serious lying-on-a-couch-across-from-a-shrink kind of help.

She pressed her forehead to the warm glass and closed her eyes. How had things gotten so fucked up? She couldn't even blame Gray. He'd actually salvaged what was otherwise an exercise in complete disappointment.

Why had she reacted to him and not Brent?

Because it had been real with Gray. Not a pretense. Not a show put on more for the spectator than the participant. Brent had merely toyed with her. Given her the appearance of dominance. Gray? He was a completely different story.

A fascinating, seductive story. One she wanted to watch unfold. Wanted to *experience* unfolding.

She didn't know what the hell was wrong with him, but she'd learned quite a lot tonight. Namely, that what she was looking for *was* well under her nose. His name was Gray. And he was more than capable of feeding her darkest, most secret desires.

When they pulled into the parking lot of the apartment complex, Faith didn't immediately move to open her door. Gray opened his and walked around to open it for her, but still, she sat there.

"Faith," he said, holding out his hand. "It's time you got home."

Her chest gave a jerk as she let out a dry laugh. Then she turned her stare on him.

"You're just going to ignore what happened?" She got down and stood toe-to-toe with him, craning her neck to look into his eyes. "Gray, we didn't just share a kiss, trade a few gropes and back away."

He turned his head upward to stare at the sky, his face drawn tight.

"It was a lot more than that, and you're pretending it didn't happen?"

He lowered his head again but didn't look her in the eye. "I need to go get your car," he said. "You go on in. I'll see you tomorrow."

"How are you going to get my car?" she asked in exasperation.

"Faith, please. Just go inside."

She threw up her hands and stalked off toward her door. Whatever was up his ass wasn't going to be dislodged tonight. But damn it, tomorrow he was going to talk to her.

She jammed her key into the lock and shoved her door open. A hand touched her shoulder as she started to go in. She turned around to see Gray standing there. A surge of hope rose within her.

"I need the keys," he said simply.

With a scowl, she slapped the keys against his chest, and without waiting for him to take them, she whirled around and left him standing in the doorway. She slammed the door behind her, fuming the entire time.

She clutched her arms around her waist and headed for the bathroom. Right now a long, hot bath was the first order of business. Sorting out her cluster fuck of an evening could come later.

CHAPTER 19

*G*ray stalked to Micah's apartment, trying to gain control of his raging emotions. He couldn't even begin to explain what had happened at the damn sex club. What demon possessed him to cross the line with Faith he didn't know. All he did know was that she had set fire to his senses in a way no other woman ever had.

Never would he have imagined she would have been so fiercely responsive. He'd intended to teach her a lesson. To prove to her that having her ass spanked wasn't what she wanted. God knew she hadn't responded to the pussy Dom wannabe.

He cringed as he remembered just how hard he'd marked her ass after he'd stepped in. He groaned as his cock tightened all over again. He'd expected her to hate it, to beg him to stop, and then he could tell her to get her ass out of the place and never come back.

Instead, she reacted wildly, wanting more. And when he'd touched her . . . Jesus. She'd come immediately, the sweet juices of her pussy flooding his hand. He didn't want to think of the implications of that.

He pounded on Micah's door, knowing he was going to get bitched at again for disturbing him. A few minutes later, Micah swung the door open, a resigned expression on his face. To Gray's surprise, Micah was dressed.

"So did you find Faith?" Micah demanded.

"Yeah, she's home." Gray shifted and shoved both hands into his pockets. "Look, I know I'm probably interrupting again, but I need you to ride over to the damn sex club with me and drive Faith's car back for her. I brought her home with me."

"You're not disturbing anything," Micah said. "I sent her home after you came over the first time."

Gray cocked an eyebrow in surprise.

"Picturing Faith at The House was kind of a mood killer," Micah muttered. "Let me get my wallet, and I'll hop in with you."

Gray nodded and walked back out to his truck. Mood killer? He wished seeing Faith bent over, ass in the air had killed *his* attraction. Instead, it had fired every single one of his kinkiest fantasies.

Micah jogged out a few seconds later and slid into the passenger side. Gray put it in reverse, and they headed out in silence. It didn't last long, however.

"You going to tell me what went on?"

Gray stared straight ahead, his knuckles white against the steering wheel. "No."

Micah grunted. "C'mon man. I'll find out later anyway."

Gray glared over at him. "I imagine if Faith wanted you to know her business she would have confided in you already."

Micah returned his glare. "I don't recall her confiding in you, Mr. Barge-into-the-Place-and-Haul-Her-Out-over-Your-Shoulder."

Gray sighed. Fucker had a point as much as it pained him to admit it.

"Look, dude, I just need to know if there's anyone whose ass I need to go kick. Is she okay?"

Some of Gray's irritation diminished at the concern he heard in Micah's voice. "She's fine," Gray said. "I stepped in before anything really happened."

Micah shook his head. "I don't know what's gotten into that girl. The House isn't a place I would have ever expected her to even know about much less go visit."

Gray was beginning to wonder just how much Micah or any of the other guys at Malone's, including Pop, knew about her. She was a contradiction, that was for sure. The face of an angel, sweet, innocent, soft and so very feminine. But she had a body that would tempt a man to sin. Wasn't that what all men wanted? A beautiful, demure woman in public and a sexy firebrand in private?

He wasn't going to speculate about what other men wanted, but he knew that scenario certainly did it for him.

"You're way too quiet, man," Micah spoke up. "What the hell happened tonight?"

"I'm not entirely sure," Gray said honestly.

Silence stretched between them again. Gray caught Micah staring at him from time to time. It was only a matter of time before, like Pop, Micah started the subtle (or not so subtle) prying.

"So what's between you and Faith?" Micah asked casually, though Gray could hear the keen interest in his voice.

Gray clenched his teeth then blew out a breath around them. "There's nothing between us."

"Bullshit."

Gray looked sideways at him and frowned.

"Look, dude, I'm sure you've already gotten the 'speech' from Pop. He gives it to everyone where Faith is concerned. Don't expect to get one from me. Faith is a big girl. Pop, well, I like the old fart, but he treats her like a piece of glass. He's way too over-protective of her, and I understand, given the shit she's gone through in her life, but she's tough. Much tougher than Pop gives her credit for. While I'm not crazy about her fucking around at a place like The House, I'm sure she's very capable of choosing the guy she gets involved with."

"Thanks for your support," Gray said dryly.

Micah shrugged. "I just wondered, that's all. Faith . . . well she's hot. A better girl you won't find. I'd think you were a fuck-ing pussy if you weren't attracted to her at least on some level."

"Can we stop with all the touchy-feely shit?" Gray muttered. "You sound like a damn woman."

Micah chuckled. "Hey, I just wanted to know if you'd staked a claim on Faith, because if you aren't interested in her, I might ask her out."

"Over my fucking dead body," Gray growled. As soon as the words were out of his mouth, he knew he'd been had.

Micah bent over laughing, looked up at Gray then dissolved into laughter again.

"Fuck you and the horse you rode in on."

"Don't you love it when a woman manages to twist you all up in knots?" Micah said around a bubble of laughter.

Gray briefly closed his eyes, as long as he could get away with as they zipped down the highway. This was a fucking mess. And he so wasn't in the mood for Micah's obnoxious joking.

Thank God it was Friday. He glanced at his watch. Or Satur-day morning. He wouldn't have to face Faith until Monday. But even then, he wasn't sure how the hell he was supposed to look her in the eye.

"I'm so fucked," he muttered.

Beside him Micah chuckled. Gray shot him another dirty look, but Micah regarded him innocently, a smug look on his face.

"Sure you don't want to tell me what all went on in there?" Micah asked.

"Nosy bastard."

"Can't blame a guy for trying," Micah said with a shrug. "Guess it's too bad I didn't choose to hang out at The House tonight."

"Yeah, that would have gone over real well," Gray said sourly. "I'm sure Faith would have been real happy to see you there."

Micah grinned evilly. "No happier than I imagine she was to see *you*."

"Just shut up," Gray mumbled. "Let it die already. I'm going to have to hope Faith has no more desire to rehash everything than I do."

CHAPTER 20

*W*hat kind of twisted, weird-ass woman did it make her that when she got up the next morning, the fact that she could feel the slight ache in her ass made her all quivery inside?

Faith rolled out of bed and flexed her muscles experimentally as she stood and stretched. A warm tingle buzzed up her midsection at the memory of the night before. Gray commanding her body, making her come.

She remembered every swat to her ass, how it made her feel, the delicious balance between pain and pleasure. But more than that, and something she was starting to realize, was that her reaction wasn't just to the stimuli, but to Gray. Otherwise, Brent would have been able to get her off just as quickly.

She yawned and trudged to her bathroom where she turned on the shower, full blast and blistering hot. Ten minutes later, she walked out of the bathroom, towel on her head and dressed in a T-shirt and gym shorts.

As she puttered around her kitchen, she gave thought to her most pressing dilemma: Gray.

If she lived to be a hundred, she'd never understand men. Women were supposed to be the enigmas, but men? Moody, brooding bastards, the lot of them. A woman with PMS had nothing on a man. Where women might get hormonal once a month, men suffered their own brand of PMS on a daily basis.

He wanted her. She could see it in his eyes, in his body language. He practically screamed possession. It made her shiver just to think about all that testosterone flowing behind those big muscles.

So what was his problem? Why did he shove her away like she was Satan's spawn right after they went at it in the hallway of The House?

She poured herself a glass of orange juice and padded into the living room, where she flopped on the couch. She glanced at the TV remote for all of three seconds before twisting her lips and redirecting her gaze.

She wasn't in the mood for television. What she was in the mood to do was brood and mull. Figure out this thing between her and Gray.

His directive to stay away from The House should have pissed her off, but she shrugged it off. He was right. And she had no intention of ever going back. Why should she, when she'd found exactly what she wanted, and it wasn't anything The House offered?

No, she was pretty certain she knew precisely what it was she wanted now. It just happened to come in the form of a six-foot-plus surly male. A man she was dying to taste again. Take in her mouth. In her body.

Goose bumps prickled over her arms, and she closed her eyes

to relish the memory of his hands on her body, his fingers between her legs.

Finally. Finally she'd found a man who was forceful. Strong. Unapologetic. A man who didn't ask. Who took what he wanted.

Now she just had to figure out how to reel him in.

She started when a knock sounded at her door. She hurriedly leaned forward to set her glass down on the coffee table and lurched to her feet.

On the way to the door, she found herself holding her breath, hoping it was Gray. But when she opened it, it wasn't Gray standing there. It was Damon. Damon from the sex club.

He smiled and held up his hand where the straps of her shoes dangled from his fingertips.

"I thought you might want these back," he said.

She blushed, and then she stammered, and finally she clapped her lips shut and prayed for a giant anvil to drop from the sky and crush him where he stood.

"May I come in?" he asked.

"No." Horrified that she'd said it aloud, she cleared her throat. "I mean yes. Yes, of course." She stepped back and opened the door wider.

She led him into her living room. "Would you like something to drink? Juice or water?"

He shook his head. "No, I don't have long."

She sank onto the couch while he took an armchair diagonal to her. She waited, not knowing what the hell to say or how to instigate a normal conversation. What could she say anyway? *Did you enjoy the show? Did you see me suck off Gray in the hallway after he spanked my ass?*

A red-hot glow seeped into her cheeks, and she looked down.

He dropped her shoes on the floor, and the sound made her look up again.

"I just wanted to make sure you were all right," he said softly.

Her gaze lifted to his eyes, and she saw genuine concern there. She relaxed slightly and gave him a hesitant smile.

"That was sweet of you, Damon, but you didn't need to worry about me. Or come all this way to return my shoes. Though I love those shoes." She gave them a longing glance, grateful to have them back.

Damon chuckled. "It was the least I could do. Somehow I don't think last night went as you thought it would. It certainly didn't go according to my plan."

She fidgeted in her seat and twisted her fingers together in her lap. "No, I don't suppose it did," she agreed. Then she looked directly into his soft brown eyes. "But I'm glad it did happen that way. It showed me . . . it showed me a lot." She refused to get more specific, but he seemed to understand.

He nodded. "I think I knew that. But I had to be sure."

She looked away again, down at her fingers. "Did . . . did you watch last night?" She wasn't sure why she even wanted to know, what demon prompted her to ask.

She peeked at him from the corner of her eye and saw the corners of his mouth turn slightly upward.

"Watching is what I do," he said nonchalantly. "It's my job to make sure no one is hurt."

"And what did you think?" she asked, tilting her head at an angle to look more directly at him.

He regarded her thoughtfully for a moment. "It's obvious he wasn't a stranger to you. He seemed to know what it was you most needed when even you were not certain. You reacted to him when Brent left you cold."

She inhaled in surprise.

He smiled gently. "Faith, I see a lot of people in the throes of passion. You were obviously not. You were obviously frustrated and disappointed. If your mysterious man hadn't stepped in when he did, I was prepared to stop things. It was apparent it wasn't the experience you expected or wanted."

She smiled ruefully. "Will it offend you if I tell you I won't ever be back?"

He laughed. "No. If I had to guess, you'd have one very angry man to deal with if you ever set foot back at the club."

She harrumphed under her breath, but she knew Damon was right. Gray might well blow a gasket if she ventured back into the club. On the other hand, if he reacted like he did the first time . . .

A delicious thrill coursed through her body at the thought.

Damon rose, smoothing hands down his neatly tailored slacks. She took in his appearance for the first time since he'd arrived so unexpectedly on her doorstep. He looked like money. He was the epitome of refinement. Apparently it wasn't just an act he portrayed for his job at the club.

"I should be going," he said. "I wanted to bring you your shoes and to see how you were doing after your experience last night."

She also stood and smiled. "Thanks, Damon. I appreciate it."

"Keep me posted, okay? Let me know how your search goes for you."

"Uh, well, okay, sure. I've got your e-mail."

He leaned over, cupped her elbow in his hand and kissed her

cheek. Then he headed for the door, leaving her standing there feeling slightly confused.

She sighed as he closed the door behind him. Then she flopped back on the couch and let out her breath like a sagging balloon.

Why couldn't she be attracted to Damon? He seemed open enough to the things she wanted. Hell, he'd even watched her suck off another man, and for some inexplicable reason, that didn't creep her out. It titillated her in an odd way.

Who knew she was a closet sex maniac? Okay, not maniac. One instance of public acts didn't relegate her to nympho status. What was surprising to her was her reaction to the various scenarios she'd witnessed last night.

She'd seen things that by all rights should horrify a girl like her. Instead, she'd watched with breathless wonder, a new awakening dawning inside her. But. The proverbial *but* cropped up. She wasn't sure she wanted to experience them so clinically. Like an exhibition at a freak show.

The club, while very enlightening, wasn't what she really wanted. What she wanted was to be taken on a similar journey, but she wanted the journey to be real. Not a trumped-up show for an audience. And she wanted a man who would take care of her every need.

A man like Gray.

No matter how many circles she turned in, she always ended up right back at the central point of all her struggles: Gray.

It seemed abundantly clear to her that Gray fit the bill on so many levels. Only problem was, he didn't seem to agree. He was fighting his attraction to her way too damn much. Why? That she didn't know. But she suddenly became very determined to find out.

Chapter 21

*F*inding out proved to be more frustrating than she'd possibly imagined. If Faith was determined, then Gray was even more so. Determined to avoid her, that is.

She'd gone over to his apartment not long after Damon's visit. He hadn't answered the door, even though she knew damn well he was home. Coward.

Later, she'd gone by Cattleman's when she knew he'd be getting together with Micah and the others. Only when she arrived, Gray had beat a hasty retreat, mumbling something about an appointment he'd forgotten. And Micah had stared intently at her, probing enough that she had no doubt he knew at least some of what she'd done.

Hell. At least now she knew how Gray got her car back to her apartment. At least he hadn't asked Connor to go with him. She would have had to kill him over that.

Faith ended up staying and having a few drinks with Nathan, Connor and Micah, since it would look pretty suspicious if she left on Gray's heels. So she hung around like she hadn't come looking for Gray at all.

And Micah had watched her the entire evening like he was trying to pry every one of her secrets right out of her head. By the time she did end up leaving, she couldn't get out quick enough.

Sunday was more of the same. She went over to Gray's apartment early. He didn't answer the door. Which was pretty silly, and it was really grating on her last nerve. She saw him leave in the early afternoon, and she was tempted to follow him until she thought about how stalkerish that would come across.

She'd catch him at work the next morning. He couldn't avoid her forever.

Monday morning she made sure she was in the office early. Coffee was made, donuts were laid out, and she waited for Gray to make his appearance.

He walked in with Micah and never met her gaze. Micah was more than happy to grab a cup of coffee and stuff his mouth full of a donut. But Gray retreated to his office, leaving Micah behind.

With a firm set to her lips, she poured a cup of coffee for Gray, snatched up a donut and headed for his office. If he'd locked her out, so help her God, she'd have someone break the door down.

It wasn't locked, but it was still difficult for her to navigate the door with her hands full. As she elbowed her way in, Gray looked up from his desk.

"What the hell are you trying to do, burn yourself?" he

exclaimed as he rushed around to take the coffee from her faltering fingers.

She slapped the donut on his desk and leveled a glare at him. "I was being nice. Friendly. You know, sociable. Something I can't say for you."

He swallowed hard and emitted a weary sigh. "Look, Faith, it's best . . . it's best if we just forget Friday night ever happened. I can't even begin to tell you how sorry I am that I stepped over the line like that."

She narrowed her eyes and put a hand on her hip. "Well, I'm not."

He blinked in confusion. "You're not what?"

"I'm not sorry," she said through gritted teeth. She planted both palms on his desk and leaned over until they were eye to eye. "You pretending it didn't happen doesn't make it true. It happened, Gray, and I want to talk about more than just forgetting it. I can't forget it."

He cupped her chin in his hand. "Faith, let it go. Please. Nothing good can come of us rehashing it. I wanted to teach you a lesson. I didn't like the idea of you being in there. You're a sweet girl. I like you a lot. I hope to hell you never go back. You weren't supposed to like it."

Flames scorched up her neck until her head threatened to boil over and explode.

Sweet girl. Teach a lesson. I like you a lot. What the effing hell was all that hogwash?

She tried to speak, but nothing came out. She was honest to God too pissed to formulate a coherent or even an incoherent sentence.

Finally she threw up her hands and made an *arrggg* sound before she stormed out of his office. By the time she made it back to the front, she was seething. Micah made a quick escape once he got a look at her. Smart guy.

Once he was out, she did something she rarely ever did. She shut her office door, a clear beacon to anyone not to enter. She could count on one hand the times she'd resorted to such drastic measures since coming to work for Pop. Now certainly qualified as a necessary time.

She tossed the donuts in the trash and poured the coffee down the drain, never mind that the others hadn't been the one to piss her off. But they'd suffer her wrath just like Gray.

When she was through with her huff, she flopped into her swivel chair and turned her gaze up to the ceiling.

She needed a vacation. A break. Something. Between her mother driving her to drink, her foray into a risqué sex club, and Gray driving her crazy, she was ready for the white suits to come bearing an I-love-me jacket and take her to a padded cell.

Running away wasn't something she'd ever been tempted to do. All her life, she'd stuck with it, even when sticking with it meant supporting an incompetent mother and her many vices. No, Faith wasn't a quitter. She had too much work ethic ingrained in her. Closest she'd ever come to running away from anything was when her mother had overdosed and Pop and Connor had come and all but dragged her home with them.

But now? Getting away from the insanity that had become her life in the past few weeks was vastly appealing. Maybe she should hit Pop up for some vacation time. She knew he'd grant it in a heartbeat, because she'd never taken any.

"Quit overreacting," she muttered.

A vacation did sound awfully good though. She'd definitely have to consider it.

A cautious tap sounded at her door, and she glared in that direction, wondering who the brave fool was who risked her wrath.

Nathan stuck his head in the door and glanced questioningly at her. "Mornin', Faith. I ah, just wanted to see if you were okay."

"PMS," she said, knowing it was the one thing guaranteed to make him haul ass in the opposite direction. And she was right. He couldn't get out fast enough.

She giggled when he shut the door in a nanosecond. Men were such pussies.

"So what the fuck did you do to piss Faith off? Apart from barge in on her night of hedonistic delight," Micah said as he and Gray got into Micah's truck to head to a job.

Micah fumbled around in the glove compartment and dragged out a pack of cigarettes. He flicked his lighter as he backed out of the parking lot then inhaled deeply, briefly closing his eyes.

"Guess you haven't quit yet," Gray observed.

Micah cracked his window and flicked his ashes. "Going to answer my question?" he asked, ignoring Gray's statement.

Gray sighed. "I'm avoiding her, and apparently, it's pissing her off."

"Can't imagine why," Micah said dryly.

"It's for the best."

Micah took a long drag from his cigarette and looked mournfully at the glowing tip. "Damn things are going to kill me, but I spent too many years smoking on the job. Hard as hell to kick the habit."

"Why'd you quit?" Gray asked curiously.

"The job or the cigarettes?" Micah joked.

Gray laughed.

Micah's expression turned serious. "Just had enough."

For a moment, Gray could swear he read deep sadness in Micah's expression. Micah tossed the cigarette out the window and immediately reached for another. His fingers shook as he fumbled with the lighter. Gray sensed there was a lot more to it than he'd "had enough," but he didn't feel comfortable prying, and Micah didn't seem inclined to offer further explanation.

They rode in silence for several minutes before Micah flicked the butt out the window and looked back over at Gray.

"You can't avoid her forever, you know. She deserves better than that anyway."

Gray didn't respond, but then what could he say?

Faith sighed when she heard a tapping at her office door. When she didn't respond, the door opened, and Nathan tentatively stuck his head around. "Is it safe to come in?" he asked.

"Will you go away if I say no?"

"Uh, no, I need a favor," he said, giving her a charming grin.

"You're either really brave or really stupid," she muttered.

His grin got bigger as he pushed farther into the room. "My mama always said I was her brightest child."

"Were your siblings particularly stupid?" she asked dryly.

He adopted a wounded look and clutched his chest. He ambled over and slouched in a chair in front of her desk, still holding his chest like she'd inflicted a mortal blow.

"What's the favor?" she asked in resignation.

To her surprise, his cheeks darkened. She raised a brow, intrigued by his reaction.

"I, uh, wondered if you'd go with me to get my ear pierced," he mumbled.

Her mouth fell open, and laughter bubbled in her throat. "You're going to get it done? Really?"

He fidgeted and rubbed his left ear. "Yeah, I think so. But I don't really know where to go. Well, not a place where I wouldn't feel like a dumb-ass anyway."

"I know just the place," she said as she reached for the phone. "I can take you where I get my hair done and let Julie pierce your ear. The girls there will love you."

"Girls?" He visibly perked up.

She laughed. "Yeah, this is a girly place."

He definitely looked interested, but then he scowled. "You're not going to tell anyone where we're going, right?"

She giggled. "You'll owe me a favor, but no, I won't tell anyone. Maybe I can sign you up for a few tanning sessions so your head catches up with the rest of your body." She let her gaze drift appreciatively over his tanned arms. Then she reached over and ran a hand over his bald head.

He frowned. "You're not turning me into some metrosexual sissy."

Her shoulders shook with mirth. "Perish the thought. Too bad you're not into the spa experience. Julie also gives a mean massage."

"Massage?"

"Yeah, but you'd have to get naked." She bit her lip to stifle the grin.

"Are there other naked women there?" he asked.

She lost the battle and snickered.

"Do you get naked when you go?" Nathan asked, as if the idea had just occurred to him.

She snorted. "As if I'd tell you."

"C'mon, Faith. Give a guy a bone here."

She grinned. "Want me to call Julie and have her hook you up with a complete package?"

He stared suspiciously at her. "I'm not so sure about this. I might get my penis revoked by the league of manly men if this shit ever gets out."

Faith rolled her eyes. "Don't be such a pussy. Who's going to find out? You could do worse than having a gorgeous woman feel you up for a half hour."

"Gorgeous?"

"Change your mind?" she teased.

"And you swear you won't breathe a word of this to anyone."

She held up two fingers. "Swear."

CHAPTER 22

*S*he'd thought about it the entire night. It had actually hit her as she sat in the spa waiting on Nathan, and once the idea had presented itself, she hadn't been able to shove it out of her mind. It had unfolded in exacting detail along with her smug assuredness that it just had to work. It was perfect.

So here she sat, the next day, waiting for everyone to leave the office so she could sneak Pop's spare key to Gray's apartment.

Of course, Connor picked today to host a client meeting in the main conference room. She glanced at her watch, knowing she had limited time if she was going to get into Gray's apartment before he finished up at his current jobsite.

She breathed a huge sigh of relief when she heard the murmur of voices in the hallway. A few seconds later, Connor and the three clients he'd met with walked by her office. She sat fidgeting in her chair until she heard Connor return.

"Hey," he said as he stuck his head in her door. "You didn't have to stay."

She smiled brightly. "Oh, no problem. I have a few things to finish up. I'm planning to leave in a few minutes."

"Want me to wait?" he offered.

She waved him away. "No, you go ahead. Nathan and Micah are waiting for you at Cattleman's."

"See you tomorrow then," he said before he ducked back out.

She waited until she was sure he was gone and then hurried back to Pop's office. She fumbled through the desk drawer where he kept all the spares until she came to the one marked with Gray's apartment number. Triumphantly, she palmed it and walked back to her office to collect her purse.

She dug out her cell phone on her way out and punched in Micah's number.

"Hey, sweet thing," Micah said when he answered the phone.

"Are you with Nathan?" she asked.

"Yeah, why?"

"Don't let him know it's me you're talking to," she hurried to say.

He paused. His tone grew serious. "What's going on?"

"I need a favor," she said. "A no-questions-asked favor."

"Uh, okay."

"Can you ditch Nathan and meet me at Gray's apartment right now?"

"I'll be right over," he said.

She sighed in relief. "Thank you. See you soon."

She closed her phone, grateful he'd done as she'd requested and asked no questions. Not that he wouldn't have plenty when he saw her, but at least he hadn't let on in front of Nathan.

She drove straight home and parked in her spot. She glanced warily down at Gray's empty parking place and hoped he stayed tied up at the job for another half hour like he was supposed to.

She sat in her car, drumming her fingers on the steering wheel until she saw Micah pull in and park a few places down. Gray's key in hand, she got out and hurried over to meet Micah.

"Hey, baby doll, what's going on?" he asked as she approached. His brow was creased in concern.

She grabbed his hand and pulled him toward Gray's door. "I'll tell you when we get inside his apartment."

"Oooh, breaking and entering. You know how to have fun, girl."

She laughed. The nut. She held up the key when they got to the door. "It's not breaking and entering if you have a key."

"Sneaky. Even better."

She hauled her purse strap over her shoulder as she inserted the key into the lock. Seconds later, she and Micah slipped into the darkened interior, and Micah closed and locked the door behind them.

"Okay, doll face, we're in. Now are you going to tell me what I'm risking a jail cell for?"

She swallowed nervously and fidgeted with her purse strap. "I want you to . . . tie me to Gray's bed. Naked." She tensed, waiting for Micah's response. She didn't have to wait long.

His mouth fell open. "Whoa. Wait a second. You want me to do *what?*"

"You heard me," she mumbled.

"Hoo boy." He shoved his hand through the hair at his forehead and pushed back until his fingers were thrust deep into his unruly mop. "Faith, honey, are you sure you know what you're doing?"

She checked her watch as panic edged up her spine. "Look, Micah, can you play armchair shrink while you're tying me to the bed? I'm running out of time. He's going to be home soon, and I'd rather he not find you here."

"That makes two of us," Micah muttered. He sighed. "Lead on."

She headed down the hallway and paused at the open door to his bedroom. As she glanced inside, she was relieved that the bed was the same model as hers. She'd been banking on the hope that Pop had similarly furnished all the apartments. If Gray hadn't had bedposts, she would've had to have done some major improvising.

She motioned Micah in and turned around to face him. "I know this is awkward, but I couldn't ask Nathan. He's too much like a brother, you know, like Connor. But you . . . you at least look at me like I'm a woman and not some kid sister."

He arched one brow.

She gave him an *oh please* look. "I see you checking out my ass," she said. "Nice to know at least one of my guy friends finds me, or least my ass, attractive."

He laughed. "Well, I guess the reward of this venture is getting to see you naked. I can mark at least one fantasy off my list."

She chuckled as she pulled her purse off her shoulder and dug for the rope she'd purchased the night before. She thrust it at Micah, and he uncoiled it as she started to slip her clothing off.

"You know," he said. "If you're wanting to get this guy's attention, which I'm assuming is the reason behind all this, I can think of less drastic measures than tying yourself to his bed."

Her hands paused as she reached around for the clasp of her bra.

"Here, let me," he offered.

His fingers brushed across her back as he unclasped the hooks, and she held the cups over her breasts with her arm. She walked over to the bed, still clad in her underwear.

"Tell me something, Micah. If you walked into your bedroom and found a naked woman tied to your bed, what would you think?"

"That I'd been a very good boy in a past life?"

She shook her head. "My point is, a woman bound, naked, offering herself to a man—it's a clear signal. She is his to do with as he wants. He's in control."

Their eyes connected for a long moment, and she saw a kernel of arousal, a spark of pure, primitive male. Yeah, he understood what she was talking about.

"What happened at The House, Faith?" he asked softly. "What did you go there looking for?"

She shivered at the intensity of his gaze. Then she climbed onto the bed, letting her bra fall to the floor. She felt him staring at her, and she felt awkward and vulnerable. Taking a deep breath, she reached for her panties and slid them down her legs.

She glanced up to see Micah standing over her, the rope in his hands. There was an odd fire in his eyes, like he was seeing her for the first time.

"What happened at The House?" he repeated.

The command was strong in his voice. It evoked a heady sensation, and awareness prickled over her skin.

"I went looking for something," she whispered. "Something I wanted. I found Gray."

Micah took one of her hands and pulled her arm above her head. He looped the rope around her wrist and tied it to the headboard.

"And what is it you want?"

His voice, buttery smooth, glided over her body, removing the awkward vulnerability and leaving vague arousal in its stead.

She licked her lips as he walked around the bed to take her other arm.

"I'm waiting," he said as he secured her other hand.

"Control," she said simply. "A man's dominance."

She heard Micah suck in his breath. In silence, he slid his hand down her leg until he looped a length of rope around her ankle.

"You surprise me, Faith," he finally said when he moved to her other leg.

He pulled gently until her legs were completely parted. Her pussy was exposed, and she closed her eyes in embarrassment. He'd see how aroused she was.

"Faith, look at me," he ordered.

She opened her eyes as he walked around to the side of the bed. She could see the bulge against his jeans. Fingers, featherlight, danced across her belly then up toward her breasts. His touch left her for just a moment before he cupped her soft mound in his palm and ran his thumb across her turgid nipple.

She shuddered and arched her body. What the hell was wrong with her?

"I had no idea you wanted a dominant man," he murmured. "A man would go crazy to have such sweet submission."

She gazed helplessly at him, confused, aroused and curious about the promise she saw reflected in his dark eyes. He bent down, leaned over her until his mouth hovered above her belly. Then he pressed his lips to her navel and ran his tongue erotically around the shallow indention.

Chill bumps raced up her body until they collided with her neck.

"You don't have to stay here," he said.

He let his hand wander down her abdomen, down to her pelvis until his fingertips brushed against the nest of curls between her legs.

"You could come home with me. I can give you what you want, Faith."

His fingers slid into her wetness, and she cried out as a jolt of surprised pleasure echoed through her groin. She was tempted. So tempted to take the easy road. Gray was avoiding her. This man was not. Micah wanted her, seemed to understand what *she* wanted. And though her mind was plenty confused, her body didn't seem to have any reservations about accepting Micah's offer.

But Gray called to her. On more than just a sexual level. If it was only about sex, then yes, she could forget this crazy plan and go home with Micah right now. But it was more than that.

She was drawn to Gray on an emotional level she didn't quite understand.

Micah's finger rolled lazily around her clit. It felt good. Her body responded, but she couldn't agree just for the physical release she'd find.

"I can't," she whispered. "Maybe Gray will toss me out of his apartment. Maybe he won't want what I'm offering, and maybe he can't give me what I need. But I have to find out."

Micah bent and tugged her nipple into his mouth just as his fingers found her sweet spot. She was going to come. She rolled her hips, wanting, needing release from the impossible, edgy tension.

Just as she neared bursting, he pulled away, leaving her aching with need. Then he moved his lips to hers and kissed her softly.

"If he tosses you out of his apartment, he's a damn fool."

He touched her cheek with his finger as she sought to control her erratic breathing.

"I hope you find what it is you want," he said. "But if you don't, you know where to find me."

Without a backward glance, he walked out of the bedroom.

CHAPTER 23

Gray left the jobsite, glad that the day was over and he could retreat to his apartment. Where there was no chance of seeing Faith.

She was driving him insane. Half the time he could smell her, and she wasn't within a country mile of him. Images of her tied, over the whipping stool, ass invitingly in the air, haunted him.

Man, that position tempted him in so many ways. He could fuck her pussy or her ass. Both were open and accessible. He could spank her bare cheeks until they reddened with a rosy blush.

He could imagine a dozen scenarios that put him in control, but he wasn't going to go there. He really didn't want to be some woman's damn Tinkertoy.

He pulled into his parking space and noted that both Faith and Micah were at home. He got out and headed toward his door, ready for a hot shower and a cold beer.

He let himself in and tossed the keys on the bar. As he headed down the hallway, the hairs at his nape stood on end. He put his hand on the back of his neck and rubbed as he entered the bedroom.

When he looked up and saw Faith lying on his bed, he damn near tripped over his feet. Naked. Tied to his bed. What the fuck?

She looked at him through half-lidded eyes. Her expression was a mixture of nervousness and arousal. At that moment, every single ounce of feeling was routed to his groin. His cock swelled against his jeans until he was certain he'd have a chafing problem tomorrow.

Finally, he got his feet in working order, and he stepped forward, shoving his hands into his pockets in an attempt to disguise the heavy bulge between his legs.

"What are you doing here?" he asked, then felt like a complete dumb-ass for asking what had to be the most obvious question of the year. Women didn't just get naked and tie themselves to a man's bed without a good idea of what they wanted out of the situation.

She wet her lips, the pink tip of her tongue darting out. He nearly groaned as he remembered that tongue on his dick, her sweet lips surrounding his flesh and how it felt when he came down her throat.

He pulled his hands from his pockets and flexed his fingers back and forth. He wanted to touch her. Taste her. Fuck her. More than anything, he wanted to peel his jeans off and dive into her, body and soul. Lose himself in her liquid heat.

He curled his fingers into his palms to control the shaking.

"Touch me," she whispered. "Please."

She stared imploringly at him, her bottom lip full and swollen as if she'd been biting it. It looked instead like someone had ravaged her mouth. It reminded him of how she'd looked after he'd fucked her mouth against the wall at the sex club. She looked utterly kissable.

He sank onto the bed beside her and leaned down to touch his lips against hers. She met his advance hungrily, open, accepting, inviting him further.

His tongue swept over hers, and he swallowed her sweet taste into his chest. He reached for her, his hand meeting the curve of her hip as he deepened his kiss. There was no breathing. His lungs screamed for oxygen, but he couldn't tear himself away from her molten touch.

A touch, a caress, his fingers danced over her skin, up her body until he felt the gentle swell of her breast. He tore his mouth away from hers, and they both gasped for air. His mouth slanted over hers again, drinking deeply of her essence.

His lips slid to the corner of her mouth, and then he kissed a line down her jaw, his breaths coming in raspy, erratic bursts. The small fleshy earlobe tempted him. He sucked it between his teeth.

She moaned and twisted restlessly underneath him. He licked then swirled his tongue around the shell of her ear. He felt her shiver against him and saw the chill bumps rise and pucker her skin.

He chased a line of those goose bumps all the way down to her breasts. For a long moment, he simply stared at the coral peaks. Her nipples were perfect. Not too pointed. Soft, velvety and round. He wanted to taste them. Wanted it badly.

He licked one, letting his tongue rasp over the silky tip. She flinched, and he turned to the other, lapping at it like it was a delicious treat. Then he nipped, grazing the nub with his teeth, applying just enough pressure so she'd feel the slight bite of pain.

She made a sound of deep satisfaction, and he smiled against her flesh.

He caressed the soft skin of her belly then moved lower to tease and twist the wispy curls of her pussy. He delved into her folds, spreading the damp flesh with his fingers.

With his middle finger, he flicked and rolled her clit. Sweet sighs whispered from her lips. Delicate, like her. It was a sound bound to inspire male appreciation. He wanted to give her more pleasure just so he could listen to the appreciative noises she made.

He slid his finger lower, circling her entrance, marking a path around the outside, teasing, hinting at a promise not yet fulfilled.

She bucked against him, a moan of contentment bubbling from her chest. In response, he plunged his finger inside her, and she nearly came off the bed.

He groaned as her inner walls convulsed and squeezed his finger. They clasped wetly to him, so tight. Hot silk. He closed his eyes as he imagined it surrounding his cock.

"No, not yet," she whimpered.

He opened his eyes to look at her. Her head was thrown back, her honey-blond hair spilling over the pillow. The muscles in her legs and groin trembled and spasmed. She was close to her orgasm. Why did she want to stop?

"I want," she gasped. "I want you to spank me, like you did the other night. I want you to tie me up and take control. Then—"

He never let her finish. He stood up abruptly, putting at least a foot of distance between them. A surge of irritation belted him square in the face.

She looked at him in confusion, her eyes burning brightly with unfulfilled need. "What's wrong?" she asked. "Why did you stop?"

He swore under his breath, kicking his ass from here to kingdom come for getting sucked into this game.

"Let me guess. You have an entire scenario worked out. First you want me to play around with you. Get you worked up a bit. Play master to your slave. Then you want me to spank your ass and fuck you senseless."

She winced at his crudity, but he didn't spare any guilt for being so bald. Slowly she nodded.

"Is that so bad?" she whispered. "I mean, if you don't want me, just say so. I thought . . . I thought we connected, that we had chemistry."

Chemistry? Hell, they had enough sexual energy to supply the entire greater Houston area with power.

He scrubbed a hand over his head and tried really hard to keep his gaze from the pointed tips of her breasts or lower it to the fine blond curls of her pussy. He could see a hint of her pink flesh between her spread legs, and it made him want to run his tongue over the folds, taste her.

"Faith, what you think you want . . ." He began as gently as he could. "I think you're kidding yourself."

Her cheeks stained red, and he could tell he angered her.

"Don't patronize me," she said. "Don't tell me what it is I want or don't want."

He held up his hand. "Let me finish. Let me see if I have this right. You want to submit to a man. You want a man to dominate you. That's what the trip to The House was all about and your allowing a complete stranger to spank your ass. In public."

She blushed and looked away.

"Faith, look at me."

She turned her gaze back to him.

"Am I right? You want to give up control to a man?"

Slowly she nodded.

"But that's not what you're doing," he pointed out.

Her brow furrowed. "What do you mean?"

"As much as you say you want a man's control, you cling to every vestige of control yourself." He gestured down her body at her tied arms and legs. "You've set the scene just as you imagined. You've scripted the role, my role, and decided how everything plays out. You've got every detail worked out in your mind. You're in complete control. No one else. I'm merely a puppet dangling on a string waiting on you to command me to command you and for you to tell me *how* to command you."

Her mouth fell open in shock. Her pupils widened.

"I don't work that way, Faith," he said softly. "I told you what I wanted. A woman who'd be content to let me call the shots. Nothing about this scenario is me doing anything but allowing you to dictate how it is we get together."

He reached down and untied her legs. Then he freed her hands. He pushed himself off the bed and looked down at her. "I'm going to take a shower. It's been a long day."

Faith watched him go, her entire world turned on its axis. Slowly, she swung her legs over the side of the bed and got up to collect her clothes. Not bothering with her bra or panties, she pulled on her jeans and shirt then sat back on the bed in stunned silence.

Her body ached from the constant state of arousal, first instigated by Micah and carried one step further by Gray. But she hadn't found completion. But Gray's words had definitely brought her down from her impending orgasm.

How could she not have seen it before? He was exactly right.

She craved a man's dominance. Wanted a man to take care of her, but she scripted every aspect of his performance. She had a detailed idea of how she wanted everything to go. Hell, if she had her preference, she'd provide him with a list of every single thing she wanted him to do to her.

She dropped her face into her hands. Oh God, what a moron she was. She hadn't wanted a dominant man. Just the opposite. She'd been trolling for a mindless puppet.

But that wasn't really what she wanted, was it? No, definitely not. Actually what she wanted was a man who didn't *have* to be coached. Someone who could reach inside her and pull out her fantasies, her needs and provide for her. Emotionally and physically.

And even when searching for a mindless puppet, she'd been a dismal failure. She'd spent more time hinting around than she had coming right out and saying what it was she wanted. Was it any wonder she was a walking case of sexual frustration?

What a mess she'd made of things. She wanted to go home and have a good cry. She'd found the perfect man, a man who wanted the same things she did, but she'd gone about it completely wrong. Now he thought she was an idiot who didn't have the first clue what she wanted and worse, thought she was playing stupid mind games.

She had obviously sat there beating herself up for longer than she thought because the next thing she knew, Gray put a hand on her shoulder.

She looked up to see him standing there, a towel around his waist.

"Are you okay?" he asked quietly.

She let her hands fall to her sides, and she looked away. "You were right. I didn't even realize what I was doing, but you're right. I was orchestrating the entire thing. It's what I've done in all my relationships. Is it any wonder I'm so fucked up?"

He sat down beside her, holding the towel up with one hand. "You're not fucked up, Faith. And there's nothing wrong with you wanting to orchestrate your sexual fantasies. I merely suggested that what you think you want and what you really want might be two different things. Maybe you need to consider that you might be better off in a situation where you're calling the shots and controlling the situation."

She let out a frustrated sigh. "But that's just it, Gray. That's not what I want. I know I'm all mixed up, but what I want is a strong man. Someone who isn't afraid to step up and call the shots, as you put it. I want, no I need that from the man I'm going to be involved with. I want . . . I want someone who will take care of me, who will cherish my gift of submission. Maybe that sounds horribly old-fashioned, but I'm tired of searching for something that obviously doesn't exist.

"Maybe I went about it all wrong, but it doesn't change what I want. I know what I want. I just haven't figured out how to go about getting it yet."

She stood, suddenly possessed with the need to get the hell out of there. After all, she'd made a big enough ass of herself for one day. Maybe she'd go cry on Micah's shoulder. Or maybe she'd just go home and try to forget this day ever happened.

She chanced one more look at him and found him staring at her in faint shock. There was an odd expression in his eyes like he was puzzling over her words. Which wouldn't surprise her, since she'd made a muck of everything else.

"I'm sorry," she whispered. "Truly, I am."

She headed for the door, only anxious to be as far away from any more self-discovery as possible.

"Faith, wait," he called, but she didn't stop.

She picked up her pace and hurried out the door.

CHAPTER 24

Gray watched her go, helpless frustration seizing his throat. Had he gotten her completely wrong? She'd looked so lost and confused, and then she'd spoken with such conviction about what she wanted.

He'd assumed she was playing sex games. Wanting her little kinky thrills without the veil of realism. But as he'd listened to her pour her heart out, he'd become more convinced that he'd misjudged her. Could it be possible that he'd found a woman who wanted the same things he did from a relationship?

She seemed unsteady, a little unsure, as if she was just spreading her wings and preparing to fly in uncharted airspace. And he'd shot her down.

What a mess. He couldn't afford to get involved with her, not at least until the whole situation with Samuels and her mother could be resolved. He was using her, which in essence was what he'd accused her of doing to him. He winced at the hypocrisy.

For the first time in his life, he felt real doubt over a woman. He needed to get back perspective. Remember why he was here in the first place. A call to Mick should do just that. He needed an update on the case anyway, because it sure as hell hadn't been uppermost on his mind for the last several days.

He rose from the bed and dropped the towel on the floor. He walked to his chest of drawers nude and rummaged for underwear, jeans and a shirt.

A few seconds later, he dialed Mick's number and waited for his answer.

"Got any news for me?" Mick asked with no preamble.

"I was hoping you had some for me," Gray said. "Other than the one phone conversation, I've come up with nothing. Her mother hasn't called back since."

Mick grunted. "Last report I got was the one where they were spotted in Huntsville. That was several days ago, so I'm sure they've moved on by now."

"How are you getting those reports, Mick? Is the department investigating Samuels now?"

Silence registered on Mick's end. "What are you insinuating, son?"

Gray blinked in surprise. "I didn't realize I was insinuating anything. I wanted to know if the department had come around and focused on Samuels or not. What's the latest on their investigation?"

Mick made a sound of disgust. "Rat bastards, the lot of them."

"Maybe I should call and see what progress has been made," Gray said.

"Nah," Mick said quickly. "You're supposed to be on leave. If they get wind of what you're doing, your ass will be in a sling. I've got a contact there, an old buddy of mine who is keeping me informed of what's going on. Or not going on as is the case."

Gray shrugged. "Well, I'm not coming up with much on my end either. While I'm convinced that Faith's mother is mixed up with some worthless piece of shit guy, I'm not sure it's the same piece of shit who shot Alex. I'm operating on little to no knowledge over here."

"You're doing me a favor," Mick said shortly. "That's all you need to know. I know the bastard shot my son. If I had left the investigation to Billings, we'd still be pissing in the wind trying to come up with a suspect."

Gray bit the inside of his cheek. He knew Mick's emotions were raw, but his grating attitude was not something Gray was in the mood for right now. Especially since he was the one down here chasing his tail around his ass.

Which begged the question; *why* was he down here chasing a hunch? Mick hadn't given him anything too substantive, but Gray owed him, and Alex was his partner. If Mick was right about who killed Alex, and the department wasn't doing shit about it, then Gray damn well wasn't going to back off.

"Look, son." Mick's voice became more cajoling. "I know this isn't easy for you, down there cozying up to a skirt who's probably as worthless as her mother. I know you're anxious to be back on the job. Just give it a little longer. My gut tells me Samuels is heading down there. Shadow the daughter for a few more days. If nothing turns up, then you can come on home and forget all about it."

Gray clenched his teeth together. He wasn't going to defend Faith to Mick, because it would only send the older man into a tizzy.

"I'll keep you posted," he said shortly.

"Thanks, son," Mick said, but Gray wasn't feeling all that charitable toward the guy. Not when he knew the use of the endearment was his subtle way of manipulating Gray.

He hung up, more irritated than ever. He clasped the back of his neck and rubbed at the tense muscles. What the hell was he going to do? He no longer had a lot of faith in the reason he was here.

If nothing else, he could stick around and see this to the end, or at least see if Faith's mother made an appearance with her deadbeat boyfriend.

Then he could return to his job, put Alex's memory to rest and hopefully ease some of Mick's grief. And maybe his own.

An odd tightening in his chest and a surge of sadness caught him by surprise. Nothing it seemed he did lately turned out any good. He hadn't been able to save his partner, and he'd just shit on a beautiful woman.

Yeah, life was real good.

Chapter 25

*I*n the last three days, Faith had been more sexually adventurous than she had in her entire life. She'd also made a complete ass of herself in front of more men than she'd slept with. Which was pretty dismal when she added that up in her head.

She sank lower in the tub and gazed down at her freshly painted toenails. But not even the bright, cheery pink managed to pick her spirits up.

Gray's words churned over and over in her head, an unending litany of just how stupid she'd been. Now that he'd laid it out for her, it seemed so clear.

Her idea of a man taking control had been handing him a checklist of activities to perform. She'd have been better off to hire a male prostitute and give him a script. But amid her lament, one single thought formed and took hold.

With the right man, she wouldn't have to give directions, and the simple fact was, she'd never been with the right man. That much was obvious. She'd responded out of frustration in the only way she saw how. But Gray had balked at her subtle control. He was a man used to doing things his own way. He would have been perfect for her if she hadn't managed to convince him she was a flighty twit playing games.

She was more confused than ever. Her gaze slid to the cordless phone she'd carried into the bathroom with her. She had two options. She could call Micah, but she was sure he'd respond with an invitation, and she wasn't prepared for that. Or she could call Damon and get his opinion. He seemed open enough, and she felt comfortable talking to him.

After a moment's hesitation, she picked up the phone and called the private number Damon had given her. On the second ring, he picked up.

"Damon, it's Faith. I hope I haven't caught you at a bad time."

"Of course not," he said warmly. "What can I do for you?"

She hesitated for a long second. "I need to talk to you. Is there any way we could meet for a late drink? I mean if you're not busy," she rushed to say.

"I'll send my driver for you," he said.

"Driver? I can just meet you."

"It's not a problem. I'll send the driver in say, an hour? Does that give you enough time? I know a great place across town where we can be assured of privacy."

"Yes," she said finally. "An hour is fine."

"Great. I'll see you then."

She let the phone slide from her fingers. Then she hoisted herself out of the tub to dry off. A driver? Who the hell sent a driver? It sounded positively decadent. Did the position of club manager pay that well, or was having a driver merely a perk of the job?

He'd said private and across town. That, coupled with the bit about the driver, had her thinking something a little more elegant than jeans and tennis shoes was in order.

Exactly an hour later, she went to answer the door. She'd chosen a classy black sheath with spaghetti straps and had worn the sexy, ultrahigh heels Damon had returned to her just days before. She'd piled her hair artfully atop her head and chosen simple teardrop diamond earrings. She checked her lipstick in the hall mirror before opening the door.

She was greeted by a large man in a somber-looking suit. He wore dark shades, even though it was well past nine o'clock.

"Miss Malone?"

"Yes, that's me," she said with a tentative smile.

He returned her smile and offered his arm. "Mr. Roche would like you to join him. I'll be driving you to your destination."

Her eyes widened when she saw the car he'd arrived in. Maybe she'd been expecting a limo, but seeing a freaking Bentley knocked her for a loop. Who the hell had a Bentley at their disposal? Were sex clubs that lucrative?

The driver assisted her into the backseat, then closed the door behind her. She sank into the butter-soft leather and closed her eyes in appreciation. As they drove away, she gazed out the tinted windows at Gray's truck. She emitted an unhappy sigh and turned her attention back to the interior of the car.

The soft strains of a classical melody filled the air. She turned her head to look out the window again, enjoying the lights of the city.

Thirty minutes later, the Bentley pulled up to an awning where a doorman opened the car door and extended a hand to help her out.

"Right this way, Miss Malone," he said.

She arched her brow, surprised and impressed by all the pomp. She was more intrigued than ever about Damon's status as the manager of a sex club.

She was escorted into a darkened, intimate restaurant, where she was promptly handed over to the maître d', who bowed and kissed her hand. He held an arm out to her and escorted her farther inside.

The furnishings screamed exclusive, reservation only. She wished she'd paid more attention when they'd pulled up, though she doubted she'd recognize the name anyway. The only place she haunted on a regular basis was Cattleman's, and exclusive it was not.

To her surprise, the maître d' escorted her past the common dining area and into a smaller, private club room in the back of the restaurant.

When they entered, Damon rose from the small table across the room and smiled. He reached out for her hand then nodded at the maître d'. "That will be all, Phillip."

Phillip smiled and backed from the room.

Damon pulled a chair from the table and gestured for her to sit. Then he circled around and eased into his own chair. He reached up and loosened his tie then proceeded to unbutton the cuffs on his long-sleeved dress shirt.

"I hope you don't mind me making myself more comfortable," he said.

"Not at all," she mumbled.

He laid his arm back on the table and met her gaze. "You look beautiful."

She shifted uncomfortably on the chair. For some reason, she felt that the Damon she'd talked with, had met at The House, was not this same man she now sat across from. And now she felt foolish for calling and asking him to talk to her.

"What would you like to drink?" he asked. "They have an excellent selection of wine, or if you prefer, something stronger."

She sighed. "I don't suppose you can get a root beer here." The last thing she needed was alcohol. Her head was muggy enough without adding liquor to the mix.

He laughed, perfectly straight white teeth flashing. "Root beer it is. I live to serve."

He gestured for a waiter Faith hadn't seen standing in the corner. When the young man moved to Damon's side, Damon requested wine Faith wasn't familiar with and a bottle of their finest root beer.

She chuckled as the waiter didn't so much as blink an eye. "I'm hopelessly gauche," she said by way of apology to Damon.

"You're delightful," he said with a smile. "Are you hungry at all?"

She shook her head, knowing her stomach wouldn't tolerate food after all of today's upheaval.

Awkward silence stretched between them, and Faith fidgeted with her table napkin to cover her unease. The waiter returned bearing their drinks, and she latched gratefully onto the cool glass.

As the waiter walked away, Damon fixed her with his gaze. "Now, what's bothering you?" he asked.

She sipped at her root beer then set the glass down with a sigh. "First you have to tell me how a man I thought to be a simple club manager has somehow turned into Mr. GQ."

He offered a wry smile. "I don't believe I ever claimed to be a simple club manager."

"No, I don't suppose you did," she admitted. "The Bentley might have been a bit overdone though."

He chuckled and took another sip of his wine. "Okay, I admit, I was trying to impress you. Did it work?"

She shrugged. "I think I'm more confused than impressed, but then I seem to be wallowing in confusion lately."

The amused twinkle in his eye faded and was replaced by genuine concern. He reached across the table and laid his hand on top of hers. "If there's something I can do to help, Faith, I will."

She slowly pulled her hand away and put it in her lap. "I admit, there were things I wanted to discuss with you, a subject I thought you might have considerable expertise in, but now . . ."

"Now, what?" he prompted.

She twisted in her seat. "Now, I wonder how much of your role as 'manager' of The House is just a game, like everything else. I'm having a hard time figuring out what's real and what isn't."

"Ah."

"What does that mean?" she asked, frustrated by the seemingly knowing look on his face.

He sat back and took a deep breath. "Faith, I *own* The House. So my position as manager or proprietor is certainly legitimate. The House is my escape. It's a place I can go where I'm free to be myself or to enjoy a different lifestyle."

"So it's a hobby?" she asked.

He gave her a searching look. "I can sense your anger and frustration. Right now you feel led on, lied to and played with."

Her brows went up. Yep, he'd nailed that one on the head. Actually, she felt more like she'd become trapped in some never-ending fantasy land where everyone was reading one of those scripts Gray had bitched about.

"I admire you, Faith. I really do."

"Huh?"

"You know what you want, and you aren't willing to settle for less, and you're willing to make mistakes while you search."

She laughed. She couldn't help it. Know what she wanted? She wished. It would make things so much easier.

He shook his head when she would have spoken. "You may be confused right now, but you know deep down inside what you want. You just haven't known how to get it. That's why you came to The House. Not because you didn't know what you wanted, but you just didn't know where to find it."

"Or how to go about it," she said glumly.

"Who was the guy?" Damon asked curiously. "The one who showed up at The House looking like he wanted to tear Brent limb from limb."

Faith looked down and grimaced. "His name is Gray."

"He seemed to know quite a lot about you," he said simply.

She sighed. "I think he understands me *too* well."

"Meaning?"

"It's a long story. A long, really messed-up story."

"I've got all night," he said lazily.

She hesitated for a moment, and then she poured out the entire story, starting with her breakup with John and her subsequent encounter with Gray, first at The House and then at his apartment.

"And the sad thing is, he's right," she said when she'd finished.

Damon gave her a thoughtful look as he refilled his wineglass.

"I'd hoped maybe you could offer some insight. Am I playing games? The very thing I despised so much about my experience at The House? Am I wanting something that just doesn't exist outside role playing and elaborate fantasy reenactments?"

He leaned over and touched her cheek. "I don't think that at all. I think, as I said before, that you're a woman who very much knows what she wants. You just haven't known how to go about it, nor have you met the right man, a man who won't have to take direction, hints or scripts."

"Am I twisted?"

"No. You're a woman most men would dream of having. Myself included. I spend a lot of time at The House, and part of it's because I too am searching. For what, I'm not even sure, but I know it goes beyond the harmless games played behind closed doors. I don't begrudge any of my patrons their sexual excesses. I'm very committed to giving them a safe environment in which to play out their wildest fantasies."

"What do you want?" she asked softly.

He smiled and shook his head. "It would shock you."

She raised a brow. "If having you watch while I sucked off another man didn't shock me, I don't see why anything you have to say should."

He choked on his wine and pulled a napkin up to cover his mouth. It took her a minute to figure out he was laughing.

"You are so refreshing, Faith. I can't seem to figure you out. You have the most feminine blush, yet you're extremely blunt."

"Well? Are you going to tell me what kind of woman you're looking for?"

He studied her for a moment then laid the napkin back on the table. "You and my dream woman share a lot of qualities, I think. But I would take things further."

She leaned forward. "Oh, now you have me intrigued."

He smiled. "I want a woman who is completely submissive. I guess in some circles, she might be considered a slave."

Faith's eyes widened. "A slave?"

"I said in some circles," he said dryly. "You see, people are too hung up on labels. I want a woman completely devoted to me and my needs. In return, I would take care of her and provide for *her* every need. But I would be in control."

"But that's what I want," she said softly.

He nodded. "I know. Sad, isn't it? Here we are, a man and a woman, both wanting the same things, and yet, you aren't attracted to me."

She started to protest, but he grinned. "C'mon, you know it's true. Yes, you responded to my touch. But when Gray stepped in, well, it was another story entirely."

There wasn't much she could say to that.

"So, do you think based on what I've told you that I don't have a chance with Gray? I mean it sounds like he's just like you. He wants a submissive woman without the games, etc. How do I show him that I want the real thing too?"

Damon shook his head. "I don't know what to tell you, Faith. It sounds to me like he's fighting his attraction to you. Why, I don't know. If you showed any interest in me, I'd have you collared and tied to my bed in two seconds flat."

Heat buzzed up her spine and surged into her cheeks.

"Like that image, do you?" he teased.

"Asshole," she muttered. "Damn, why do I have to be hung up on him? Why does he do it for me and no one else? Do you know since I've started pursuing this whole wanting a man to take care of me thing, that I've had more offers than I've ever gotten in my life?"

"Men love a submissive woman," Damon said simply. "Even when they say they don't. There's something about a beautiful, soft woman looking to them to protect and take care of them that inspires a man to greatness."

"It seems like there's a lot of room to abuse that power, though," she remarked.

Damon nodded. "That there is. If more men acted responsibly, then more women wouldn't mind allowing them a lead role."

"Oh my God! I can't believe you said that. That's what I said! I told Gray that last week. That if more men didn't abdicate their responsibility, women would be more willing to let them be the head of the house."

Damon smiled at her, and again, she cursed the fact that Gray dominated her thoughts and desires. Here, again, was a man willing to show her the things she wanted. And again, she would walk away after spending so much time looking for such a man in the first place.

It was enough to make her howl in frustration.

"I need a vacation," she said. "I need time to figure out what the hell I'm going to do with my life."

He took her hand in his and rubbed his fingers over her palm. "I have a beach house. I could give you the key. You could spend a few days there, have some time to yourself. No one would bother you."

She studied him, tempted to take him up on his offer. A few days away at the beach sounded like heaven. And it would prevent her from having to see Gray until she'd fortified herself.

"I'll have my driver take you down in the Bentley," he wheedled with a mischievous grin.

She laughed. "Okay, deal. Damon, I don't know how to thank you."

"Don't thank me. I have an ulterior motive."

"Oh?"

He grinned. "Yeah, if things don't work out between you and Gray, I'm hoping you'll come to me."

A warm shiver rolled over her arms as his fingers continued to stroke her palm.

"I'll keep that in mind," she said. And she was serious. If she gave Damon half a chance, she might find that they were compatible.

"When would you like to leave?" he asked. "Name the time, and I'll have my driver pick you up."

She checked her watch. "Honestly, I have no desire to go home just yet, so you're stuck entertaining me for a while. And if your driver isn't too tired, he could just run me home later and wait for me to pack a bag. I can always sleep when I get there."

Damon smiled. "Good, that's settled. Now, can I get you some more root beer?"

CHAPTER 26

Gray spent a restless night arguing with himself. In the early hours of the morning, he gave up on the idea of sleep and sat in his kitchen nursing a cup of liquid caffeine.

Had he fucked up any chance he had with Faith? And just when was it that he'd actually started entertaining the idea of a relationship with her anyway? Relationship? He had to be out of his damn mind.

First there was the fact that he was lying to her and using her. She was a means to an end. Then there was the fact that his life, what little he had, was in Dallas. Funny that he hadn't given much thought to his career since arriving in Houston, but the fact remained he was a damn good cop.

There's no reason you can't come clean. Tell her the truth. She's an intelligent woman. She doesn't want anything to do with her mother anyway. Quit making excuses. She wants the same thing you do.

When put that way, it seemed perfectly simple. He'd simply tell her the truth about why he was here. Then, with that out of the way, hopefully she'd cooperate. He could investigate Samuels's involvement in Alex's death, and then maybe he and Faith could explore the attraction between them.

Attraction. Hell. The word didn't do justice to this entity between them.

Mick would shit a brick, but he'd have to deal. It wasn't his ass down here on the line; it was Gray's. As long as justice was served, it shouldn't matter one iota to Mick how it came about.

Now that he was finished convincing himself, he was eager to get to work and figure out how he was going to break things to Faith. He honestly didn't know how she'd react. But he wasn't willing to take the deception any further. Not when he very much wanted to explore a relationship without any baggage.

There was that damn word again. But if he was honest, he knew he wanted something other than a casual fuck. And the sort of relationship she said she wanted was exactly what he wanted as well, and assumed he'd never find.

He collected his keys and walked out to his truck, feeling lighter than he had in a while. He glanced down to see Faith's car still parked, which he thought odd, considering she usually beat everyone in to the office. A quick glance at his watch told him he was earlier than usual, though.

He briefly thought about going to her apartment to talk to her, but she was likely getting ready, and he didn't want to ambush her. He'd just wait until he could get her alone at the office.

When he got to the office, he found Pop and Connor already there. Pop looked up when Gray walked by his office then called out to stop him.

Gray backed up and stuck his head in the door. "What's up?"

"Faith's not coming in this morning," Pop said. "Connor and I are going out on a bid, and Micah and Nathan won't be in until later. Can you sort the mail and hang around here for a phone call I'm expecting? I have to be back around ten for a conference call with an important client, so I could use the help around the office."

Gray blinked in surprise. "Faith's not coming in?"

"Yeah, I know; no one knows where a damn thing is but her," Pop grumbled. "She's spoiled us rotten. Gonna be a bitch without her today."

"Is she okay?" Gray asked, half fearing the answer to that. Had he upset her? That was an asinine question. Of course he'd upset her, but was he why she wasn't in, or was it something completely unrelated?

Pop shrugged. "Said she wasn't coming in. She doesn't call in enough for me to question her the one time she does."

Gray frowned then said, "Sure, I can get the mail and hang around here. It's not a problem."

"Thanks. I'm expecting a call from Sherman Winston. When he calls, patch him through to my cell. I'd originally planned to be here, but this bid came up, and I need to handle it."

Gray waved and headed on to his office. He guessed Faith had enough of his shitting on her. Not that he could blame her. He had a lot of groveling to do, and that was only if she'd even speak to him after he told her the truth about why he was here.

At nine, the postman carried in a white tub full of mail and heaved it onto Faith's desk. Gray thanked him then grabbed handfuls of envelopes and began sorting out the obvious checks from the other correspondence.

He was halfway through the pile when he came across an envelope addressed to Faith Martin. He frowned as he took in the scrawled name and address. There was no return address, and it obviously wasn't from a business.

Faith Martin? Martin was Faith's mom's last name. No one who had any dealings with Faith would have called her anything but Malone.

The hair on his neck stood up. Not sparing an ounce of guilt for opening her mail, he eased a letter opener into the corner and sliced the top. He didn't want to disturb the seal in case DNA could be taken.

He was careful to only handle the corners of the paper as he opened it. His gaze darted over the nearly illegible handwriting, and as he took it in, red-hot rage billowed over him.

Give us the money, bitch. Your old man has a lot of it from what I hear, and I bet he'd be willing to part with quite a bit of it to keep his pretty daughter from being hurt. We can do it the easy way or we can do it the hard way. Either way, we'll end up with the money. Your choice.

Gray stuffed the paper back into the envelope then folded it and shoved it into his pocket. Goddamn bastard had just threatened Faith. He had to get to her apartment right away. Make sure she was okay and then make sure she wasn't left alone. There was no time like the present to have their come to Jesus moment.

Faith leaned back in the leather seat and lazily watched the scenery fly by in a blur. It was a beautiful morning. Already hot, but the sun was shining, and the farther they got out of Houston, the bluer the sky got.

They drove through Galveston and headed west. The traffic and number of houses lessened as they got farther down the island. Finally, they pulled into the drive of a large beach house, the only house for at least a mile stretch of the coastline.

She stepped out and breathed in the salty air. It was perfect. She'd have complete privacy. No one to bug her or intrude. It was heaven.

The driver, who had identified himself as Sam, carried her suitcase up the two flights of stairs to the front door and unlocked it for her.

He set the luggage inside the door then dug in his pocket for a card. "Here's my number. If you need anything, just give me a call."

She took it from his hand and smiled. "Thank you, Sam. I really appreciate this."

He nodded and headed down the stairs back to the Bentley, leaving her alone in the spacious house.

She walked through the living room to the back deck and stepped out of the sliding glass doors. The breeze caught her hair and flipped it around her head.

The gentle sounds of the waves rolling in soothed fraught nerves. She raised her shoulders then relaxed them with a great big sigh.

A lawn chair beckoned, and she couldn't resist sinking down onto it. She propped her feet up and gazed out over the stained waters of the gulf.

Remembering she needed to call Pop and give him a better explanation than that she just wasn't coming in, she dug around in her pocket for her cell phone and hoped she got service this far out of Galveston.

"Why are you calling on the cell?" Pop asked when he answered.

She smiled. "Because I'm not at home."

"Everything okay? I assumed you were sick. You don't sound sick, but you don't sound okay either."

"I'm fine," she managed in a wavery voice. "I just need . . . I need a vacation, Pop. I hope you don't mind me taking a few days. I know I should have planned ahead but—"

He cut her off before she could delve further into her explanation. "You don't need to justify a vacation to me, girl," he said gruffly. "You deserve one, and you should take it. I don't want to see you in here for a week at least."

"Are you sure?" she asked, though she'd already committed to doing just that.

"We'll manage just fine around here. Coffee won't be worth a damn, but we'll get by."

She laughed. "Thanks, Pop. You're the best."

"You just take care. You haven't been yourself lately."

"I love you," she said softly.

"Love you too, girl."

Gray left the office and tore out of the parking lot like he was heading to a fire. He needed to call Mick and tell him things had escalated and that Samuels was most assuredly in Houston or close, but first, he had to make sure Faith was okay and square things with her.

He saw her car still in the parking lot and wheeled in beside it. He rushed to her door and knocked loudly. When he got no response, he knocked again. "Faith, it's Gray. Open the door. It's important."

Again he waited but got no response. Dread tightened his chest. Her car was here. Why wasn't she answering the door?

He knocked one more time in case she was in the shower and waited several long seconds. Then he did what any other cop would do in the situation. He kicked the door in.

It flew open and hit the opposing wall with a bang. He rushed in, wishing like hell he'd brought his gun. Her apartment was dark. Not a single light was on. The only sound he could hear was the humming of the refrigerator.

He hurried through the apartment, searching each room, but came up empty. Panic surged in his stomach, leaving him with a nauseated feeling. Where the fuck was she? Had Samuels already gotten to her?

He raced back out to his truck and pulled out his cell phone. He called Mick on his way back to the office. Hopefully Pop or Connor could provide a perfectly sane reason why Faith's car was at her apartment and she was not.

When Mick picked up, Gray quickly outlined the letter he'd intercepted. Mick's breathing hitched up several notches.

"He's there. I knew the son of a bitch wouldn't be able to resist hitting the daughter up for money. This is a perfect opportunity, Gray. We can use her as bait, draw Samuels out and nail his ass to the wall."

"Whoa, wait just a damn minute, Mick. We aren't using Faith as bait. Use your head. She's an innocent victim here. No way I'd place her in that kind of danger."

"*You* use your damn head," Mick growled. "She's our best chance at nailing this bastard. You shouldn't even think twice. You know it's a good idea."

Gray had to swallow the angry retort. He sucked in a breath

and tried to remain calm. "Mick, you're worked up. You need to calm down and think rationally about this. No way catching Samuels is worth putting an innocent woman in harm's way."

"You're thinking with your goddamn dick," Mick said furiously.

"I will not involve Faith in this," Gray ground out. "I think it's best that I go to Pop and tell him everything. Get his help. He has a daughter to protect, and we have a killer to catch. We can bring in the local authorities and do this by the book."

A string of curses erupted over the line.

Gray gritted his teeth and counted to ten. "I'm right, and you know it, Mick. I can't believe you'd even consider using Faith like that. You've lost all perspective. I think you should step away and let me handle this."

Silence fell over the line. "No, no, you're right of course. Do what you need to do. I'm coming down there. I can be there in five hours. I'll call you when I get in."

Gray started to say that it wasn't necessary, and actually preferable if Mick stayed in Dallas, but Mick had already hung up.

Gray bit out a curse and tossed the phone onto his seat.

He'd screwed everything up. Mick was way over the line, and Gray should have seen it before. He never should have let Mick talk him into this crazy-ass scheme.

But a small voice inside his head reminded him that if Mick hadn't asked him to come down, Faith would still be in danger. A danger that no one would know about if Gray wasn't here. If he could just find her before Samuels did, if he hadn't already, then he could make things right. And make damn sure she stayed safe.

When he arrived back at the office, he barreled down the

hallway to Pop's doorway. He threw open the door and met with the irritated stares of Pop, Connor and Nathan.

"Where's Faith?" Gray demanded as he strode in.

Pop quickly pushed the speakerphone button and picked up the receiver. Then he covered the mouthpiece with his hand and glared at Gray.

"This is an important call," Pop bit out.

Gray put his hands on Pop's desk, ignoring Nathan and Connor, and leaned toward Pop. "Faith could be in a lot of danger. Do you know where she is?"

"I'll have to get back to you," Pop said right before he hung up the phone.

Connor and Nathan surged to their feet about the time Pop's feet hit the floor.

"What are you talking about, son?" Pop demanded. "I just talked to Faith a while ago. She seemed well enough."

Gray nearly wilted in relief. He sagged into a nearby chair and blew out his breath in a deep sigh.

"I need to know where she is."

Connor folded his arms over his chest and stared menacingly at Gray. "I don't see that it's any of your business where she is, but I'd sure like to know why you think it is."

"I want to get back to the part where you think she's in danger," Pop interjected.

In response, Gray pulled out the letter he'd opened and flipped it onto the table. "Careful," he said when Pop reached for it. "That's evidence."

Pop scowled but carefully slid the paper out of the envelope and gingerly opened it. His frown deepened as he read, and Nathan and Connor crowded over his shoulder so they could see as well.

"What the fuck?" Nathan said.

Pop's hand shook as he set the letter back down. "What do you know about this, and where did you get it?" he asked Gray.

Gray twisted his lips and shook his head knowing he'd have to come clean with the entire story. "Faith's mother has been calling her and asking for money," he said, after deciding to start with the more pertinent information. He'd get to his deception in a minute.

"Goddamn it," Connor swore. "I knew something was bothering her."

"But what does her mother have to do with this?" Nathan asked. "You don't think she—"

Gray shook his head. "Celia is mixed up with a man who is suspected of murdering my partner," he said softly.

Three sets of eyes drilled holes in his skull.

"I have a feeling I'm not going to like what I'm about to hear," Pop said in a near growl.

"No, you probably won't," Gray said. "I came down here as a favor to my partner's father. Alex, my partner, was killed in the line of duty. The investigation wasn't going anywhere, and there was a lot of finger pointing, most of it directed at my partner.

"Mick did some poking around on his own and came up with Eric Samuels, a man who happened to have hooked up with Faith's mom right before the murder. Then they both disappeared."

"That doesn't explain why you came down here," Nathan pointed out.

Gray met Nathan's gaze then looked back at Pop. "Mick's investigation also turned up the fact that Celia Martin liked to lean on Faith for money when she was in dire straits."

"That much is true," Pop muttered. "Damn bitch. I should have known better than to think she'd get out of Faith's life permanently."

"So you came down here to get close to Faith, hoping Celia would turn up," Connor said in a dangerously low tone.

Gray sucked in his breath and took the last plunge. "Mick arranged for me to get a job here through a mutual acquaintance of his and Pop's. I bugged Faith's office and home phone and waited for her mother to call. She actually called the first day I met Faith, but I hadn't gotten the tap in place yet."

"Son of a bitch," Connor seethed. "And you didn't think to tell us any of this?"

"You've been using her," Nathan observed quietly. "I knew something weird was going on between you two. Just how close did you get to her in this little investigation of yours?"

Connor took a menacing step forward, and Pop put his arm out to halt him. "Not now, damn it. I want to hear the rest of this."

Gray stood, meeting Connor's unspoken challenge. "A few days after that first phone call, she called again, and I found Faith in her office extremely upset. Later, when I listened to the playback, I could hear Samuels in the background making threatening remarks to Faith's mother. Mick gave me a report that he and Celia had been spotted in Huntsville, so we thought they might be headed this way."

Pop bit out an uncharacteristic swear word.

"This morning I found this in the mail," Gray said, pointing to the letter on the desk. "The bastard is here, which is why we have to find Faith and keep her safe."

Connor clenched his fists at his side and his neck muscles

bulged and flexed. "She wouldn't be in any danger if you had been honest with us from the beginning. It's kind of hard to protect her when we're kept in the fucking dark."

Pop picked up his cell phone and punched in a number with trembling fingers. He stuck the phone to his ear and stood, twitching impatiently. A few seconds later, he bit out another curse before he closed the phone and dropped it on the desk.

"I got her damn voice mail."

"You don't know where she is?" Gray asked incredulously.

"No, I don't damn well know where she is. She called and said she needed a vacation. I told her to take one. I didn't even think to ask her where she was. I didn't think it was important at the time." Pop sank down in his chair and rubbed a hand over his hair. "I need a minute to think, damn it."

"Do you have any contacts with the Houston PD?" Gray asked. "We need to have Faith's apartment watched. Maybe even set up a decoy. If Samuels is watching, he'll likely go for her there. Faith has a set routine that she normally doesn't deviate from."

"Yeah, you'd know wouldn't you," Nathan said with a grunt.

"We could set a trap for the asshole," Connor said. "Sounds like he's pretty damn desperate."

"That was my thought," Gray said. "We need to find Faith, tell her what's going on and stash her someplace safe."

Pop shook his head. "No."

Gray, Connor and Nathan all looked at him in surprise.

Pop stared back at them in turns. "I don't want her to know about any of this."

Gray shook his head in confusion. "How are you going to keep it from her? And *why* would you keep it from her? She needs to know."

"Just give me a damn minute to think," Pop growled. He put his forehead in his hands and looked down for a long moment.

"I've got a plan," Gray said slowly, his brow furrowing as he gave more thought to the idea forming in his head.

"Maybe you should let us handle this," Connor said acidly. "I'm not too crazy about your plans so far."

Pop held up his hand. "I'm not too happy about any of this myself, but right now, the most important thing is making sure Faith is safe. Everything else can wait."

Gray cleared his throat uncomfortably and continued. "I can't be involved in this, not officially, I mean. We find out where Faith is, and I go to her. Keep a close eye on her until this is re-solved. You can coordinate with the Houston police here and work out a way to catch Samuels. Maybe even go with a decoy like we mentioned earlier. I'll let Faith know what's going on, and you can keep us posted on your progress."

Again Pop shook his head. "I don't want her to know about this."

"She has to know," Gray said. "There's no way to keep this from her."

"You don't goddamn tell me what I will or won't tell my daugh-ter," Pop said in an explosion of anger. His lips tightened, and he appeared to be trying to regain control of his temper. "Look, Faith is the most tenderhearted girl I know. Even with all her mother has done, it would break her heart to know her mother was in-volved in something like this. I can't let that happen to her again. She's already been let down too many times by that bitch."

"You can't protect her from everything," Gray argued.

Pop looked him straight in the eye and held up a finger. "I'll protect her from as much as I can. There is no need for her to know. She's on vacation. I told her to take a week. We'll find out where she is, and then you can go make sure she stays put and is safe."

"I don't like it," Connor interrupted. "I don't want him anywhere near her."

Pop held up his hand. "I'm not any happier about this damn mess than you are, Connor, but Gray's right. He can't be involved in this, and I need you and Nathan and Micah here if we're going to catch this son of a bitch. Someone has to make sure Faith stays safe." He stared Gray down. "Can I count on you to do that?"

"I don't like lying to her," he said through gritted teeth. "Not about something like this."

"But you'll lie to her about everything else," Nathan pointed out with a scowl.

Gray's fingers curled into fists. "I did what I had to do to find the man responsible for murdering a cop. That bastard killed my partner. I had a responsibility to do whatever was necessary to bring him to justice. I didn't like deceiving any of you, and I don't want to lie to Faith any more than I already have. I . . ."

"You what?" Connor demanded.

He ignored Connor and looked Pop in the eye. "I care about your daughter. I've tried my best not to. I've tried to stay away from her. I'm the reason she took this damn vacation. I upset her, and now it's time for me to make things right. I can't make it right if I'm stuck lying to her some more."

Pop didn't so much as flinch. He met Gray's stare with a steady gaze. "You can make it right when the bastard who is threatening her is behind bars. There's no sense upsetting her needlessly. Her mother has caused her enough grief. If she knows what her fool mother has done, you won't be able to keep her away from here.

She'll worry that Celia is in trouble. It could be days before we catch this guy. There's no sense in having her worried sick the entire time."

"I don't like it," Gray said.

"I'm not that crazy about it either," Connor muttered. Gray noticed the sideways glance Connor threw at Pop.

"She's not a child," Gray pointed out.

"You didn't seem to have any problems keeping the truth from her when it suited your purpose," Pop said, anger rising in his voice again.

Gray looked up at the ceiling in frustration. They were wasting so much valuable time in a ridiculous pissing match. He needed to find Faith and make sure she was protected. He returned his gaze to Pop. "Look, when I got here, I had no idea if Faith was innocent or not. How was I supposed to? For all I knew, she was completely aware of her mother's situation. I didn't *know* Faith. I had to treat her like any other potential suspect. I know now that she's not involved, and I don't like lying to her any more than I already have."

"And I don't want her hurt," Pop said quietly. "She's my daughter. I love her. If I can keep the knowledge that her mother was willing to allow her latest boyfriend to harm her own daughter over money, then by God I will."

Gray closed his eyes. "All right. Fine."

What an impossible situation. His mind raced to find a way to make everything work. How was he supposed to just show up, crash Faith's vacation and act like he didn't have an ulterior motive for being there? He doubted she'd be overjoyed to see him. He imagined being able to level with her but instead he'd be going to her with more deceit.

But everything else would have to be real. He'd have to show her what was real. And what was real was his attraction to her, his need to see if they had any shot at the kind of relationship they both wanted.

Could he pull that off as the real reason for tracking her down? That part wouldn't be a lie. He'd very much wanted to level with her and then pursue this thing between them. Only now, he'd have to go about it bass-ackwards. *Pursue*, then level.

Hell.

CHAPTER 27

The office building resembled the monthly meeting of the SWAT team just an hour later. Policemen, friends of Pop's, littered the offices of Malone's, and the buzz of a dozen different conversations reverberated through the building. Amid the chaos Micah walked cautiously in, a bewildered expression on his face.

"What the fuck is going on?" he asked from the doorway of Pop's office.

All four men turned around, their cell phones to their ears. Pop tossed his aside. "Do you know where Faith is?" he demanded.

A peculiar look crossed Micah's face. "Uh, why do you ask? What's going on?"

Gray rose and walked over to where Micah stood. "If you know where she is, tell me. She's in a lot of danger."

Micah's gaze sharpened. He lowered his voice so only Gray would hear. "She's at Damon's beach house."

"Who the fuck is Damon?" Gray growled.

"He's the manager of The House, the guy who set Faith up to visit. You probably saw him when you went to get her."

"Yeah, I saw him," Gray muttered. *What the hell was she doing with the sex club guy?*

"She's alone," Micah said as if reading Gray's thoughts.

"Would you two care to share with the rest of us?" Connor demanded. "Micah, if you know where Faith is, then you better spill it."

"I know where she is. Now who's going to tell me why our office looks like a policemen's union meeting and what that has to do with Faith being in danger?"

Gray quickly related the story to Micah. Micah frowned and glanced over at Gray. "So all this time you were jacking us around?"

Gray sighed. "I had a job to do, man. You were a cop. You understand."

A dull shadow crossed Micah's eyes. "Yeah, I do."

A commotion in the hall had them all looking up. A few seconds later, Mick came barreling past several policemen. He hadn't shaven in at least a week, and he looked like hell.

"Damn it, Mick, what are you doing here?" Gray demanded.

"Where else would I be?" he ground out. "Now tell me what's going on."

Gray sighed. "I can't be involved in this, Mick, and neither can you. I'll give you the key to my apartment. You can go stay there. The police will notify you when an arrest has been made."

"The hell you say! And where the hell are you going?"

"I'm going to make sure Faith stays out of harm's way," he said evenly. "Hopefully this will all be over quickly."

"You're leaving?" Mick asked incredulously. "You're going to

let some piece of ass deter you from catching your partner's—
your brother's—killer?"

In a blur, Connor flew past Gray and shoved Mick against the
wall, his hand twisted in Mick's shirt. "Listen to me, you son of a
bitch. That's my sister you're talking about. Why don't you do
what Gray told you and get the fuck out of here."

Pop strode over and pulled Connor away. Though he appeared calmer than Connor, his eyes blazed with anger. "Back
off, son. Me and Mr. Winslow here will have a little chat. And
then he's going to clear his ass out of my office." He turned to
Gray. "You need to get on out of here. You're supposed to be protecting my daughter."

Gray started to dig around in his pocket for a key to his apartment, but Pop waved him on. "I'll take care of making sure Mr.
Winslow has a place to stay. You focus on your job, and we'll do
ours. I'll be in touch and let you know how things are going and
when it's safe to come back home."

Gray nodded then turned to Micah. "I need you to tell me
where."

Micah walked out to the front with Gray and picked up a
tablet of paper and a pen and jotted down an address. He tore off
the piece of paper and handed it to Gray. "Just head straight
down Seawall Boulevard out of town. You can't miss it. Just about
the time you think you're going to fall off the other end of the island, you're there."

"Thanks," Gray said. "Look, keep me posted okay? You
weren't here this morning, and the guys are pretty pissed over
this. I don't blame them, but I need to be kept in the loop, and
Pop is adamant that Faith not know any of what's going on. If I
had to guess, he's not going to be calling much."

Micah nodded. "Will do, man. Let me know if you need anything."

By the time Gray arrived at the beach house, it was close to sunset. He pulled onto the paved circle drive and parked outside the steps leading up to the front door. As he got out, he eyed the bags he'd packed but decided to wait and bring them in later.

He jogged up the steps and tapped at the door. Déjà vu settled over him as he recalled doing the exact same dance at her apartment earlier that morning.

This time when she didn't answer, he didn't waste any time letting himself in to make sure she was all right. He stepped into the spacious living room and took in the masculine decor. Definitely a bachelor pad. Didn't have a woman's touch at all. He briefly wondered if Damon had planned to join Faith here and scowled at the thought.

When his gaze lighted on the French doors leading out to the deck, he saw an arm draped over the side of a lounger. Faith's hand dangled and brushed the floor.

He hurried, and when he got close enough, he could see that she was curled up asleep. Quietly, so as not to wake her, he eased outside, closing his eyes in appreciation when the gulf breeze blew over his face.

But as his gaze lowered to Faith's sleeping form, his appreciation only grew. She looked beautiful. One hand dangled from the lounger, the other curled underneath her chin. Her chest rose and fell gently with each breath, and the breeze lifted the blond strands of her hair and blew them around her face.

All the way down here, he'd convinced himself that he'd tell her the truth no matter what Pop wanted. But now that he looked at her, so fragile and innocent, he understood why Pop wanted to protect her. Hell, *he* wanted to protect her. Wrap her in cotton and make sure nothing ever hurt her.

She wanted to be taken care of, and what man wouldn't want to? She was sweet, soft and delicate in all the right places. As he stood watching her, she stirred and moved restlessly on the lounger. Her eyes fluttered open. She blinked as she looked at him, and then her eyes widened in surprise.

"Gray?" she asked sleepily. "What are you doing here?"

He bent and ran a finger down her arm. "I hope you haven't been lying out here all day. You'll burn."

"Was in the shade most of the day," she mumbled. "What are you doing here? How did you know where I was?"

She shifted and sat up in the seat and continued to regard him with sleepy eyes.

"I wanted to talk to you," he said simply.

Her expression was disbelieving.

"I know I've acted like an ass," he said. "The fact is, Faith, you threw me for a loop."

He knelt on the wood deck, shifting his weight to alleviate the discomfort on his knees. She placed a gentle finger over his lips, and he was shocked into silence.

"Let's go inside to talk," she said.

He rose and held out his hand to help her up. Her hair, tousled by her nap, blew in the breeze, and he reached out to snag a tendril, unable to resist touching the silky tresses.

She turned and walked inside, leaving him to follow. He watched the gentle sway of her hips, and he imagined himself between her thighs, his hands curled around those hips as he thrust into her.

His throat tightened, and he swallowed against the uncomfortable sensation.

When she entered the house, she turned and looked over her shoulder at him. "You coming?"

He moved forward, the knot growing a little larger in his stomach at the thought of what he was about to embark on. He was continuing, not ending, his chain of deception, and he was looking to start a relationship steeped in those lies.

The cooler interior air brushed over his face as he stepped inside. Faith padded barefoot into the kitchen and opened the fridge.

"You want something to drink?" she asked. "There's beer, wine and some juice."

He shook his head then said, "No, I'm fine."

She poured herself a glass of juice then walked back into the living room where he stood. "So what did you want to talk to me about?"

He observed the slight tremble of her lips, something she tried to disguise by raising the glass to her mouth. She was nervous. Hell, so was he, but he didn't want her to feel uneasy with him.

He reached out and cupped his hand under her elbow. "Let's sit down."

She gazed at him with troubled eyes as if fearing what he'd say. Unable to help it, he leaned in, cupped the back of her neck with his hand and pulled her to him. Her glass pressed into his stomach, mashed between them as he captured her lips with his.

He swallowed the whispery sound of surprised pleasure that escaped her mouth. He tasted the tangy orange on her tongue, absorbed her flavor and savored it with every swipe of his tongue over hers.

When he pulled away, her unfocused gaze met his, confusion outlined in the depths of her eyes. Her mouth, now puffy from his kiss, tempted him again. Later, he told himself. He'd sample every inch of her skin.

He nudged her backward until her legs met the edge of the couch. Then he sat her down. Opting to stand, he moved a few steps back and began pacing, unable to control the anxious energy flowing through him.

"I made a mistake in pushing you away," he said.

Her green eyes widened. She set her glass on the end table then folded her hands in her lap, clutching at her fingers until the tips were white.

He stopped pacing and looked directly at her. "I want what you want, Faith. You, in my bed, in my arms, my way."

Color surged into her cheeks as she reacted to his blunt statement.

He moved toward her, kneeling in front of her. He gathered her hands in his and raised her fingers to his lips. "I'm not easy, Faith. I'll push you. I'll demand things of you that you may not be sure you can give. If we do this, you'll give everything to me. In return, I'll cherish your gift. I'll see to your every need. I'll take care of you."

A slow blaze began to burn in her eyes as she studied him. "You want this?" she asked huskily. "You want me? This isn't some game? Some role you think I want you to play?"

He cupped her chin in his hand and stared into her eyes. "No games. You're off for a week. As it turns out, so am I. This is the perfect opportunity for us to explore this relationship."

Her chin trembled in his hand. He rubbed his thumb over her velvety lips before he stood and began pacing again.

"There are some things you need to understand, Faith. If we do this, I will be in complete and utter control. There are no safe words, no playacting, no 'lifestyle' books to read. That's all bull-shit. I've never lived by anyone else's rules and certainly not a bunch of rabid lifestylers all spewing what people do or don't do according to their list of guidelines.

"If that's what you're expecting, then you need to walk now. You can forget about anything you've read or experienced, be-cause what I will demand from you bears no resemblance to what a bunch of role players screwing around with sex games would."

He paused to let his words sink in. Then he walked forward again, kneeling once more in front of her. He threaded his hand into her hair, twining the strands around his fingers as he caressed her scalp.

"You'll be mine. *Mine.* You'll give your everything to me, and in return, I'll give you more than you can ever imagine. I'll take care of you, pleasure you, provide for you."

"Wow," she said after a shaky breath.

"Is that a yes?" he asked as he stroked through her hair.

Slowly she slid her hands up his chest and around his neck. Her fingers curled at his nape, and she dug her fingers into his hair. "Yes," she whispered.

He carefully extricated his hands from her hair then touched her face with his fingers. They fanned lightly over her cheeks, and he pressed his lips to hers.

When he pulled away, they were both breathing heavily, though the kiss had been tender. He slid his fingers over her shoulders and down her arms, enjoying the sensation of her skin on his.

"Let's drive into Galveston. Go someplace nice to eat. When we come back, we can start all over again."

She rubbed her hand over her mouth nervously and nodded. "Okay," she said huskily.

CHAPTER 28

*F*aith took a shower and hurriedly dressed. Her stomach was a mess, and she wasn't sure she was going to be able to eat a thing. She dried her long hair then brushed it and let it hang loose over her shoulders. She knew Gray liked it that way.

Mine.

His declaration still echoed in her mind and sent sparks to her girly parts every time she pictured the possessive look on his face when he'd said it.

Deciding on a pair of jeans and a short-sleeved pink top, she dressed and searched out a pair of heels. She gave herself one last once-over in the mirror, and then she walked into the living room where Gray waited.

He was standing by the French doors, thumbs hooked into his pockets. His blue eyes sparked in appreciation as he let his gaze drift over her.

"You look beautiful," he said.

She smiled. "I'm ready if you are."

He dug his keys out of his pocket then walked toward the door. When he got to her, he held out his hand. She slid her small hand into his much larger one, and his fingers curled tight around it.

Together, they walked out to his truck, and as he'd done the night at The House, he settled her into the passenger seat. During the drive into Galveston, they were silent, but Gray tucked her hand into his and rubbed his thumb across her knuckles.

She took comfort in the intimate gesture. It made her less nervous. Like this was a date like any other. As soon as that thought crossed her mind, she nearly laughed. This was nothing like any other date. This was what she'd been looking for, waiting for, wanting. Not much pressure there.

"Seafood sound good?" he asked, breaking the silence.

She nodded.

He slowed and made a left then eased into a parking spot. Then he squeezed her hand and looked into her eyes. She smiled shyly at the approval she saw reflected in his gaze. He leaned across the seat and kissed her, warm, soft, nonaggressive. Then he drew away and stepped out of the truck.

When they walked in, Gray spoke quietly to the hostess, who gave him a quick smile and nodded. She glanced past him to Faith and smiled again. Then she collected two menus and motioned them to follow her.

"What did you tell her?" Faith whispered as they walked behind the hostess.

"Just that we wanted some privacy."

And sure enough, the hostess sat them in a corner booth toward the back of the restaurant. The closest people were at least six tables away.

As they sat, a waiter appeared to take their drink order. A few seconds later, they were finally alone.

Gray reached across the table and twined his fingers with hers. "We've . . . well, I've spent too much time avoiding you. Things have been crazy between us, moved way too fast. I want to slow things down just for tonight so we can learn more about each other."

A contented glow warmed her chest. "I'd like that," she said softly. "I don't know much about you. Just what Pop's told me. You're a cop. You live in Dallas. You lost your partner earlier this year, and you're taking a break to sort things out. I'd like to know more."

He looked a little chagrined, as if he'd been expecting her to volunteer information on herself first.

"When was your last relationship?" she asked.

His mouth turned down into a frown. "Relationship? I'm not sure I'd call my encounters with the opposite sex relationships."

She arched one brow. "What would you call them then?"

"Sex," he said bluntly.

"And is that what I am to you? Just sex?" she asked softly.

He stared at her for a long moment. "No. And that's what scared the shit out of me. Why I put you at a distance and tried like hell to stay away from you."

"Why do guys freak out so much over the idea of a woman being more than sex?" she asked curiously. "It's become positively cliché. Did your mother never hug you or something?"

His eyes widened in surprise, and then he laughed. "No, I can't blame my mother for my issues with relationships. I didn't know her well enough for her to turn me off or on to the female populace."

She waited for him to go on, not sure what part of that statement she wanted to tackle first.

He let go of her hands and leaned back in his chair. He lifted his glass to his lips and took a long swallow before setting it back down. "My issues with relationships stem from my frustration with not finding what I want."

"We seem to have that in common," she said.

He nodded. "I saw in you things that appealed to me. I saw a woman who I imagined being a perfect fit, but the old adage too good to be true kept coming to mind."

"I hope I don't disappoint you," she said wryly. "I can only be myself. Just like you don't want a script to adhere to, neither do I."

"I wouldn't ever want you to change, Faith. I like you just the way you are. Even if we don't work out."

"But you don't know anything about me," she pointed out.

He shook his head in disagreement. "I know that you're beautiful. Loyal. Intelligent. Feminine. You know exactly what you want, and you won't settle for less. You're not afraid to surrender to a man." He leaned forward again, pinning her with his earnest gaze. "There are two kinds of women I could never get involved with."

She cocked her head to the side in blatant curiosity. The inner workings of a man's mind . . . well that was definitely worth the price of admission.

"A woman who plays games. Mind games, sex games, whatever. I like a woman to be honest, not to hide behind a mask. The second is a woman who isn't strong enough to surrender."

That earned him another raised brow. She too leaned forward, her curiosity growing.

"I don't want a woman I become involved with to become a

mindless puppet any more than I want to become one. It takes a very special woman to submit to a man but still retain everything that makes her strong and unique. Her own person."

"You've given this a lot of thought," she mused.

He shrugged. "It's what I want."

"And what about out of the bedroom?" she asked. "Does your control extend to every aspect of the relationship? I gathered that the game players you referenced are those women who only want good, kinky sex and then want to step out of the role as soon as they get out of the bedroom."

He looked intently at her, his expression one of absolute seriousness. "I have no desire to be a tyrant. I just know me. I'm a control freak. I'm comfortable when I'm making the decisions. When you pair that with the kind of woman I'm most attracted to—a soft, feminine woman who I can protect and take care of—then I suppose I do want an all-encompassing relationship where I call the shots in and out of bed. Does that alarm you?"

She smiled. "No. Does it make me weak to admit that I want a man who can take care of me?"

A gleam of satisfaction shone in his eyes. He stared at her with promise reflected in every facet of his face. "I think you're probably one of the strongest women I've ever met, Faith."

She felt warmed by the praise and the admiration in his voice. And she'd have to be a blind fool not to see the lust in his eyes. Every time he looked at her, it was as though he was peeling her clothing off, inch by inch. She'd waited forever for a man to look at her like this. Like she was the only woman in the world. No, she didn't feel weak. At the moment, she felt very powerful.

They were interrupted when the waiter brought their food.

They relaxed and began eating. From time to time, Gray offered her a bite of his food, and he seemed to enjoy feeding her.

When they'd had enough, the waiter took their plates and left the check, but still, they lingered at the table. Faith was nervous about the return to the beach house. Not a bad nervous. She was still unsure of what to expect but was relieved that she wouldn't have to make the moves. That was clearly Gray's territory.

They chatted about innocuous things. Gray told her about growing up in a crime-infested neighborhood and how that influenced him to become a cop. He told her about his partner and Mick, his pseudo father figure.

She'd already suspected Gray was a very black-and-white kind of guy, and after hearing him talk about his job, justice and his partner's death, she was more convinced that he wasn't one to see anything in shades in between. Everything was either right or wrong.

Gray motioned for the waiter to refill their drinks. Then he regarded Faith intently as he sipped from his glass. "When you went to the sex club . . ."

She winced at the description. It seemed so tawdry. "The House," she corrected.

He shrugged. "When you went to *The House*, what did you want to happen?"

"I would think it was obvious," she said. "You saw what happened."

"I was only there a few minutes," he said. "You'd obviously been there for a while. Did what you saw interest you?"

Her face warmed. "Some of it," she admitted.

He raised an eyebrow. "What parts?"

She looked down for a moment. "It was in part shocking. I mean

I've watched porn movies, but I've never seen or experienced anything like that in person."

"Did it arouse you?" he asked.

She slowly nodded. "Very much so."

"Some of it more than others?"

Again she nodded.

"What parts did you like?" he pressed.

Her tongue lay thick in her mouth. Her lips parted as she worked to overcome her awkwardness. "When I first got there, in the downstairs rooms, there was a woman sitting between two men. Their attention was focused solely on her. It was obvious they both wanted her. I was jealous of her."

He watched her, keen interest in his expression. "Go on."

"Then when we went upstairs there were two men. I'd never seen two men having sex, not even in a movie. It was shocking, yet I was so transfixed I couldn't look away. It was one of the most erotic scenes I ever remember seeing. And then there was a woman who was having sex with two men. In that moment, I wanted to be her so badly."

"Having two men intrigues you?" Gray asked.

She flushed.

"Don't be embarrassed. Would it surprise you to know that a lot of men fantasize about sharing their woman with another man?"

She cocked her head, intrigued by his statement. "Really? Do you?"

He shrugged. "There's something primitive, not to mention erotic and arousing, about allowing another man to possess what's yours, to fill more than one of a woman's orifices. Simultaneously."

Her face grew even hotter.

"You're turned on by that," he observed.

"What woman wouldn't be?" she blurted.

"What else did you see at The House?"

"The spanking."

"You liked it."

She shifted in her seat. "It wasn't so much the spanking. It was his control over the other woman. His authority. It was so dark and sexy. It started a yearning in me that made me feel like I was turning my skin inside out."

"Yet when you took her place, the spanking did nothing for you," he said quietly.

She shook her head. "How did you know?"

He smiled gently. "It was obvious. I could see your disappointment and your frustration. You needed more than what he was giving you."

"Yes," she whispered. "It wasn't real, and I knew it."

He leaned forward, reaching for her chin, cupping it in his hand. Their gazes met and locked. "This will be real, Faith. I don't play games."

She shuddered delicately as the huskily rendered promise slid over her body. "I know."

They sat in silence for a while, sipping at their drinks. Faith relaxed and let go of some of her nerves. The evening had been perfect. The idea that they had an entire week to explore each other gave her a thrill. She couldn't wait to discover if Gray was truly the man who could give her everything she'd dreamed.

At one point, Gray set his drink down and looked over at her again. She could sense the forthcoming question. She looked inquisitively at him.

"Are you on birth control?" he asked bluntly.

"Yes," she said calmly.

"My last sexual encounter was over six months ago," he said. "I've had a physical since then. And there's the fact that I've never not worn a condom when I've had sex with a woman."

She shifted a little uncomfortably. "Well, my last checkup was a couple of months ago. The guy I was seeing until recently had blood tests before I would sleep with him. But we also used condoms."

Gray nodded. "My question is how you would feel about us not using them."

A whole host of colorful images flashed through her head. The idea of taking Gray into her body, skin to skin, was extremely arousing.

"You've never not worn a condom?" she asked.

"No. And if you'd prefer, I can have the results of my last set of blood tests faxed down tomorrow morning. I'm not some horny teenager willing to say anything to get into your pants."

She smiled. "I believe you. And the thing is, I'd love not to have to mess with condoms." She wrinkled her nose. "Without a good amount of lubricant, they're extremely uncomfortable for me. But I have to be honest. The last time I had sex was right before you and I met for the first time. We used condoms. We're both clean, but you deserve to know the situation you're getting into," she said plainly.

"I very much want to feel every delicious inch of your pussy," he said in a husky voice.

An uncontrollable quiver rolled over her body.

Gray looked down at his watch, and she knew their dinner was over. So many things bubbled up. Desire. Excitement. Curiosity. Fear. Her hands shook as she bunched them together in her lap.

"Are you ready?" he asked softly.

She nodded and stood when he got out of his seat. He touched his hand to her back and ushered her out of the restaurant.

The warm, salty breeze hit them as soon as they stepped out. In the distance, intermixed with the sounds of passing traffic, the soft music of the ocean filled the night.

"Let's get back," Gray said close to her ear.

She nodded, and they climbed into the truck.

CHAPTER 29

*W*hen they returned to the beach house, Gray laid his keys on the table and watched as Faith walked to the French doors and looked out. She was nervous. Her body language screamed uncertainty.

He walked quietly to the bathroom, leaving her for a moment. He knelt by the huge sunken tub and flipped the lever for the stopper. Then he turned the bathwater on and ran his fingers under the tap to test the temperature. When he was satisfied with the heat, he rose and walked back into the living room.

She was where he'd left her. He walked up behind her and slid his hands over her shoulders. Brushing her hair to the side, he lowered his head and pressed his lips to her neck. She shivered beneath him, and a soft sigh escaped her lips.

He lifted his gaze and stared out at the rising moon. It was nearly full and reflected off the distant water. It was a perfect night.

"Come to the bathroom," he murmured against her ear. "I'm drawing you a bath."

She turned in his arms, and his hands slid to her waist. "That sounds heavenly," she said.

He hooked his fingers in the front waistband of her jeans and pulled her close to him. He fumbled with the button then undid it. Next he eased the zipper down and started shoving the denim over her hips. When the pants finally tumbled down her legs, he curled his fingers around her hips and eased his palms upward, caressing the soft line of her curvy figure.

Her shirt rose with his arms, inching its way up her body. "Raise your arms," he said.

When she complied, he gently pulled the shirt over her head and tossed it aside. She stepped out of her jeans, tugging the cuffs with one foot and then the other.

He looked down at the lacy, feminine underwear. Pale lilac bra and matching panties. Sheer. Beautiful like her. He placed his hands on her shoulders then slowly pulled at the straps, sliding them over the curve of her shoulder until they fell down her arms.

He reached around and unhooked the clasp and let the bra fall away. The full globes of her breasts shone pale in the distant moonlight. He couldn't resist touching her nipples. He rolled them between his fingers, plucking lightly at the stiff points.

He let his hands fall down her waist until they met the waistband of her panties. Tucking his fingers inside until they brushed the tiny curls between her legs, he pulled until the lace slid down her hips.

When the tiny scrap of material fell to the floor, she stood naked before him, her body illuminated in the luminescent glow of the moon.

She looked like a goddess. All his.

"Mine," he growled.

Tiny little chill bumps danced over her skin, raising the hairs on her arms. He smoothed his hands down her arms to soothe the prickle.

Knowing the bath would probably be full by now, he bent and scooped her up into his arms, eliciting a surprised gasp from her. He silenced her with a kiss and started down the hallway to the bathroom.

The bath was full, so he slowly lowered her into the steaming water then reached over to turn the faucet off.

Faith laid her head against the side of the tub and let out a sound of satisfaction as the hot water lapped over her body. Beside the Jacuzzi, Gray knelt and reached for a bottle of shampoo.

"Turn around so I can wash your hair," he directed.

She repositioned herself in the square tub so that her back was to Gray. He pushed her up so that there was adequate space between her body and the side and then he dipped water into a small ice bucket.

He poured the water over her hair until it was wet, and then he leaned her back once more. She heard the squirting noise of the shampoo bottle, and then his hands delved into her hair. He rubbed and massaged, working up a lather.

He was gentle, and his fingers worked over every inch of her scalp until her eyes rolled back in her head at the exquisite sensations. She closed her eyes and gave herself over to the magic of his touch.

For several long minutes, he rubbed and stroked her head until she was sure she would fall into a pleasure-induced coma. Finally he pushed her forward and began rinsing the soap from her hair.

When that was finished, he nudged her shoulder and murmured

for her to turn back to her original position. She flushed a little as the globes of her breasts peeked above the surface of the water. His eyes tracked down her body, and she found herself hoping that his hands traveled the same path.

He reached for the bottle of body soap, and instead of using one of the washcloths stacked on the side of the tub, he squirted the liquid into his hand. Then he reached with his other hand to let the water out.

He waited as the water tracked downward, exposing more of her body. When her chest was bare, he smoothed the soap over her breasts, rubbing lightly as lather built.

He cupped first one, and then the other, rubbing a thumb over each puckered nipple in turn. As the water fell lower still, he massaged the skin of her belly, kneading lightly.

When his hand returned to her breasts, she moaned and arched her back. His finger traced circles around the taut nubs then flicked lightly at the points. Each twinge sent a bolt of awareness straight to her pussy.

She squirmed in the water. Her legs parted, and the warm water lapped between her folds, whispering over her clit. Soon the blond curls at the V of her legs appeared.

He refilled his hand with the soap and slowly, gently cupped the soft mound between her legs. His finger found the sensitive bundle of nerves and strummed it with light precision.

She spread her legs wider. "Please," she whispered. "Oh, please."

His finger delved lower until it circled her tender opening. The blunt tip breached her entrance, pushing inward the teeniest bit.

She panted lightly as her body tightened, and an unbearable ache began deep inside her pelvis.

"Tonight is for you," he whispered. "All for you."

At those words, his thumb found her clit as his fingers sank deeper into her pussy. Her hips lifted, and she convulsed. She bit her lips as the words "Don't stop" came screaming to the surface.

Thankfully he didn't.

His middle finger caressed the wall of her vagina as his thumb massaged her throbbing little button. Then he pushed inward, finding her G-spot. Her world exploded in a kaleidoscope of color and sensation.

Her orgasm burst upon her with the speed of a freight train. Her palms braced on the slick bottom of the tub, and she would have slipped if he hadn't cupped the back of her neck with his other hand.

It was several long seconds before she became aware of her surroundings again. She lay against the tub, gasping for breath as the world gradually returned to rights.

She slowly turned her gaze to see him staring at her with glittering eyes. Eyes that screamed primal possession. Eyes that staked their claim with every stab. She shivered weakly, her muscles a puddle of goo.

He lifted her into his arms, and he carried her to the shower, where he rinsed the remaining soap from her body. Then he carefully dried her from head to toe, his touch gentle yet commanding.

He tugged her into the bedroom, where he retrieved a robe from the closet. He helped her into it and then tied it in front. He left her for a moment while he changed out of his damp shirt. When he returned, he collected her hands in his.

"Let's go out and sit on the deck. I'll brush your hair for you."

She walked behind him on shaky legs. The aftermath of her orgasm had her as weak as a kitten. All she really wanted to do was curl up in his arms and let him hold her.

He opened the French doors and put a hand to her back to guide her outside. Warm sea air tugged at her still-damp hair. She closed her eyes and breathed deep, inhaling the tangy breeze.

It was a gorgeous night.

Gray sat down in the lounger then pulled her down in front of him. He settled her between his legs, and for a moment, she leaned against his chest, her head resting underneath his chin.

She savored the intimate contact, loved being nestled against his big body. Her body hummed, sweet desire flowing through her veins. At this moment, everything seemed so right. As if nothing could ruin such a perfect moment.

The moon shone bright in the sky and cast a brilliant glow over the calm waters of the gulf. Like a sheet of glass, the water wasn't disturbed by so much as a ripple. Closer in, small waves lapped at the shore and cast a cascade of foam over wet sand.

Gray's hand tangled in her hair, separating the locks with his fingers and tugging downward. He reached around her for the brush in her lap and let his hand linger close to the knotted belt of her robe, as if he contemplated untying it. Slowly, teasingly, he withdrew his hand.

She moaned softly as he began brushing the now-drying tresses. As he continued his downward strokes, he wrapped the ends around his hand and let them slide over his fingers. Each tug elicited another purr of pleasure from her.

"You have such beautiful hair," he said. "It suits you perfectly. Vibrant. Free-flowing. Soft."

She turned her head so she looked at him over her shoulder. "I'm tempted every so often to cut it all off."

His hands stilled. "You wouldn't."

She shrugged. "It can be a real pain in the ass sometimes."

"I can't wait to see it spread out over the bed while I'm sliding my cock between your thighs," he said huskily.

Her clit throbbed, and her nipples hardened, sending little tingles of pleasure buffeting through her body.

"I've imagined you on top of me, my dick buried so deep inside you. You leaning over me, your hair like a curtain over my chest. Then I wrap both hands in the strands and hold on while you ride me."

She sucked in her breath and closed her eyes as she imagined the scene he portrayed. He continued his gentle strokes with the brush, each one lulling her deeper into semiconsciousness.

"But my favorite?" he whispered close to her ear. "Is you on your hands and knees, my hands wrapped all up in your hair, holding your head back as I fuck you from behind."

Was it possible to orgasm simply from erotic talk and having your hair brushed? She didn't know, but she wanted to find out.

He grew quiet, and once again, the only sound that could be heard was the distant sound of the ocean. She relaxed against him as he alternated threading his fingers through her hair and sliding the bristles of the brush through the long strands.

She leaned farther back, turning her chin up and closing her eyes. Whispered sounds of pleasure escaped with each breath. She couldn't ever remember being so content. Couldn't ever remember having a man so focused on her. It was exciting, satisfying and a little terrifying all wrapped up in one.

"Why don't you ever talk about your mom?" he asked.

She stiffened and cursed the fact that she had thought nothing could ruin this moment.

"I don't like to talk about her."

The brush moved down her hair, the bristles scratching lightly at her back. He was silent for a moment as he continued his careful attention.

Her shoulders fell. She supposed it wasn't fair. She'd asked him personal questions. If they were going to make a go of any sort of a relationship, she had to be honest. Even if the thought of him knowing about her childhood and her mother gave her hives.

"That wasn't fair of me," she said in a low voice. "I'm sorry. I just hate to talk about her."

"I understand," he said.

"It's such a long story."

"We have all night," he said simply.

The quiet acceptance in his voice bolstered her spirits. He wasn't pressing for more than she wanted to give. Which only made her want to give nonetheless.

He dropped the brush on the deck but continued to play with her hair. Soon he worked his fingers deeper until they massaged her scalp.

"Mmmm. You keep doing that, and I'll tell you whatever you want," she said.

He chuckled but continued kneading. He worked his way down to the nape of her neck and then out over her shoulders. She sighed in sheer bliss.

"Pop isn't my real father. Wait, that's not true. He's very much my real father—the only father I've ever known. But he isn't my biological father."

If she thought he'd be surprised, he didn't show it. He continued his soothing massage, and she relaxed her tense muscles. He didn't say anything, didn't react, just waited for her to continue.

"My mother . . . I'm not even sure how to describe her. She's lived her entire life with her head in the sand. Bad decisions are second nature to her. She's impulsive and reckless, and she's simply unwilling to accept the consequences of her actions."

"Sounds like a lot of people I know," he said dryly.

She nodded. "From an early age, I was the emotional support in our 'family.' At the time, I didn't understand that our relationship was so much different than other mother-daughter relationships. I was just trying to be the best daughter I could.

"When we didn't have food in the house, I did odd jobs, babysat for neighbors so we'd have the money to eat. I can remember holding her head as she puked her guts up after a night of drinking. Of course, I didn't realize that's where all our money was going."

Gray made a sound of disgust. "Christ, Faith. How old were you?"

She shrugged. "Nine, ten, I don't really remember."

His hands tightened on her shoulders and his rubs became more soothing as if he understood the difficulty she had in talking about her mother.

"When I was fourteen, she met and married Pop. I was so excited. I loved Pop on sight. He was so kind to me. Accepted me as his daughter. I had a major crush on Connor. What fourteen-year-old girl wouldn't? He was twenty-four, fresh out of the army, and he was nice to me. Didn't treat me like a nuisance. For the first time, I really thought that I'd landed in the kind of family I wanted."

"What happened?"

Faith sighed. The memory of that night still held such power over her. It had been the worst feeling in her young life. Worse than the disappointments her mother had thrown her way.

"She got a bug up her ass one night. Got me up in the middle of the night and left. I was devastated. I didn't want to leave. I even asked her if I could stay. She made me go with her, and I know it was because she had no one else to take care of her. It pissed me off. Pop was so good to her. He would have taken care of her if only she'd have let him. But like everything else, she fucked things up. Wouldn't allow anything good to happen to us."

His hands stilled on her shoulders, and his fingers dug into her skin. He leaned forward and pressed a kiss to her neck. "Where did you go? What did you do?"

Tears pricked her eyelids. "Back to our old life. Moving every few months when we got evicted. Going back to school wasn't an option. I was too busy trying to feed us and keep a roof over our heads."

Gray cursed.

"A year or so later, she started taking drugs. I wasn't surprised. I had to hide money from her, or she would have used everything we had on drugs. I hated her. I wanted to leave her."

"Why didn't you?"

"I was young. Scared. I had no place to go. No one I could count on. And at the heart of everything, she was still my mother. I couldn't leave her because I knew she wouldn't survive without me."

Gray wrapped his arms around her and pulled until she was tight against his chest. He reclined until they were both leaning back staring up at the night sky.

She closed her eyes and savored the strength in his embrace. The comfort and acceptance. The understanding.

"So what happened?" he asked.

She knew he meant how she ended up here, with Pop, away from her mother. Her lips trembled at the memory of that night.

"When I was twenty, I was working two jobs, so I wasn't around much to babysit her. I bought food, paid the bills and never gave her money. I thought by doing so, she wouldn't have a way to pay for drugs. I underestimated how far she'd go to get what she wanted.

"When I got home from my second job, I found her passed out in the living room of our tiny apartment. She wasn't breathing. I called 911 and did as much CPR as I remembered. When the ambulance got there, they were able to resuscitate her and take her to a hospital.

"I can remember sitting in the waiting room at the hospital feeling guilty because I wasn't sure if I wanted her to survive or not." She shuddered, trying to wipe away the guilt she still felt. "How horrible is that? Wishing my own mother dead."

Gray's arms tightened around her. "Not horrible. It's human."

"They found Pop's phone number in her purse and called him. When he and Connor showed up, I bawled my eyes out on Pop's shoulder. Connor took me to a hotel and stayed with me while Pop got Mom sorted out. He set her up in rehab and what else I'm not even sure. At the time I didn't care. I was too relieved not to have had to deal with it myself. He and Connor took me back to Houston with them, told me I was part of their family. Pop gave me a stiff lecture about not enabling my mother and told me to wash my hands of her."

She shifted against Gray, turning slightly so that her cheek rested on his shoulder. He looked down at her, his eyes soft with sympathy.

"Do you have any idea how relieving it was to have someone say it was okay to take myself out of my relationship with my mother? It sounds silly, but I needed someone to tell me it was okay, that I wasn't a bad person."

Gray nodded and touched a finger to her chin. "Most people wouldn't have done all you did for her."

"When Pop told me he wanted to adopt me . . . I can remember staring at him, so stunned. Then I burst into tears and cried a river. He thought he'd upset me, but it was the most wonderful thing anyone had ever done for me. For the first time, I felt like I truly belonged. He and Connor were my family. Here I was, twenty years old, and I felt like a child all over again."

Gray kissed her forehead and touched his fingers to her cheek, running invisible lines from her cheekbone to her ear.

"So you've been with Pop ever since."

She nodded slightly, not wanting to knock his hand from her face. "He moved me into one of his apartments, gave me a job at Malone and Sons, and gave me a stern lecture about ever allowing my mother back into my life."

"But she's calling you," he said quietly.

She tensed, but he continued stroking her cheek, and she gradually relaxed. "Yes. She's calling again. Same routine. She wants money. In her defense, I've always come through for her, even after Pop told me never to give her anything. He once said that if you give a dog a handout, they'll never leave you alone. He was right. Only this time I refused to help her."

She lowered her voice and looked away. He touched the cheek she now presented as she looked out toward the ocean. "She's in trouble, and all I want is for her to go away. I've tried ignoring it. I haven't told Pop about the phone calls, and if he knew, he'd be hurt and angry that I hadn't told him. But I didn't want to keep burdening him with my problems. He's done enough for me. I knew it was time for me to draw my line in the sand. Only this time I think she really does need help."

"You can't fix her life," Gray said gently. "Pop is right. If you keep bailing her out of trouble, she'll never go away. And the thing is, she may never get her act together. Then where does that put you? Always in a position of being her crutch."

She nodded. "I know. I keep telling myself that, but then I go back to the fact that she's my mother. If you have no one else in the world, you're supposed to at least have your mother, right?"

"You don't have no one," he pointed out. "You have Pop, Connor, Nathan, Micah . . . you have *me*."

A warm glow lit and bloomed within her. It swelled in her chest, expanding outward until it encompassed her soul. He was right. She wasn't alone.

She gazed at him, a sheen of tears blurring the lines of his face. She turned her body until she curled sideways in his lap then raised her hand to his face. "I should have told Pop about the calls. I realize that now. But some part of me is still afraid to rock the boat and cause any problems. I don't want Pop to ever regret taking me in. He's given so much to me."

"Have you ever stopped to consider how much you've given him?" Gray asked.

She stared at him, perplexed. "No, I—"

"He adores you, Faith. Hell, they all do. Connor, Micah and Nathan. Don't ever think you haven't contributed to that relationship. You're not some charity case. You're as important to them as they are to you."

"Know so much, do you?" she asked with a slight smile.

"It's obvious. In the time I've been here, it's been easy to see how much you mean to them. They're all very protective of you."

His words warmed her heart. "Thank you for saying that. I needed to hear it. I've been so stressed out over the phone calls and worrying over whether I made the right decision."

He shushed her with his finger. "No more worrying. This week is for us. Besides, who knows? Maybe by the time we get back things will be resolved."

His cryptic statement was meant to be reassuring, she was positive, and she allowed herself to grab hold of the confidence she heard in his voice.

"You make me forget my worries," she confessed.

"Good. I want our time together to be without stress. I want to take away your unhappiness. I want you to shine. For me."

She curled her hands around his shoulders and pressed her face into the curve of his neck. His pulse thudded against her forehead.

"Are you ready for me to take you inside?" he murmured.

Oh, but she loved the way he said that. She nodded.

He eased her off his lap and maneuvered his way out of the lounger. Then he bent and hoisted her into his arms. He carried her inside and walked to the bedroom. Once inside, he lowered her to the king-size bed. "I'm going to go take a shower," he said. "I want you naked and in bed when I get back."

Her stomach did a complete somersault as she saw the raw desire in his eyes. He stared at her for another long moment before he turned around and walked into the bathroom.

Gray turned the shower on and immediately unbuttoned his jeans. He was going to suffer a permanent cramp in his dick because he'd had a hard-on the entire evening, and his jeans had cut so tight across it that he'd existed in a state of pain.

As he pulled his jeans down, his erection sprang free, and he felt immediate relief. How on earth he was going to survive the night was beyond him. He sure as hell wasn't going to bed with a hard-on the size of Texas.

When he stepped into the shower, he grasped his stiff cock in his hand and worked it up and down in an attempt to alleviate the ache. Warm water sluiced down his body as he worked the foreskin back and forth over the swollen head.

He closed his eyes and turned his face into the spray as he felt his balls gather and tighten. His orgasm rose in his groin. His grip tightened around his thick shaft, and he gave two more jerks.

A jet of semen erupted from the tip and was quickly washed away by the spray of water. He ducked his head and sucked in mouthfuls of air as his pulse pounded at his temple.

He continued to stroke his softening cock until finally the waves of pleasure subsided. He quickly soaped his body and rinsed off. Then he stepped out of the shower and reached for a towel. After he'd dried off, he pulled on a clean pair of boxers and walked back into the bedroom.

When he saw Faith lying on the bed, her hair spilled out over the pillow, just like in his fantasies, her naked body illuminated by the glow of the bedside lap, his cock stiffened all over again. He cursed under his breath. So much for his plan to give himself relief from the relentless ache she stirred within him.

He walked over to the bed and climbed in beside her. She looked at him, her beautiful eyes aglow with desire, but more than that, her gaze conveyed trust. He reached for her, pulling her into his arms. Then he reached down for the covers and tugged them over their bodies.

He knew she expected him to make love to her tonight, but he also knew how important it was not to rush into things. Tomorrow would be soon enough to begin their sexual relationship. Tonight was all about finding their comfort level and developing trust between them.

He felt like a goddamn hypocrite for placing so much importance on trust when he was deceiving her at every turn. But in this, their relationship, he would be nothing but honest. He had to hope that in the end it was enough.

He tucked her head beneath his chin and held her close, enjoying the feel of flesh on flesh. "Go to sleep," he said softly. "We have all the time in the world."

Her body trembled against his, and then he felt the tension leave her as her body melted into his. He kissed the top of her head then reached behind him to turn off the lamp.

CHAPTER 30

$\mathcal{G}$ray opened his eyes to silky, blond hair tickling his nose. He blinked and pulled his head slightly away. Faith was securely snuggled into his chest, her head still tucked beneath his chin. Her hair was bunched up on the pillow next to his cheek, and he could smell the faint scent of the shampoo he'd used to wash her hair.

The room was still dark, and he raised his wrist to look at his watch. Not obscenely early. It should be getting light soon.

Careful not to wake her, he extricated himself from around her and eased out of bed. He needed to make a phone call, and this seemed a prime opportunity.

He picked up his jeans off the floor at the foot of the bed and dug in his pocket for his cell phone. Then he walked out of the bedroom. He opened his phone and punched in Mick's number as he opened the French doors and stepped into the early morning air.

"Where the hell are you?" Mick demanded.

"Good morning to you too," Gray said, irritated already by Mick's tone.

"Good morning, my ass. You should be here, helping to catch Alex's killer, not off fucking around with the girl."

"Mick, don't start," Gray warned. "I called to see what the hell was going on. You may not like how we decided to do things, but that's too damned bad. You're reacting emotionally, and if you had your damn head on straight, you'd know I'm right."

"We. Since when did this become we. I can't figure out why you brought in Malone and his crew. His only concern will be for his daughter. He won't give a fuck that Samuels killed my son."

"Just like your only concern is for your own interest," Gray said quietly. "Faith is an innocent victim, Mick. I won't allow her to be used any more than she already has. If that pisses you off, too fucking bad."

"I never imagined you'd sell out," Mick said harshly. "I never thought you'd turn your back on Alex this way."

"Damn it, Mick. Quit trying to yank my string. You've been doing this shit from the start, and I let you. I'm done allowing you to play the guilt card. If Samuels makes a move for Faith, Pop and the others will nail him. That should be all that concerns you. By the book. No legal loopholes for him to fall through."

A long pause ensued, and the only sound was Mick's harsh breathing. Finally Mick broke the silence. "If you won't help me bring Alex's killer down, I'll do it myself. I'm not going to stand by and watch him get away. Not when we're so damn close."

"Mick, quit talking out your ass and calm down," Gray said in exasperation. "Mick. Mick?"

Damn it, he'd hung up. Gray closed the phone and swore long and hard. Mick was losing it. He was too eaten up by grief and rage to think rationally. He needed to get his ass back to Dallas, but Gray knew there was no chance of that happening.

He opened his phone back up and punched in Micah's number. He shook his head and tried to blow off his anger as he waited for Micah to pick up. For all Mick's faults, Gray knew he was a good guy.

"Hey, man," Gray said when Micah answered.

"Hey," Micah returned.

"What's the latest? Any word on Samuels?"

"No, nothing yet. Cops have got a double to stand in for Faith. She's staying at Faith's apartment and will be going in to the office like Faith does."

Gray sighed. It was probably too soon, but the letter told him that Samuels was close. Even if he wasn't yet in Houston, he soon would be.

More than ever, he was glad Faith was removed from the picture where he could keep her safe. He didn't have a good feeling about any of it. Mick, Samuels or the mother. Faith stood to get hurt, if not physically, than certainly emotionally.

Again, he was hit square in the face with the reasoning behind Pop wanting to keep this from her. Though he'd vehemently disagreed, he wasn't so sure now that Pop hadn't been right.

"Look, buddy, I have to run. Things are a bit nutty around here. Nathan, Connor and I are keeping an eye out at the apartments. We have a few plants keeping watch, but we didn't want to spook Samuels off and let him know we're on to him. Faith's double is due to leave her apartment in a few minutes, and it's my turn to follow her to the office."

"Okay, man, keep me posted, okay?"

"Will do. You just keep Faith safe and happy."

Gray chuckled. "I'll do my best."

He slipped back inside and went in search of a piece of paper and a pen. After jotting a note for Faith, he eased back into the bedroom. He stared down at her sleeping face for a long moment, studying her features and how beautiful and peaceful she appeared.

Unable to resist, he leaned down and trailed a finger down her cheek. She stirred and leaned into his touch but didn't awaken. He reluctantly drew away from her then left the note on the pillow next to her head.

When Faith awoke, Gray was no longer beside her. Bright sunlight blazed through the window, and she squinted against the glare.

When her gaze dropped to Gray's pillow, she saw a single sheet of paper propped against it. She picked it up and saw Gray's almost indecipherable scrawl.

When you wake up, come into the kitchen. I'll have breakfast ready. Don't put anything on.

She let the paper drift back down to the bed, and she felt the beginnings of a full-bodied blush coming on. Naked. If she was honest, she had no idea what to expect. He'd managed to keep her off balance so far. Instead of having sex, he'd spent the entire previous evening showering her with attention. She'd never felt so pampered and cared for in her life.

"Don't be a chickenshit," she muttered as she climbed out of bed.

She walked into the bathroom and quickly ran a brush through her hair. It didn't need much. Gray had brushed it until it had shone. Now it fell down her back in soft waves.

She gazed at herself in the mirror. The woman who stared back fascinated her. There was a softness about her. A happy, radiant glow that was reflected in her eyes and smile.

She took a deep breath and left the bathroom. As she got closer to the kitchen, her pulse sped up, and a nervous tickle started rolling in her stomach.

He was standing by the bar, holding a skillet in one hand as he spooned eggs onto plates. When he looked up and made eye contact, her first instinct was to cover herself.

She halted several feet away and swallowed against the knot in her throat. He set the skillet down and wiped his hands on a dishrag. Then he stepped around the bar, his gaze roving up and down her naked body.

As the distance closed between them, her arms crept up to cover her breasts.

"Good morning," he murmured as he bent to kiss her.

His hands circled her wrists, and he pulled them down to her sides.

"Don't hide. You're much too beautiful for that. I want to look at you."

Satisfaction was mirrored in his face as she blushed. Why he liked that about her, she'd never know. It seemed a little silly for a grown woman to blush as much as she did.

"Come, sit down, and we'll eat," he said as he tugged her toward the bar.

She followed him, her confusion building. She sat down, and

he shoved a plate in front of her. Bacon, eggs and toast. And a tall glass of orange juice.

He sat down across from her and stared up at her with his gorgeous blue eyes. He was dressed, which put him at a distinct advantage in her mind. T-shirt and jeans, though he was barefooted, and for some reason, she found that sexy.

It was hard to concentrate on eating when she had no idea what to expect or what would happen next. He'd hardly fallen into the role of the dominant male. Quite the opposite, actually. He'd been clear that he expected things to go his way. What she hadn't expected, however, was that his way had been to lavish attention on her. She'd worked herself up into quite a knotted mess when Gray looked over at her. He put his fork down.

"Faith, just ask. I can see a million questions running through your head."

She smiled ruefully and set her fork down as well. "I guess I don't know what to expect. I mean, I'm a little confused. It's driving me crazy."

He raised a brow and stared intently at her. "Did you expect to be kneeling? Have to ask permission to speak? Did you expect me to beat you before fucking your brains out?"

She winced at the crudity of his description, but she also knew he was partly right. A little embarrassed, she lowered her head and nodded.

She heard him sigh. When she looked back up, he was shaking his head.

"Faith, I'm not an asshole. I'm not going to treat you like a piece of garbage. Ever. You don't ever need permission to speak, for God's sake. Kneeling is just dumb. There are lots of ways to show your submission and your respect and for me to return it as well. None of those include humiliation or ill treatment."

A warm prickle spread over her cheeks as his eyes bored into her. He spoke earnestly, and it was clear he meant every single word.

"No doubt, there will be times when I push you," he continued. "We both have fantasies. I like kink as much as the next guy, and I'll expect you to do as I tell you, but this isn't a game. I can't stress that enough.

"I'm not your parent. Have no desire to be placed in that role. We're both adults, and the petulant master/slave game bores me to tears. The little fake disobedient act so the master will punish the naughty little slave—it's ridiculous. If and when I spank you, it'll be because I like seeing my mark on your ass and because you'll enjoy it. Not because you disobeyed me. You're an adult with a mind of your own."

Her stomach tightened, her pussy clenched and her nipples formed achingly hard points. She had to open her mouth and force herself to breathe.

"Any more questions?" he asked calmly.

She shook her head and tried to stop her legs from trembling.

The corners of his mouth turned up into a smile of pure male appreciation. A predatory gleam shone in his eyes as his gazed raked over her body.

"Good. Now, yesterday was all about you. Today? All about me."

CHAPTER 31

*F*aith swallowed, then swallowed again. She'd never wanted another man as much as she wanted Gray. Ever. She wanted his touch. His mouth. His cock. Every inch of him.

Her food was long forgotten. Not that she would have tasted it anyway.

"Are you finished?" he asked.

She nodded, not trusting herself to speak.

He got up and gathered the plates. "Go on in the living room and have a seat on the couch. I'll be in as soon as I get the dishes picked up."

She rose unsteadily and all but fled the room. She needed as much time as possible to regroup before he finished. When she got to the couch, she sank down onto the soft leather and covered as much of herself as she could by hunching forward.

If she was braver, she'd spread out in a provocative pose, play the seductress. But the truth was, she was nervous as hell.

She heard the bang of dishes, then all went quiet. Anticipation licked up her spine. She looked up and saw him standing in the doorway watching her.

She curled her fingers until her nails dug into her palms as he started toward her. He stopped a mere foot away, his thumbs hooked into the pockets of his jeans.

He radiated power. A sensual heat that made her nerves tighten in anticipation. With slow, methodical movements, he reached for his fly and undid the button. She watched, mesmerized, as he lowered the zipper.

He reached into his pants with his right hand and pulled out his cock. Her eyes widened in appreciation. Before, in the dark hallway of The House, she'd only been able to feel and taste. Now she could see the thick, ruddy member jutting outward from a nest of light brown hair.

His hand gripped the base, and the broad head was directed at her mouth. She licked her lips. His breath escaped in a hiss. "You have the sexiest mouth," he said.

He reached for her with his other hand and curled it around the back of her neck. Then he pulled her forward as he positioned his cock at her mouth. "Open for me," he rasped.

She parted her lips, and he slid inside. She closed her eyes as she processed the bombardment of sensations. He was thick in her mouth, soft on her tongue and rigid across her lips.

He thrust deep, stealing her breath. He moved his hand from his cock and threaded it through her hair until it met his other at the base of her skull. He held her in place as he thrust deeper.

The head brushed the back of her throat, and she inhaled deeply through her nostrils. "Swallow," he commanded. "Swallow with the thrust and relax your jaw. Take it deep."

She did as he directed, and on his next thrust, he strained

forward, sliding deeper with her swallow. He held himself deep. His fingers curled into her scalp.

Finally, he withdrew and then he released her head. He gripped his cock again as it hovered close to her lips.

"Lick it," he said hoarsely.

She ran her tongue around the satiny crown and lapped at the small opening at the tip. He groaned, and she smiled in satisfaction.

"Happy with yourself, are you?"

She responded by circling the head with her tongue, pausing to pay special attention to the seam exposed when she shoved at the foreskin.

"Suck it," he growled.

She parted her lips and coaxed the tip into her mouth. She sucked lightly as he held still in front of her.

"Now take it deep."

She opened her mouth wider and sucked him inside.

"F-fuuuck," he gasped out.

He put his hand on top of her head and grasped his cock with the other.

"Hold still," he said hoarsely.

He began jerking at his cock with rapid back-and-forth motions. She closed her eyes and relaxed, allowing him to take over. A light spurt hit the back of her mouth just as his movements became more frantic.

He pulled from her mouth, and a hot jet of cum splashed onto her breasts. She opened her eyes to see his head thrown back, a look of pure agony on his face.

His hand jerked over his cock as he directed the spray onto her chest. The creamy fluid slid over her breasts and lower to her belly.

When he opened his eyes, they glittered with satisfaction. His gaze stroked up and down the same path his cum had landed on. He reached a finger out and trailed it up the underside of her breast to her nipple, where he collected a droplet that had tracked downward. Then he held his finger to her lips. He nudged her mouth open, smearing the cum on her lips and then over her tongue.

"Lick it clean," he said huskily.

She tasted the light, musky essence and sucked at his finger until he eased it out again.

He stepped away. Her body ached and trembled. She wanted his touch. Needed the release. She was more aroused now than she had been last night when he gently fingered her to orgasm.

"I love the way you look," he said. "Sexy as hell with my cum all over you."

His eyes gleamed with male power, a man self-assured of his control. And if she was honest, the idea of him marking her gave her a delicious thrill. It sounded silly said aloud, which is why she allowed the thought to remain unspoken.

He held out his hand for her, and she reached up and allowed him to help her up. His gaze lowered one last time to the trails of cum down her chest before he tugged her toward the bathroom.

Once there, he turned on the shower, and after the water had warmed, he drew her in with him. He bent his head and captured her lips with his. His mouth moved hard over hers as water rained down on them both.

His hands cupped her elbows and slid slowly up her arms until he grasped her shoulders. He didn't overpower her, but he overwhelmed her senses. His kiss was gentle, but she felt him in every nuance of her soul.

There was no one else. Nothing but him and her. And how he made her feel.

She slid her arms around his waist and she splayed her hands over his muscled back as his lips moved from her mouth to her jaw and then her neck.

His cock pressed into her belly. She stepped back an inch and slid one hand between them, wanting to touch him, caress him, but he grasped her wrist and halted her progress.

"Not yet," he murmured. "If you touch me, I won't last."

She stared at his face, absorbing the way he looked at her, as if she was the only woman who'd ever mattered to him. She was transfixed by the unguarded emotion she saw there. It sent a host of butterflies winging their way from her stomach into her throat.

"I love how you look at me," he said, as he reached for the soap.

She cocked her head to the side. "How am I looking at you?"

His blue eyes blazed as he returned her gaze. "Like I'm all-powerful. Like I'm the only man. Like if you ever look at another man like that, I'd kill him."

Her cheeks grew tight, and she smiled. "I was just thinking that I loved the way you looked at *me*."

He arched a brow. "And how is that?"

"Like I'm beautiful," she whispered. "Like I'm the only woman who's ever affected you this way. Like in a room full of other women, you'd only see me."

"All true," he said as he stepped even closer to her.

He began soaping her body, his touch alternately firm and gentle. When he was done, she wrestled the soap from him, despite his protests, and she began soaping his big body.

As her fingers glided over each sleek muscle, she marveled at the perfection of his physique. Not an inch of spare flesh dotted his body.

She traced the lines of his six-pack then followed the path of the line of hair leading from his chest down to his navel.

"Watch it," he growled, when her hand dipped lower.

She giggled and jumped when he smacked her on the ass.

"If you're done playing, let's get out of here," he said as he reached for the knobs to turn the water off.

They dried off together, though he did most of the work. When he was finished, he tossed the towel aside and swatted her playfully on the behind.

"In the bedroom. On the bed."

She didn't waste any time. She turned and hurried out of the bathroom and crawled onto the bed to wait.

He sauntered out a moment later and stood watching her as she propped herself up on her elbow. His legs were slightly spread, and his cock was semierect. In a word, he looked perfect.

Gorgeous. Hard. Lean. Like a predator. All man. All hers.

He walked slowly to the bed where she lay. He put his hand on her leg and let it glide over the curve of her hip. With a firm push, he nudged her over on her back.

The bed dipped as he crawled onto the mattress with her. He hovered over her, looking down with his intense gaze. He lowered his head and kissed her belly.

"I've waited long enough to taste you," he said as he backed down her body.

He gripped her hips then slid his hands around to her ass until he cupped the globes in his palms. Then he worked his hands down until they gripped the backs of her thighs. He rotated his hands until they rested on top of her legs, inches from her pussy. Then he slowly spread her thighs.

He pushed outward and then up, forcing her knees to bend. She closed her eyes and dug her fingers into the covers at her sides. His mouth was so close to her clit. If he so much as breathed on her, she'd come.

She ached, she pulsed. Every part of her body tingled like a sparkler spitting in fourteen directions.

With one finger, he parted her folds. Then he added another finger as he held them apart.

"So beautiful," he murmured. "Pink and so feminine. Soft. I bet you taste just as sweet as you look."

She shuddered and arched her hips, wanting more, wanting him.

Then he licked her. Her eyes flew open, and her head jerked upward as his tongue swiped across her entrance and upward to her clit.

Every muscle in her body tensed then spasmed as if her brain no longer had any control over their movements.

"Mmm, I was right. You taste delicious," he purred.

"Oh God," she gasped.

He lapped at her again, and she clenched her teeth as a bolt of exquisite pleasure rocked her core. She needed more, just a little harder.

But he seemed to realize just how close she was and just how much it would take to send her over the edge, because he held back. Light, teasing, he licked and nibbled along her tender flesh.

She moaned and twisted restlessly beneath him.

He raised his head to look at her. "I can see I'm going to have to tie you down if I have any hope of keeping you still."

Oh, he knew what effect that statement would have on her. She could see the smug light in his eyes when her nipples puckered and a shiver racked her body.

He lowered his head again and gently sucked her clit into his mouth. She tried not to move. God, she tried. But when he started sucking rhythmically, she lost all control.

She arched into him and was shocked to hear herself begging. Had she opened her mouth? She was close. So close. She needed . . .

He released the sensitive nub and licked his way downward until he rimmed her entrance with his tongue. She crumpled back to the bed as her urgency diminished from her almost orgasm.

All too soon, it started mounting again as he tongued her opening. Tension began rising in her groin. Her pelvis tightened. Her stomach clenched.

Her hands curled into fists, gathering the sheets with them. She squeezed her eyes shut as his featherlight caresses met her most sensitive regions over and over.

Almost . . . almost.

He raised his head, and she cried out in disappointment as he left her hanging. One touch. It was all she needed. Her hand automatically went to her pussy, needing something to catapult her over the top. But he gripped her hand and chuckled softly.

"Oh no, Faith. Not yet. This is about me, remember? And I'm very much enjoying myself."

She sighed in frustration.

He kissed the skin of her pelvis just above the nest of blond curls. From there, he kissed a line up her belly until he positioned his body between her spread legs.

Still in no hurry, he bent and lazily ran his tongue around one nipple then turned to the other and gave it equal attention.

She hummed in contentment. She loved to have her nipples stimulated. His teeth grazed the sensitive point and then he nipped harder, causing her to cry out as a burst of pleasure exploded in her belly.

He sucked the tip into his mouth and worked it back and forth, tugging it with his teeth then soothing it with a swipe of his tongue.

He captured her other nipple between his fingers as he continued to suck. He plucked at the stiff peak then pinched it between his thumb and middle finger. Then he rolled it and tweaked it again.

She was gasping for air when his mouth finally left her breasts and moved up to capture her mouth. He settled his thick cock between her legs as he kissed her with an intensity that bordered on violent.

He sucked the breath right from her lungs. She burned. She ached. She'd never experienced such volatile passion.

Her pussy cupped his erection, and no matter how much she shifted and arched, she couldn't position him so that she could take him into her body.

He kissed her lips, her cheeks, her eyes, her neck. He nipped at her earlobes in turns, and then he sank his teeth into the curve of her neck, and she let out a wail.

She was desperate for him. On fire. Out of control. And still, he was tender, fierce, controlling and dominant. It was a combination she'd never experienced.

Finally, *finally*, he reached between them and positioned his cock at her opening. He propped himself up on one elbow and gazed down at her, his eyes awash with things she couldn't begin to describe.

The head breached her opening, and she closed her eyes as he began to work himself into her body. Slowly. Reverently almost. He was thick. He was hard. He stretched her until she wondered how much she could possibly take. And still he pressed on.

Tears streamed down her face as he patiently took his time, his hips arching forward. He gathered her upper body in his arms, cradling her to him as he finally came to a stop deep within her pussy.

"You're so tight," he whispered. "You fit me like a glove. Made for me. Only me."

He trailed tender kisses from her ear, up her jaw to her lips. His mouth slid down her neck, sucking and licking at her pulse points.

She wrapped her arms around him, her fingers spread over his tightly bunched muscles. His hips rocked forward, retreating only to slide forward again.

How could he be so utterly gentle and yet bristle with so much power and command? It seemed inexplicable to her, and yet with every thrust, with every touch, caress, kiss, he made her feel cherished, protected, *loved*.

He planted his forearms on either side of her head as he held his weight off her body. They fit like two complementing puzzle pieces. He was wedged tightly between her legs, and he brushed his fingers over her cheeks, smoothing away the damp tendrils of her hair.

He gazed down at her, his eyes seeming to absorb every facet of her. There was an odd mixture of tenderness and raw possession in his expression. She reached up to cup his face, and he closed his eyes as her fingers feathered over his cheekbone.

When he opened them again, need glittered, bright, unrelenting. He flexed his hips, driving deeper. "Wrap your legs around me," he said.

She hooked her ankles around his waist, and he slid his hands down her body to cup her ass. He thrust harder. His hips pressed into the backs of her thighs as he worked himself deeper.

He closed his eyes as if in the throes of the sweetest agony. Her orgasm lurked. She was on the fringes of a slow-building hurricane. She'd been up the peak, to the edge so many times and been backed away. Now she wouldn't be denied.

He picked up his pace and the slap of flesh meeting flesh filled the room. She curled her hands around his neck, twining her fingers together at his nape. She held on for dear life.

"Please don't stop," she whispered.

"No, love, not this time," he said. "Let go. I'll catch you. I've got you."

His words sent her the final distance. Her heart lurched at the tender endearment. Her body exploded in a million different directions. For once, her heart and her mind were in unison with her body. Never had she felt so complete. So satisfied. So content. So convinced that this was where she was supposed to be.

Fresh tears rolled down her cheeks as every single muscle in her body tightened unbearably. And finally her release flooded her, relaxing the tension. She floated, weightless, cradled in his arms.

She became aware of him kissing her ear and murmuring soothing words. And then he tensed against her. He began thrusting impatiently into her, as if he couldn't get deep enough fast enough.

He whispered her name just as he collapsed onto her body. She gathered him to her, loving the feel of his weight, his heartbeat against her chest.

For a long moment, he lay there, breathing raggedly in her ear. Then he propped himself up and kissed her lingeringly.

"I didn't hurt you, did I?" he asked gruffly when he pulled away.

She smiled and caressed his hard jaw with her hand. "You were perfect."

"There you go looking at me like that again." He flexed his hips, sliding his still-hard cock against the walls of her pussy.

He eased off of her, sliding out of her body in a warm rush of fluid.

"Let me get a towel," he said. "Stay right there."

She watched as he walked naked to the bathroom. There was such confidence in his stride. No arrogance. No fake swagger. Just the walk of a man who was supremely confident.

She closed her eyes and relived his lovemaking. Her body was sated. A warm, sleepy glow surrounded her. Ultimate contentment. Pleasure.

The bed dipped again, and he gently spread her legs and pressed the towel to her still quivering flesh. She pried her eyes open to see him watching her.

He tossed the towel aside and climbed up beside her. "I love the look of a well-satisfied woman," he murmured as he pulled her into his arms. "There's no bigger rush for a man than to know he's responsible for putting that kind of look on a woman's face."

She snuggled into his chest and wished to hell she could purr like a cat. He wrapped both arms around her and positioned her head on his shoulder. His hand smoothed down her back until he cupped her bottom possessively.

"Get some sleep," he whispered.

She yawned, only too willing to follow his dictate. As she drifted off, he folded one leg over hers, and she dimly registered that there wasn't one part of her body that he wasn't wrapped around in some manner.

She fell asleep with a smile on her face.

Chapter 32

*I*n the hazy world between asleep and awake, Faith hovered, content and lethargic. Warm hands glided over her chest then gripped her shoulders. Her eyes flew open just as she flipped over and her face met the pillow.

Both hands were pulled behind her until they met at the small of her back. Gray held them in one hand, and then she felt the rasp of rope coiling around her wrists.

Her heart thudded against the mattress, and her breath came in shallow spurts as she struggled to process what was happening.

When his hands left her wrists, she pulled experimentally, but the rope held tight. She turned her cheek to the pillow and tried to relax, but the excitement stirring in her veins kept her tense with anticipation.

Firm hands kneaded and massaged her buttocks. Her legs were spread, and she was exposed. Her ass, her pussy. And she was helpless against whatever he wanted to do.

She closed her eyes and panted as an adrenaline rush like she'd never experienced crashed through her body.

Where would he take her? Her pussy? Her ass? Just the idea of him taking her so primitively had her skating precariously close to release.

Her question was answered when he lifted her just enough that he slid into her quivering pussy. She moaned as he pressed into her, stuffing every inch of his cock into her tight passage.

He leaned over her, placing his hands on either side of her head. His body covered her as his hips arched into her ass. His tight belly brushed against her bound hands as he worked his cock back and forth into her body.

His mouth brushed against her ear. "Tell me, Faith, has anyone ever fucked your ass?" he whispered. "Would I be your first?"

Tiny little goose bumps dotted her arms. "Yes," she panted.

"Yes, what?"

"You would be the first," she said in a low voice.

His hips rocked forward, thrusting hard and urgent into her. He made a sound of satisfaction as he nipped at her ear.

"Do you want me to fuck your ass?" he asked. "Does the idea of something so naughty and forbidden turn you on?"

"Yes," she groaned. "Yes!"

"Do you want me to untie you?" he asked. "Or do you want me to fuck you just like this? Helpless. Unable to move. At the mercy of however I want to take you."

His erotic words slid over her, tightening every single nerve ending in their wake. His hips stilled as he waited for her answer. She felt full, stretched. How much tighter would he feel in her ass?

He collected her hair in his fist and pulled slightly. "Answer the question," he directed.

"I want you to fuck me just like this," she whispered.

His hold loosened, but his hand stayed in her hair, fingering the strands as he resumed the slow, measured thrusts. Then he withdrew.

The bed dipped as he leaned over, and she heard a light squirting sound. Lubricant? Fingers parted the globes of her ass, and then she felt the cool shock of the slick gel.

He eased one fingertip over the opening then slowly inserted the tip. She moaned at the sensation as he lazily worked the finger in and out. One finger and it felt like he'd stuffed his entire dick through the small opening.

He withdrew, added more lubricant and then inserted two fingers. He stretched the tight channel, preparing her for what was to come.

She curled her fingers into her palms at her back and tensed when he removed his fingers. He spread her legs wider and leaned over her. His arm brushed over her buttocks as he reached between her legs to position his cock.

It slid between her cheeks, and then he took both hands and spread the globes. The head pressed against the ring of muscle, and she instinctively tensed against the invasion.

He groaned as she squeezed the tip of his cock, but he didn't relent. His fingers dug into her behind, spreading wider as he pushed into her.

He leaned forward, forcing his cock deeper. "Relax," he murmured. "It's going to hurt. But I'll make you feel so good. Let me in, baby. Take all of me."

The sensual words flowed over her like warm honey, and she willed herself to relax. As soon as he sensed her surrender, he rammed forward, seating himself to the hilt.

She bucked upward, the bite of pain unsettling her. She squirmed and bit her lip as shards of unbearable pleasure followed closely on the heels of the edgy pain.

"Faith, baby, you have to stop," he groaned. "Be still, or I'm going to lose it. You're killing me."

He smacked her ass lightly to reinforce his agonized plea, and she stilled, sucking in deep mouthfuls of air as she fought against the rising force inside her.

He grasped her hips in both hands and partially withdrew. He stopped there, and she could feel him trembling.

"Do you have any idea how fucking hot you look with your sexy ass wrapped around my dick?" He pushed forward again, and she gasped at the sensation. "It doesn't even look possible that you can take me. You're stretched so tight around me. It feels un-fucking-believable."

He scooted up farther on his knees, and he lifted her hips with him. Then he pulled out.

"Beautiful," he murmured.

Before she could beg him not to stop, he flipped her over, and she struggled to position herself on her bound hands. For the first time since she woke up, she looked him in the eyes. She shivered at the possession she saw so clearly outlined.

He spread her legs wide and pushed them back toward her body until her ass was clearly accessible again. He slid his hand over her pussy and fingered her clit just as he shoved his cock deep into her anal opening.

She cried out.

"Let go of the hurt," he said in a raspy voice. "Embrace the pleasure. Reach for it."

His thumb rubbed and strummed at her clit. Then he worked his finger lower and thrust into her pussy. She arched into him, wanting him to move, to thrust. But he held still against her, buried as deeply as he could go.

"Please," she begged.

He slowly withdrew and then eased forward. He closed his eyes, and his jaw was clenched tight as he seemed to struggle for control.

"I can't go slow," he said. He rammed forward as his finger stroked over her clit. "Oh, God, Faith."

He began thrusting, his hips slapping against her ass. Moisture flooded her pussy as her orgasm built and blew out of control. There wasn't one slow buildup to one big bang, instead there were several explosions, one after the other. Each one was wrung out of her in a mixture of pain and edgy pleasure. It all mixed and swirled together until she was mindless in her ecstasy.

And then when he buried himself one last time, and she felt the hot rush of his release deep in her body, she lost all semblance of time and place.

She screamed as her body flew apart.

He continued to thrust against her until finally he stopped. He leaned against her for a long moment as his cock jerked and spasmed the last of his release. Then he eased out of her body with a gentle pop. She felt the warm slide of his seed spill over her aching flesh as he left her.

With gentle hands, he turned her over to her side. She curled her legs until her knees tucked into her stomach. Her muscles ached, and she trembled from head to toe. But she felt more alive than she'd ever felt before. Excited, exhausted and completely sated.

He bent and kissed her hip before sliding from the bed. She closed her eyes, too exhausted to do anything more than lie there and wait for him to return.

In a few seconds, he tugged at the rope at her hands. When her hands fell free, he rolled her over onto her back and gathered her in his arms. He picked her up from the bed and kissed the top of her head as he walked toward the bathroom.

The water was still running when he lowered her into the bathtub. She sighed contentedly as the hot water lapped over her body.

He knelt beside the tub and ran a hand through her hair. "Are you okay?"

She smiled, allowing the sheer joy coursing through her to show. "I've never been better."

His eyes glittered, and she could see the satisfaction her answer had brought.

He washed her, gently tending to every inch of her body. When he was finished, he reached down and picked her up from the water. He set her down outside of the tub and reached for one of the large towels hanging on the rack.

As he wrapped the towel around her, he clutched her shoulders and pulled her close to him. He nudged her chin up with his knuckle then lowered his mouth to hers.

His kiss was tender, loving. He fanned his fingers out over her face as he deepened his kiss. She let out a contented sigh that he swallowed up as soon as it escaped.

"You're so unbelievably sweet," he murmured. "So perfect."

She warmed under his approval, and she offered a shy smile when he drew away.

He tucked her hand into his and pulled her out of the bathroom. She followed him into the living room, and he stopped at the couch.

Without a word, he wrapped an arm around her and positioned her at the end of the sofa. The arms were big and fluffy and she had to stand on tiptoe when he bent her over the plump cushion.

Her feet left the floor as he pushed her back until her cheek rested against the seat cushion. Her ass stuck high in the air as her abdomen cradled the arm of the couch.

He left her for a moment then returned and pulled her hands behind her back as he'd done earlier. He wrapped the rope around her wrists and tied them together. Then he spread her legs so that her pussy and ass were exposed and vulnerable.

"Just like that," he murmured. "I'm going to jump in the shower. I expect to find you just like I put you when I get back."

The clear warning in his voice sent a delighted chill over her skin. She heard the soft thud of his feet as he walked back across the hardwood floor to the bathroom.

She lay there, her body already humming with heightened arousal. She didn't think it was possible to have recovered so quickly from her last orgasm. It had been a force like she'd never experienced. No one had ever been able to give her so much, been able to take so much.

Was Gray the one? Her mind, her heart told her yes. Unequivocally yes. Her body told her yes. Did she dare to hope that she and Gray could forge a relationship?

She closed her eyes, afraid to hope, afraid that this was one disappointment she couldn't bear if things didn't work out.

Sensing his presence once again, she opened her eyes to see him standing beside the couch. Her vision focused on his hand at his side and the crop resting against his leg.

Heat flooded every pore of her body. He was going to spank her.

He extended the crop to touch her cheek, the leather tip trailing down her jawline. It followed a line down her neck and over her shoulder. He traced her spine down her back, and she shivered when it caressed her buttocks.

It left her body and then a split second later it struck her ass. Red-hot pain scorched the spot where the crop landed, leaving her breathless. Just as soon, though, the pain was replaced by a sensual heat as it radiated over her ass. It went humming through her body, tightening her nipples and making her pussy clench with need.

Another blow fell on her other cheek, and she flinched as a surprised cry spilled from her lips.

Two more landed in quick succession until she writhed, suspended between pain and deep arousal.

"You like the pain," he said.

She moaned softly in response. She did. She couldn't explain it. With each blow came initial discomfort, but at the same time, each strike gave her more pleasure than the last.

"I love seeing my mark on you. I love how red your ass gets with each slap of the leather. I love seeing you squirm in pain and then give over to the pleasure that follows."

"More," she whispered. "Please."

He struck the soft globe of her ass again, harder than before. She cried out then shivered when his hand caressed away the burn. Again the crop descended, and the sharp snap of leather meeting flesh cracked across the room.

"But you want to know what I love even more?" he asked softly.

She whimpered softly.

"The idea that after I've turned your ass red I'm going to fuck you. I'm going to ride you hard while your ass is still burning, while my mark is still visible on your skin."

She was going to come. Simply from his words, the spanking. She was going to blow out of control.

"How many more?" he asked. "How many blows do you think I should give you before I stuff my dick so far up your pussy that you taste me?"

"Please, please," she panted. "I need . . ."

She flinched when he struck her again. Then again. *Oh God.*

"A dozen more? Can you take it, Faith? Should I stop?"

"No!" she cried. "Please, don't stop."

"That's what I like to hear," he purred.

He brought the crop down on her ass then moved an inch in the other direction and struck her again. Five, six, seven times. She lost count as her ass caught fire. She was lost in a world of edgy pain and euphoric pleasure.

Harder. Each blow was harder than the last. He had begun light and increased the intensity with each strike. Unbearable heat bloomed until all she could feel was the tingle in her ass.

Then he stopped. The crop fell to the floor, and he roughly grabbed her ass in his hands, spreading her.

Before she could process what was happening, he rammed into her pussy. Her entire body burned with a fire only he could give her.

He reached up and curled his fingers tightly around her bound hands. He held on as he fucked her from behind.

No way she could withstand it a second longer. Pushed to the edge long before he penetrated her body, now she fell over in a cataclysmic burst.

She screamed and screamed again as he rode her mercilessly.

"Come for me," he commanded.

She felt a gush of wetness and realized it was her. The smack of his hips meeting her ass filled the room. Wet, erotic sounds that only spurred her orgasm higher.

"I can't . . ." she began, begging for something she didn't even understand or comprehend.

His grip tightened on her hands and he slammed forward again. Her ass, tender from the spanking, tingled with every thrust.

"Let go," he said gently, his tone at a direct contradiction to the power of his thrusts.

And she did. Her stomach clenched. Her pussy tightened and spasmed around his cock. She closed her eyes and pressed her lips together as a terrifying force built and raged inside her, demanding to be let out, forcing its way out.

Just when she thought she couldn't take another second of the unbearable tension, the world exploded around her. The room shifted and fuzzed out of focus. Her body took on a life of its own as it shook and trembled.

Tears slid from underneath her lids as her body popped like a rubber band at full stretch. Relief. Such sweet, aching relief.

As she slowly came down from her orgasm, she registered him still rocking against her ass, his cock probing the depths of her pussy.

It was almost painful. She was too tender, too sensitive from such a volatile orgasm. He was stretching her, filling her. She whimpered against the painful ache of his attentions.

Then he withdrew and rotated her body until her hip rested on the arm of the couch. She drew in her legs to alleviate the awkwardness of the position as he walked around the side of the sofa. He bent his knees and lowered himself to her face.

He slid his cock into her mouth and held himself deep. He leaned over and grasped the back of the couch with his left hand and braced himself on the seat cushion beside her head with his right. Then he began thrusting into her mouth.

"Swallow it," he growled.

It was all the warning she got before the first splash of cum flooded her mouth. He paused to let her swallow before thrusting again, deep, and he held himself at the back of her throat while his cock pulsed more warm seed.

He rode her mouth just like he rode her pussy. Hard, deep and unrelenting. Her lips stretched around the base to accommodate his size. He didn't let up until he'd poured every drop down her throat.

Slowly and with seeming reluctance, he pulled away, but he paused as his cock slipped from her lips and dangled a mere inch away.

"Lick it clean," he said huskily.

He lowered it until she sucked it back into her mouth, swirling her tongue around her head.

He groaned as he pumped his hips forward. When she'd licked every drop of the moisture from his skin, he pulled away and stood to his full height beside the couch.

He reached behind her to untie her hands then pulled her up until she was in a sitting position. "Give me one second to get some shorts on, and I'll be right back," he said.

She sat there, body shaking, numb, her ass still on fire from the spanking he'd given her. He returned just a minute later and sat down on the opposite end of the couch. Then he stretched out and reached for her.

She went willingly into his arms, and he pulled her up on top of his body. He positioned her back against the back of the couch and wrapped his arms around her as she nestled her cheek into his chest.

"You're incredible," he whispered into her hair. "Never did I imagine finding someone like you."

She smiled and burrowed deeper into his embrace. He continued to run his fingers through her hair, gently pulling the strands apart.

"I was wrong about you," he continued. "I treated you badly, and all because I believed something about you that wasn't true."

She raised her head to look him in the eye. Sincerity blazed in his blue eyes. And regret. She lowered her head to his until their lips touched. She kissed him sweetly, gently, too tired to infuse more passion into the act. He didn't seem to mind. He gathered her tighter in his arms, and kissed her back, exploring her mouth with his tongue.

Then he turned so she slid down the back of the couch and they faced each other.

"You wore me out," he confessed. "You're way too young for me. I can't keep up."

She laughed. "Thank God you're worn out, because I can't move another muscle."

"Then go to sleep," he said softly. "I just want to hold you for a while. I'll fix us something to eat when you wake up."

Her heart swelled, and she felt a giddy thrill as he rubbed his cheek to hers. Nothing in her fantasies, in her most vivid dreams had come close to the reality of their lovemaking. He was the perfect combination of strong and tender.

She nuzzled into his neck and pressed a kiss to his warm skin. He squeezed her a little tighter, and she closed her eyes, content to let him do exactly what he wanted: hold her.

CHAPTER 33

*G*ray slowly opened his eyes and registered immediate contentment. He glanced down to see Faith's head burrowed in his chest. His right arm was asleep, but he hated to move. She felt right in his arms. Like it was the only place she belonged.

He kissed the top of her head and stroked her hair with his left hand. She stirred and rubbed her cheek against his chest. He felt her yawn against him, and he smiled.

"Want to go swimming?" he asked. "I assume you brought a bathing suit, but I wouldn't care if you went naked."

She raised her head and looked at him with sleepy, contented eyes. "I brought a suit. I don't want sand and salt up my woo woo, thank you very much."

He laughed. "Sand up the woo woo would be a tragedy indeed. Especially since I plan to spend a lot of time up that woo woo."

Her brow crinkled. "Yeah, wouldn't that be like screwing sandpaper?"

His entire body shook with laughter, and he smacked her on

the ass. He left his hand there and glanced down to see the faint red marks still on her behind. The sight turned him on all over again.

He shifted until she was positioned underneath him on the couch. He struggled out of his shorts and tossed them to the side. Then he nudged her legs apart with his knee and was deep in her pussy in two seconds.

This was no gentle lovemaking session. His need was urgent, and he wanted to fuck her senseless. He gripped her hips in his hands and rode her hard and deep. Her pussy wrapped around his cock. Sucked him deeper, heated, silky. As tight as her sweet ass had been, her pussy gripped him just as hard.

His balls drew up and tightened painfully. He elicited tiny gasps from her every time he pounded home. He ran his hands up her sides to her arms then up to her wrists. Gripping them tight, he pulled her hands above her head and held them there as he drove deep and locked himself against her.

He wanted to come inside her this time. Mark her his in the most primitive way a man can. He wanted to empty himself as deep in her as possible.

Her velvet pussy spasmed around his cock, and to his surprise, she orgasmed. She cried out, arching her chest forward as he held her captive against the couch. The sound of her pleasure pushed him over the edge. He hammered home one more time, clenched his teeth and came deep inside her welcoming heat.

As he felt the last jerk of his cock, he collapsed onto her. He let go of her arms and curled his arms around her, gathering her closely. He was holding too tight. She probably couldn't breathe worth a damn, but in that moment he didn't care. He wanted her as close to him as possible.

He kissed her temple and suddenly wanted to tell her more. Wanted to make her promises he wasn't sure he could keep but wanted to make nonetheless.

As he became aware of her struggling for breath underneath him, he pushed himself off her. His cock slid from her body in a rush of fluid. He gazed down at her pussy, pink and swollen from his lovemaking. His fluids glistened against her pinkness, and he felt a deep satisfaction. His. She was his.

He held his hand down to her. "Let's go take that swim," he said.

She slid her small hand into his, and he was struck by the trust the gesture implied. It was all there in her eyes for him to see. Vulnerability, like he had the power to hurt her or pleasure her in a way no other man could. For the first time, he was uncomfortable with the idea of having complete power over her.

He helped her up, and she surprised him by wrapping her arms around his stomach and hugging him tight. As she laid her head on his chest, he raised his arms to hug her back. He stroked a hand over her hair and kissed the top of her head.

When she drew away, she looked up at him, her green eyes sparkling with happiness. "Give me a few minutes to get my suit on."

He walked to the bedroom with her and while she was putting on her bikini, he dug his swim trunks from his suitcase. When he looked back over at her, she was struggling with the strings to her top.

"Let me," he offered as he moved over to where she was standing.

She relinquished the ties, and he secured them in a quick knot. His gaze wandered downward to the tiny scrap of material charged with covering her ass. He raised a brow as she turned around to face him.

"Not that I'm complaining, but I really doubt that thing you call a suit will keep the sand out of your woo woo."

She grinned. "I guess I'll just have to be very, very careful."

He cupped her chin in his hand and kissed her. With reluctance he pulled away and reached for her hand. "Let's go before I become a complete animal and fuck you senseless again."

She blushed, but he could see the spark of desire in her eyes before she quickly looked away.

They walked out the French doors and out on the deck. The sun beamed hot on them as they walked down the wooden ramp leading to the beach.

Faith gazed out over the water as her feet hit the sand. Today the water was greener, not as muddy as it had been the first day she'd arrived. There was a sparkle to the water that was inviting.

She glanced down at Gray's hand entwined with hers and couldn't help the surge of happiness that filled her. With a mischievous smile, she broke free of his hand and dashed toward the water.

"Last one in is a rotten egg!"

He took off after her, and she ran shrieking into the water. Water splashed in all directions as she charged into the surf. She slowed when the waves reached her knees but continued to wade out into the warm water.

Gray caught up to her and scooped her up in his arms. She let out a yelp as he grinned evilly down at her.

"I may be a rotten egg, but you're going to be a drowned rat."

"You wouldn't," she dared.

He arched one sexy brow before tossing her into the air. She sailed several feet and landed with a splash in the deeper water. Her head went under, and she came back up, sputtering and coughing.

He was there, wrapping his arms around her. He hauled her up against him and kissed her. She wrapped her arms around him and returned his kiss. When he pulled away, she launched herself at him, knocking him over into the surf.

She laughed as he dragged her with him and they both fell under the water. She got a mouthful of salty water again, but it was worth it to see the look on his face when he'd fallen.

They laughed and they played. Faith couldn't remember a time when she'd felt so happy and carefree. And Gray had lost the driven, intense look he'd worn so often since his arrival. She harbored a teeny tiny hope that she was responsible for the relaxed expression he now wore.

After an hour of swimming, they dragged themselves back onto the beach. She was waterlogged, and her tender bits were starting to chafe from the salt and the sand.

Gray wrapped an arm around her waist and kissed her temple. "Let's go shower and wash the sand off, and then I'll make us dinner."

She moved closer to him and wrapped her arm around his waist as well, as they headed back up to the beach house. She shivered when they stepped into the air-conditioned interior. Gray rubbed his hand up and down her arm and hurried her toward the bathroom.

While he turned the shower on, she stripped out of her bikini and waited for the water to warm. Then he gestured for her to step in with him.

The steam rose from the heated water, and she sighed in sheer bliss when he pulled her into the spray. He soaped her body with gentle hands, taking care to get all the sand.

She closed her eyes and let the water spill over her face while he soaped himself. A few seconds later, he cupped her cheek, and she opened her eyes to see him staring at her.

"Ready to get out?" he asked.

She smiled and nodded.

He turned the water off and stepped out. He reached his hand back to her and pulled her out beside him. Once again he dried her, taking his time as he rubbed the towel over her body.

When he was done, he pulled her up and kissed her lightly on the lips. "You go get dressed, and I'll start dinner. We'll eat out on the deck."

While Gray cooked, Faith sat in the kitchen and kept him company. They talked about unimportant things. Laughed. Chatted. It was comfortable. No awkward lapses.

He handed her plates and utensils, and she walked out onto the deck to set the small table. The sun had set, and the breeze blowing off the water was cooler now. She arranged the plates and turned back toward the doors. She met Gray, who was carrying a platter of pasta in one hand and a bottle of wine in the other.

"The bread's on the bar if you'll get it," he said.

When she returned with the small basket of rolls, he had dished out portions of the food onto their plates and was sitting at the table waiting for her.

She sat down and glanced at the wonderful-smelling pasta. She picked up her fork and took a bite. It melted on her tongue, and she made a sound of appreciation.

"I feel so spoiled," she admitted.

He raised a brow in question.

"I've done nothing since you got here. I haven't lifted so much as a finger."

He smiled lazily, his eyes glittering as he stared back at her. "You're doing exactly what I've asked you to do. I couldn't ask for more, and I couldn't be more satisfied."

Warmth surged to her cheeks. She swallowed at the fierce look in his eyes.

"Eat," he said huskily.

They ate as night fell around them. As the stars popped across the sky and the moon, now full, rose over the water, she sipped at her wine and sat back in her chair.

Her gaze drifted across the table to Gray when he stood and began collecting the dishes. When she started to get up to help, he motioned her back down.

"I'll be back in just a second. You sit here and relax. It's a beautiful evening."

That it was. Waves crashed in the background. The moon cast its pale glow over the beach. The sand crystals winked and glistened as the water chased up and down the shore.

A few minutes later, he returned carrying a blanket. She looked curiously as he settled onto one of the loungers. Then he looked up at her and crooked his finger.

"Come here."

She rose and walked over to him. He patted his lap and

motioned for her to turn around and sit. He spread his legs and pulled her down into the chair with him.

As she settled against his chest, he tossed the blanket over them and pulled it up to her chest. Then he slid his arms underneath and wrapped them around her body, cradling her to him.

He held her tightly and rested his chin on top of her head as they both stared out over the water.

"Gray?" she asked in a low voice.

"Yes, baby?"

"Can I ask you something?"

"Of course."

She hesitated, not sure how to voice what she wanted to ask.

"Is this . . . is this just sex between us?"

His arms tightened around her, and she could feel the breath catch in his chest.

"No, Faith. It's definitely not just sex."

She wanted to press. Wanted to ask him more, but she contented herself with his answer. She didn't want to push him away.

So she relaxed against him, content to enjoy the night in his arms.

CHAPTER 34

$\mathcal{G}$ray woke to a buzzing vibration in his pocket. He blinked, disoriented, as his surroundings came into focus. The pale light of predawn lay soft over the ocean. In his arms, Faith sighed and snuggled deeper under the covers.

They'd slept all night on the deck.

The buzzing stopped, and he realized it was his cell phone. Carefully, so he didn't disturb Faith, he eased his hand into his pocket and dug out his phone.

He flipped it open to see who had called. Micah. He punched the Send button to call him back and shoved the phone to his ear.

"Hey, man," Micah said. "Hope I didn't wake you and Faith."

Gray grunted. "You woke me. Didn't wake Faith."

"Ah good. Look, I just got into Galveston, and I'm headed your way. Just wanted to give you a heads-up."

Gray frowned. "Is everything okay?"

"Yeah, just wanted to give you a report and see how you guys were doing."

Gray looked down at Faith. "That's fine. There's something I wanted to run by you anyway. I have a feeling you might be interested."

"I'm intrigued now. I'll see you in a few minutes."

Gray closed the phone and set it down beside the lounger. He gathered Faith a little closer in his arms and kissed her soft hair. He was curious as to how she'd react to what he had planned. She'd been so open to everything else so far.

With infinite care, he maneuvered out of the lounger then bent to pick Faith up. He carried her into the bedroom and laid her on the bed. She stirred when he began undressing her, but he murmured soothingly to her, and she never fully woke.

He pulled the covers back so that she was exposed, and then he retrieved the rope he'd tossed aside. He gently eased her arms above her head and bound her wrists together. Then he took the long end of the rope and stretched it to the bedpost, wrapping it around it several times.

Satisfied that she'd be comfortable but wouldn't be able to move from the bed, he headed for the bathroom to take a shower. Five minutes later, he dressed and peeked into the bedroom one last time. She was still sound asleep.

He walked into the kitchen and put a pot of coffee on. He'd just poured his first cup when a knock sounded at the front door. He ambled over to open it and saw Micah standing on the porch.

"Want coffee?" he asked by way of greeting.

Micah followed him inside. "Yeah, sounds great. I was up way too damn early this morning."

Gray poured him a cup and slid it along the bar. Micah grasped it in both hands and sipped at the hot brew.

"So what's going on?" Gray asked in a low voice.

Micah looked up at him and then around. "Faith still asleep?"

"Yeah, she won't be walking in until I go get her, so you won't have to worry about her hearing."

Micah raised one brow.

Gray laughed. "I tied her to the bed."

A flicker of interest stirred in Micah's eyes. One that didn't go unnoticed by Gray.

"Well, so far, the plan to bust Samuels hasn't gone too well," Micah said.

"Tell me," Gray said tersely.

"He made the decoy we put in place. Not sure how. He followed her to the office one morning. I thought he was going to make his move, but then he gave us the slip."

Gray swore. "Has he made any contact since then?"

Micah shook his head. "For all we know, he's in Mexico by now."

"He'd be stupid to hang around," Gray said. "He has to know we're on to him now."

"That's my thinking. You're buddy Mick isn't taking it well."

Gray sighed. "Mick needs to go the hell back to Dallas and let the locals handle it. He's lost all perspective. He's crazy with grief and can't see beyond his need for revenge."

Micah nodded. "At any rate, I wanted to let you know what was going on. And I needed to get away from that place for a few hours. The tension is thick. Pop is pissed. Connor is on edge. Nathan and I are just trying to stay the hell out of the way and let them do their thing."

Gray studied Micah for a long moment. "You might as well

stay for a while. I have a proposition for you that you might find interesting."

Faith yawned and opened her eyes. When she tried to roll over, her arms twisted above her and held fast. She pulled slightly and realized that her hands were tied to the bed. Her second realization was that she was naked.

She smiled. The last thing she remembered was going to sleep on the deck in Gray's arms. Sometime during the night he must have carried her to bed, stripped her naked and tied her to the bed.

Which could only mean he planned more naughty things.

Arousal hummed low in her groin. Her stomach fluttered, and her nipples tightened in anticipation. Would he spank her again? Fuck her ass?

She moaned low and twisted her legs as she remembered the way he'd taken and mastered her body. Owned it. There wasn't an inch of her body he hadn't marked in some way, and it gave her a delicious thrill to remember in exacting detail the way it had made her feel.

A sound at the door made her turn her head in that direction. Her mouth fell open in surprise when she saw Micah standing there. His gaze raked over her body, and a primitive light gleamed in his eyes.

Suddenly she felt way too naked and way too vulnerable.

"Gorgeous," Micah murmured.

He started forward, walking with slow, measured steps as if he didn't want to frighten her. She wasn't frightened. That didn't aptly describe what she was feeling. Confused. But aroused. Where was Gray?

Her question was answered a few seconds later when Gray walked in. Her gaze went to him in question.

Micah stopped at the foot of the bed while Gray sat down on the bed beside her head and leaned in close to her ear. He reached up to fumble with the rope around her wrists.

"If you don't want this, all you have to do is say no," he whispered in her ear. "If you don't want this to happen, I'll make him leave, and it'll be just you and me."

Excitement curled in her veins and raced through her body. She searched his face for any sign of what he was thinking. Her deepest fear wasn't of having sex with Micah. If she was honest, the idea turned her on. Her fear was of how Gray would react. Would she lose any chance she had with him if she consented to being with another man?

"You're okay with this?" she whispered back.

He touched her face, stroked her cheek with his fingers. "If I wasn't okay with it, Micah wouldn't be here. We all have kinks. This just happens to be one of mine."

He bent and sucked her nipple between his teeth and gave it a sharp nip. Then he reached up and tugged the remaining rope from her hands and backed off the bed.

She glanced over at Micah, who was unzipping his pants. Her heart pounded, and her mouth went dry. Her gaze flitted back to Gray, who was watching her with simmering eyes.

"Do as he tells you," Gray said in husky voice. "For now I'm giving you to him. You're ours to do with what we want."

She shivered, and nervous excitement curled in her stomach. She looked back at Micah, who'd pulled his cock from his pants and walked to the edge of the bed.

She stared, unable to drag her gaze away from the dark hair at his groin. Black and silky. His hand wrapped around the base and still, a few inches remained above his hand. He wasn't as thick as Gray, but he looked longer.

"Come over here, baby doll, and wrap your mouth around my dick," Micah said, his voice low and husky.

She got to her hands and knees and slowly crawled to the edge where he stood. She was nervous. How much of the initiative should she take? With Gray, she knew she didn't have to make any awkward decisions, but she wasn't sure how forceful Micah was.

She didn't have to wait long to find out.

As soon as she got close enough, he reached out and tangled his hand in her hair. With one hand on his cock, guiding it to-ward her mouth, he bunched her hair in his other and pulled her with a sharp yank until the head of his cock slid past her lips.

He removed his hand from his erection and arched his hips, thrusting deep within her mouth. He threaded both hands through her hair now and held her head as he fucked her mouth with forceful thrusts.

He moaned appreciatively as she relaxed her jaw and took him deeper.

"Faith, baby, seeing you naked may have been in my top-ten fantasies, but fucking you definitely topped the list. I have very vivid fantasies of all the ways I'd like to take you."

She moaned around his cock and closed her eyes.

"You like that?" he murmured as he stroked to the back of her throat.

She nodded her head.

He ran gentle hands through her hair, fingering the strands. And then without warning, a stinging pain rocketed over her ass. She gasped, and Micah sent his cock even deeper into her mouth.

Behind her, Gray brought the crop down again on her ass, and she jumped as the crack filled the air.

"Oh goddamn," Micah muttered. "You have the sweetest ass, Faith. It looks so pretty with those red welts on it."

Gray struck again, and she whimpered even as the burn disappeared and the flush of pleasure radiated over her heated skin.

He set a rhythm, one destined to push her to the very edge of her limits. Caught between two men, she was mindless in her pleasure even as she gave them pleasure in return.

She lost count of the blows as they rained down on her behind, each one harder than the last. She was no longer aware of anything but the cock sliding in and out of her mouth and the crop landing on her ass.

Micah's hands tightened in her hair, and he yanked himself from her mouth. She gasped for breath as the blows subsided.

"Turn around," Micah ordered.

Gingerly, she rotated, positioning herself on her hands and knees with her aching ass to Micah. She looked up to see Gray standing at the bed, the crop still in his hand. He stared at her with stark approval in his eyes.

She heard the crinkle of a wrapper. Then Micah roughly grabbed her ass in his hands, causing her to moan as jagged pleasure shot to her pussy. He spread her, and thrust inside her. No workup, no teasing. He was balls deep. Urgent. Impatient.

She dropped her head, but Gray touched the crop to her chin, nudging it upward.

"Look at me," he directed. "I want to see your eyes while he fucks you."

She locked gazes with him as Micah grasped her hips in his hands and began riding her hard. It was too much for her. Each slap of his thighs against her tender ass sent a spasm of ecstasy rocketing through her body. His cock probed deep, touching her deepest recesses.

Just when she was poised to explode, once again, he pulled from her body. She whimpered in protest, and Micah smacked her already sore bottom.

Gray reached over and picked up the lubricant from the nightstand then tossed it over her head. Her breath caught deep in her chest, and she worked to expel it.

Gray reached for his fly and began unzipping his jeans. As she watched, he pulled his cock out, holding it in his hand. He walked forward and got on his knees in front of her on the bed.

"I'm going to fuck your mouth while he fucks your ass," he said. "Can you take him, Faith? Can you take him like you did me?"

She nodded wordlessly, unable to say anything.

Micah grasped her ass in his hands, spreading the cheeks. The head of his cock nudged her opening just as Gray cupped her chin in his hand and squeezed to open her mouth.

Micah surged forward, and she let out a cry. It was quickly silenced as Gray slid to the back of her throat.

"That's it, baby," Gray murmured. "God, you look beautiful. Do you know what a huge turn-on it is to see another man buried in your ass because I gave it to him?"

She closed her eyes as his words washed over her. Ownership. God, the idea of belonging to him unfurled dark, forbidden desires.

Micah stretched and plundered her ass as he reamed her with his cock. Gray filled her mouth, butting against the back of her throat as he matched the intensity of Micah's thrusts.

Micah shoved forward and stilled against her, his cock buried as deeply as he could go. "I'm going to take this condom off and come all over you, baby doll," he rasped. Then he ripped himself out, and she flinched as the head slipped past her tight ring.

Gray thrust deeply then he too tore himself from her mouth. He began working his cock with his hand. As the first splatter hit her face, she felt a hot stream of cum splash onto her ass.

It ran down the crack of her ass and slithered inside her still-open anus.

The two men groaned as they directed more cum onto her body. She was edgy with need. She'd been so close, and now she trembled, wanting nothing more than to finish what they'd started.

Gray reached out and wiped the cum from her lips with his thumb. She looked up to see him gazing at her, a fierce, possessive look on his face.

He stuffed his cock back into his pants then hastily zipped his jeans. Behind her, Micah smoothed gentle hands over her ass. He pressed a tender kiss to the small of her back. Then Gray reached for her, picking her up as though she weighed nothing. He carried her into the bathroom and started a shower.

He hurriedly stripped then pulled her into the shower with him. He gave her a quick rinse, and then he picked her up and placed her back against the wall of the shower. He positioned his arms underneath her legs and pushed her even higher up the wall until her pussy was at the level of his mouth.

"I didn't allow you to come for him," he murmured, his breath blowing over her wet curls. "Your orgasms are mine and mine alone."

She trembled at the raw possession in his voice. He nuzzled between her folds and began licking her clit. She reached down to grasp his head, moaning as he sucked the tight little bud between his teeth.

As the water sprayed over his back, he tongued her entrance, lapping and sucking like he was starving. Her thighs began to shake uncontrollably as the sensations became unbearable.

His hands slid to her buttocks, and he squeezed as he deepened the assault with his tongue. He licked, sucked and then he thrust his tongue into her pussy.

She yelled hoarsely as, finally, her orgasm flashed, hot and painful. She gripped his head, holding him close as he lapped at the flood of juices from her pussy. He continued eating her until she could stand no more. She whimpered as he tongued her sensitive flesh, and he pulled away, allowing her to slide down the wall of the shower.

Her legs wobbled underneath her, and he grabbed her waist to steady her. He reached behind him to turn off the water, and then he turned back to her, his expression serious.

He nudged her chin upward with his finger. "Tell me the truth. Did I go too far?"

In that moment, she realized that she loved this man. No matter how forceful or dominant, he was only willing to go as far as she was comfortable with. Despite his concern that she was playing games, his desire was still to please her.

She cupped his face in her hands and pulled him down to kiss him. Their wet bodies met, and she wrapped her arms around him, wanting to absorb him.

"You were perfect," she whispered. And it was the truth. He was taking care of her. It wasn't about dominance. She didn't have an overwhelming need to submit. What she wanted was a strong man to take care of her, to see to her needs, to satisfy her desires.

What she'd mistaken for submission was in actuality a need to connect to a man on an emotional as well as a physical level. The emotion had been what she lacked in her previous relationships. Without it, the sex didn't measure up. Now she realized why.

Tears pricked her eyelids as she hugged him close. He squeezed her and kissed the top of her head before tugging her out of the shower with him.

He dried her, and all she could do was stand there numbly, overwhelmed by the depth of her feelings. She wanted to tell him what he meant to her, but she knew this wasn't the time. Not with Micah here. No, this would be saved for when it was the two of them again. In the meantime, she'd enjoy having a man fulfill all her fantasies.

As he dried the last of the water from her body, he kissed her and pushed a damp tendril of hair behind her ear. "Watching you with Micah was unbelievably hot. Watching another man take what's mine . . . I can't even explain the turn-on. It may seem weird to you, but it's indescribable."

"You like to watch."

He nodded, his eyes blazing with blue heat.

"I like to watch you watch me," she said with a slight smile. "If you're weird, I guess so am I."

He slid his hand down her back and gently cupped her ass. "Are you sore?"

She flushed. "A little."

He kissed her again. "We'll let that part of your body rest for a while. This was your first time, and I don't want to hurt you."

Her heart melted just a little more at the gentle concern in his voice.

"Go into the bedroom and lie down on the bed," he said. "I think Micah would like to taste your sweet little pussy."

Her knees shook as she stepped around him to do as he'd told her. When she walked into the bedroom, she saw Micah lying on the bed, naked, his hand stroking his semierect cock.

He watched her with sultry eyes as she hesitantly made her way to the bed. His earring winked at her, and his shoulder-length dark hair fell over his ears, slightly damp from sweat.

She looked nervously over her shoulder to see where Gray was and whether he was coming. When she saw him standing just a few feet away, she relaxed.

"Come here," Micah called from the bed. He held out his hand, crooking his finger.

She walked to the edge of the bed. Micah scooted down until his head lay in the middle of the bed and his feet dangled off the end.

"Climb up, baby doll. I want to taste that pussy."

A low shudder rolled over her body as her nipples tightened, and she felt a surge of wetness between her legs. She got onto the bed, and he reached for her waist. He helped her straddle his face and slowly lowered her to his waiting mouth.

When his tongue touched her, she bucked upward. His grip tightened around her hips as he pulled her back down. As his tongue delved between her folds and found her clit, she turned her head toward Gray.

He stood across the room, and their gazes locked. Remembering what he'd said about watching, she became determined to give him a show he'd enjoy.

She slid her hands up her belly and to her breasts. She plumped them up and out with her palms and then rolled the tips between her fingers. Gray's eyes flared, and he shifted his position.

She continued to roll her nipples, massaging and caressing her breasts. Her breathing picked up as Micah continued to lap hungrily at her. She was close. God, she was close. But she also remembered what Gray had said about coming only for him.

She opened her mouth to speak, but Gray had already crossed the room and stood next to her. He held out his hand, and she grasped it as he helped her off of Micah.

"Lay down," he ordered.

When she complied, he pushed her toward the other end of the bed until her head dangled off the edge. Then he crawled up between her legs and spread her wide. His cock, hard, turgid, like steel, probed between her thighs and then shoved inside her with one impatient thrust.

Micah positioned himself over her head and tilted her head downward until she viewed his cock in an upside down position. He rubbed the head of his erection over her lips and then pressed inward until she relented and opened her mouth. He immediately slid in and began fucking her mouth in long, hard thrusts.

Gray pushed her legs upward, spreading her wider as he pushed deeper into her pussy. She moaned deep in her throat, vibrating against Micah's cock. He began fucking her harder in response.

"Inside you, baby," Gray uttered harshly. "This time we're coming inside you. We're going to fill you with our cum. Do you want that?"

It was a needless question. She was twisting and writhing, anticipating their release, wanting hers as well. It was freeing, not having to dictate, coordinate or direct the action. They gave her precisely what she wanted without her having to outline it in detail. All she had to do was lie back and feel. Allow herself to be taken care of.

Micah reached down and twisted her nipples between his fingers. She whimpered and squirmed restlessly as she skated closer to the edge of her orgasm. Gray slid back and forth, the friction he caused with his larger circumference sending exquisite shards of pleasure to her groin.

"Come for me," Gray growled. "Only for me, baby. Let it go."

As both cocks thrust to their limits inside her body, something within her snapped. Like a bowl of spilled sugar, her body crystallized and flew in ninety different directions. She jerked and heaved as the two men buffeted her body between them. The slap of flesh meeting flesh echoed loudly in the room along with their heavy grunts.

She opened her mouth to scream only to have Micah muffle it when he drove deep. Gray gathered her legs over his arms and yanked her back to meet his thrust. It hurt. It was pleasure like she'd never known. It ached. It was the most exquisite ecstasy of her life.

Her mouth filled as Micah flooded her with his release. She swallowed as more splashed onto her tongue. At the same time, she felt the heated spurts of Gray's orgasm deep in her pussy.

They held her, they owned her, they filled her.

She lay there limply as she came down from her orgasm and the men above her eased back and forth as they finished within her. Micah was the first to withdraw. He reached down, lifted her head and kissed her forehead.

Gray slowly slid out of her pussy, a warm flood following his retreat.

"Stay right there," Gray said huskily. "I'll get a washcloth and clean you up. Then you can take a nap while I fix us something to eat."

Micah sat down on the bed beside her head and looked down at her. His fingers trailed over her cheek as he pushed her hair away from her eyes.

She didn't say anything, but neither did he. There was really nothing to say. She supposed she should feel awkward, but then he'd already seen her naked, touched her intimately.

Gray returned a moment later and gently wiped between her legs. When he was finished, he patted the pillow at the head of the bed. "Come on, baby. Crawl up here so I can tuck you in. We've worn you out."

She wouldn't argue there. She yawned and moved up then curled up and laid her head on the pillow. Gray tugged the covers up then leaned down to kiss her.

"I'll wake you up in a little while."

She smiled and nodded, but her eyes were already closing.

CHAPTER 35

"You're a lucky son of a bitch," Micah said as the two men stood in the kitchen.

Gray shoved a beer at Micah and nodded. "I know. Believe me, I know."

"If she wasn't so hung up on you, I swear I'd drag her home and tie her to my bed. I'd never let her out of my bedroom."

Gray chuckled. He could understand that sentiment, because it was very much the way he felt. His smile disappeared when he remembered just how much he was deceiving her.

"What's wrong, man?" Micah asked as he sat down on a barstool.

Gray took out a skillet and put it down on the counter with a bang. "I just hope she understands when I tell her the truth about why I'm here."

Micah went silent for a moment. "I think she will. I mean, I'm with you, I didn't see a need to keep what was going on from her, but I also understand Pop's desire to protect her. Who could blame him? Faith just inspires a man to protect and shelter her."

Gray nodded. "Exactly. I came here determined to tell her the truth and fuck what Pop wanted, but when I got here, I just couldn't. I found myself willing to do whatever I could to keep her from any hurt."

"You love her," Micah said quietly.

Gray paused for a moment, prepared to deny it. But no, he couldn't. Not when it was true. "Yeah, I do."

"That certainly complicates things."

Gray jerked his gaze to Micah. "What do you mean by that?"

Micah shrugged. "You live in Dallas. Your job is there. Faith lives here. Family is important to her."

Gray stared at him for a long moment then looked away. He didn't reply. He wasn't sure what to say. Part of him was ashamed of the fact that since coming to Houston he'd thought very little about his job or Alex. He'd actually been able to get up every morning without having to force himself out of bed. He'd greeted his job with enthusiasm, not dread.

And then there was Faith.

"Hey, I didn't mean to be a downer," Micah spoke up. "Just saying you have a lot to think about."

"Yeah," he said grimly. "It would seem I do."

Micah drummed his fingers on the bar. "Look man, I'm going to get on out of here. You two could use the time alone, I think, and I need to get back and see what the hell is going on."

Gray nodded. "Give me a call. Keep me posted. I don't want to take Faith back to Houston until we know it's safe."

"Sure," Micah said as he got up. "And hey, if you ever want to do it again, let me know. Faith . . . well, I don't have to tell you how hot she is."

Gray smiled. "See you." He gave a slight wave as Micah headed for the door.

When he heard the front door close, he looked down at the pan in front of him. Suddenly he had no desire to cook. What he wanted to do was talk to Faith. Tell her he loved her. Tell her the truth about everything.

He glanced at the clock and saw that only a half hour had elapsed since Faith had gone to sleep. She was tired. He and Micah had been hard on her. She needed the rest. As much as he itched to wake her up, he was going to let her sleep.

Instead, he'd cook her a good meal and pamper her when she woke up. And then they could have a long talk about their relationship.

Faith stretched and yawned. Her body protested her movement, but she loved each little twinge and ache. It was too easy to remember how she'd gotten those aches.

She sat up and let her legs dangle off the bed. Gray hadn't said whether she could dress or not, but with Micah here, she wasn't comfortable parading around in the nude. They could always undress her later.

With a grin, she stood and walked over to her suitcase where she rummaged for a pair of shorts and a tank top. She slipped the shirt on then shoved her feet into a pair of flip-flops lying on the floor.

Before she left the room, she took in her appearance in the

dresser mirror. In a word, she looked rumpled. Well loved. Her lips were swollen, and her eyes glowed with supreme female confidence. The kind you could only get from knowing how well you'd satisfied a man.

She ran a hand through her hair then shoved the locks behind her ears before finally turning to leave. When she walked into the living room, she saw Gray standing at the French Doors, staring over the water.

She watched in silence, enjoying the outline of his powerful body. Then, as if sensing her presence, he turned and saw her.

His face softened, and his eyes lit up. A thrill shot up her spine as she saw his reaction to her.

"Hey," he said softly. "Did you sleep okay?"

She smiled and nodded.

He held out his arms. "Come here."

She went gladly, and she closed her eyes in pleasure as he wrapped his arms around her and pulled her tight against him. He threaded his fingers through her hair and let the strands slide through his fingers. Then he pulled her away.

"Micah's gone."

She felt a surge of elation. As much as she'd enjoyed the erotic experience of having two men, she wanted so much for it to be just the two of them now.

"Come sit down on the couch with me. I want to talk to you," he said quietly as he guided her toward the sofa.

He sat her down and took a spot across from her. He picked up her hand and kissed her fingertips before slowly lowering it to his lap.

She stared inquisitively at him. It was obvious he wanted to say something. Anticipation beat heavy in her chest.

"Faith, the last few days . . . they've been just incredible. I don't have words to describe them."

She smiled. "I know," she said. "For me too." She took a deep breath and knew that this was it. She wanted to tell him how she felt. It was the perfect opportunity.

She looked down for a moment as she collected her courage, but Gray nudged her chin upward with his finger.

"I hear a *but* in there somewhere," he said.

She shook her head. "No *but*." She looked him directly in the eyes and hoped he could see the love shining in hers. "Gray, I love you."

Fire surged in his eyes at her declaration. He started to speak, but she laid a finger over his mouth. "Let me finish. I have so much to say."

He nodded, and she let her finger fall away.

"I should feel weak right now. Giving up control the way I did should make me feel smaller somehow. But I don't. In fact, I've never felt more empowered than I do right now. More in control of my own destiny. Maybe I didn't really know before exactly what I wanted, but I do now. I want *you*. And I realized why another man has never been able to satisfy me. It's because I didn't make the emotional connection with them that I did with you. I didn't *trust* them. And trust is everything. Without it I couldn't really let go of that control, and as long as I was holding fast to it, I was destined to remain disappointed."

He gathered her hands in his again and lifted them both to his mouth. He kissed first one and then the other. "You are such an incredible, honest woman," he said in a shaky voice. "Weak? I don't think you could ever be weak. What could possibly be more powerful than admitting your needs and not being ashamed or afraid to embrace them? People spend their entire lives hiding from their true selves, living out farces and fantasies, never embracing reality. By offering your surrender, by meeting your needs and desires head-on, you've freed yourself from the worst sort of bondage. And nothing is more powerful than that. Or more courageous."

He reached out and touched her cheek with the back of his finger. "I love you, Faith. Lord knows I've tried not to. I wanted to believe that you were playing games. That you couldn't possibly give me what I wanted. But you're what I want. What I'll always want."

She stared at him, too overwhelmed to do anything more than gape numbly in shock. She closed her eyes and willed the tears not to come. But one slipped down her cheek.

He tenderly thumbed it away. "Open your eyes, Faith, and look at me."

She blinked, his face a shimmery glare as she looked at him through a tear-thickened sheen.

"There's something else we need to talk about," he said quietly.

She frowned at the worry she heard in his voice. Before she could ask him why, the front door exploded inward. Gray shoved her to the floor and bolted to his feet.

"Don't move a muscle, or your buddy here gets it."

Faith looked frantically around Gray from her position on the floor to see a strange man holding a gun to another man's head. Fear and desperation radiated from the gunman, and his hostage looked pissed. But strangely unafraid.

Gray held his hands up in a placating manner, but on the inside he was cursing a blue streak. Beside him, Faith scrambled up from the floor. Gray grabbed her wrist and yanked her behind him. His first priority was her safety.

"I'm going to take a guess here and say you're Samuels?" Gray said in an even voice.

The gunman sneered. "Does it really matter who I am?"

"It does if you killed my partner."

Faith huddled close to Gray's back, clutching at him with her hands. He still had a hand on her wrist as he held it behind his back, and he rubbed up and down her skin in a soothing manner. He could feel how frightened she was, and it pissed him off all the more.

How the hell had Samuels found them? And for that matter, how did Mick end up mixed up in this? Mick's threat about taking Samuels down himself echoed in his mind. Damn fool was going to get them all killed.

"What do you want?" Gray demanded. "How the hell did you get here?"

"I want the girl," Samuels said.

Gray felt Faith tremble against his back, and he squeezed her hand reassuringly.

"That's not going to happen," Gray said in a dangerously low voice.

"Let her go," Mick said bitterly. "She doesn't matter."

"Shut the fuck up, Mick," Gray growled. "What were you thinking, going after Samuels alone? Are you just trying to get us all killed?"

"Both of you shut up," Samuels barked. "The bitch's mother is anxious to see her. I'm sure her old man will be willing to cough up some cash if he wants to see her alive again."

Faith stiffened, and before he could pull her back, she stepped from behind him and stared at Samuels. "What does my mother have to do with this? What's going on?"

"Faith, get behind me," Gray said slowly.

Samuels tightened his grip around Mick's neck and pointed the gun at Faith. "Move over," he ordered, gesturing to the left with his gun. "Move, or I'll shoot you."

Faith stood stock-still, whether out of fear or the fact that she was in shock. "How do you know my mother?" she demanded. And then understanding flashed in her eyes. "You're the man my mother was with. Why she was calling and asking for money. You're the one I heard in the background." She turned her confused gaze to Gray. "But what does that have to do with your partner?"

"They used you as bait, *sweetheart*," Samuels said. "Too bad they're so incompetent. Now, get moving. I don't have time for all the drama."

Gray's heart clenched at the confused, hurt look in Faith's eyes. But more than that, things were getting desperate. He couldn't take Samuels down, not when he was pointing a gun at Faith.

"What do you mean, used me as bait?" she said.

"I sent him to Houston," Mick said, his face growing red as his anger exploded.

"Mick, shut up," Gray said.

"Sent him to Houston why?" she asked softly.

"To get close to you."

"But why? I don't understand." Her voice echoed her bewilderment.

In a flash, Samuels shoved Mick, sending him stumbling across the living room. He reached out and yanked Faith to his chest, repositioning the gun at her temple.

"Now, that's better," Samuels said, satisfaction lining his voice. "Let me make this simple for you, sweetheart. Just so you know what a bastard your lover is. The old man over there sent lover boy to Houston to cozy up to you because he knew I'd hooked up with your mother. And then lover boy brings you out here to lure me out."

Samuels looked over at Gray. "Were you planning to take me out yourself? Bet you didn't tell your buddies in Houston that. Quite the sting operation they were running. The decoy looked remarkably like Faith. I probably would have fallen for it if the old man hadn't let it slip where you were holding her. But then I guess that was all part of the plan. Only I decided to change things up a bit. I'm not entirely stupid."

Faith looked shell-shocked. Hurt and confusion emanated from every part of her body. "Is it true?" she whispered.

Gray wasn't going to waste time begging for her understanding. That could come later. Right now his focus was on keeping Samuels from taking her. He ignored her question and tuned out the betrayal in her stare.

"You won't get very far," he said evenly. "You're on an island, for God's sake. How do you think you're going to get off with a hostage?"

"The same way I got on with one," Samuels said with a chuckle.

Out of the corner of his eye, he saw Mick make a move. Gray tried to reach him, to prevent the stupid action, but Mick hurtled himself forward, like an out-of-control lunatic. He didn't care about Faith or whether she got hurt, he only saw his son's killer.

It all happened so quickly. The loud report of gunfire. Faith's scream. Mick crumpling to the floor. It was the night of Alex's shooting all over again, and he was powerless to stop it. Another shot sounded, and a searing pain blazed through his arm. The last thing he remembered as he crumpled to the floor was the look of fear and betrayal in Faith's eyes.

CHAPTER 36

*P*ain. It was the one thing he was aware of as he opened his eyes and stared up at the ceiling. Gray blinked, and then the memory of what happened came roaring back.

He flipped himself over, ignoring the surge of agony that blasted through his chest. He put an experimental hand up to his shoulder, and looked as he pulled it away again. Red. Bright red blood. Fuck.

He scrambled over to where Mick lay. He rolled the older man over, his chest tightening when he saw the massive chest wound. He knew before he felt for a pulse that he would find none.

Tears burned his eyes. He was so goddamn angry. Mick's death was as pointless as Alex's. And now Faith's life was in danger.

The room swam in his vision. He felt light-headed and weak from the blood loss. In his pocket, he felt his phone pulse and vibrate. Ignoring the screaming pain shooting through his body, he thrust his hand into his pocket to retrieve his phone. He flipped it open and shoved it to his ear just as he collapsed back to the floor.

Micah didn't even wait for him to mutter a greeting. He started sounding off, cursing a blue streak.

"Slow down," Gray said weakly. "What was that about a news story?"

"Your fucking buddy Mick set you up. You have to get the hell out of there, Gray. He went on the goddamn news going on about the operation and how you and Faith were in hiding—"

"It's too late," Gray managed to rasp out. "He's been here. He has Faith. Mick's dead. I've been shot. Need help."

"Oh Christ. Fuck. Man, are you okay? Talk to me. Hold the line while I call the damn ambulance."

"Not dying. Just feel like it. I think."

Again Micah cursed. Gray heard him yell at someone in the background and then vaguely heard him tell a 911 operator the situation and the address of the beach house.

Micah's voice grew dimmer and dimmer. He gritted his teeth and tried to hold on. At some point, Nathan got on the phone, but none of what he said made sense. It was all a garbled mess.

"Find Faith," he whispered. "Don't worry about me. You have to find Faith."

He faintly registered someone shouting his name, but he wasn't strong enough to hold the phone to his ear any longer. It clattered to the floor as the room went dark once again.

Blinding light pierced his eyeballs as someone peeled back his eyelids. He shook his head and snapped his eyes shut again.

"Come on, son, wake up."

Gray let his eyes flutter open.

"Ah, that's better."

The room came into focus, and Gray realized he was in a hospital bed. A man he presumed was a doctor stared at him from a few feet away, clipboard in hand.

Gray's gaze skirted around the room until he saw Micah standing in the far corner, phone to his ear.

"Where's Faith?" he rasped.

Micah snapped the phone shut and hurried to the bed. "Shit, man, you scared the hell out of me. It's about damn time you woke up."

Gray looked between him and the doctor. "How long have I been out?"

"A little over twenty-four hours," the doctor replied.

Gray let out a stream of curses, and he struggled to get out of the bed.

"Whoa, son, where do you think you're going?" the doctor demanded as he put a hand on Gray's chest and shoved him back down on the bed.

Gray looked desperately at Micah. "Faith. Where is she? Have you found her?"

Micah's expression was grim as he shook his head. "Sorry, man. Nothing yet."

Gray shut his eyes and thumped his head against the pillow. "I have to get out of here. I have to find her."

The doctor frowned and turned his disapproving stare on Gray. "You won't be going anywhere today."

"How bad is it?" Gray demanded, as he gestured toward his heavily bandaged shoulder.

"Not nearly as bad as it could be," the doctor said in a placating voice. "Just a flesh wound. I stitched you up. Our main concern was the loss of blood. Sometimes the simplest wounds bleed badly."

"If it's just a flesh wound, then I can get the hell out of here," Gray growled.

"You need to rest. I might consider letting you go tomorrow, although I'd prefer you to stay a few days. We have to monitor you for infection."

"I'm leaving today," Gray said through gritted teeth. "Write me a damn prescription for some painkillers and some antibiotics, and I'll be good to go."

"If you leave, you'll have to sign as AMA."

"I don't give a shit. I'm walking out of here, with or without your permission."

He glanced at Micah, expecting to get grief from that corner, but Micah stayed silent.

The doctor sighed. "All right, but I'm going on record that you're leaving against strict medical advice. I'll write the prescriptions. Be sure and take those antibiotics. If you start running fever or your wound gets red and inflamed or swells more, then you get your ass back here."

Gray shoved himself into an upright position and nearly passed out as a wave of pain hit him. He groaned and reached down with his free hand to steady himself.

Micah gripped his arm. "Hang on to me, and don't try to stand up too fast."

Between the two of them, they managed to get Gray out of bed. The doctor returned a moment later and handed Micah a piece of paper with the prescriptions on it. Then he shoved a clipboard at Gray.

Gray took it and didn't bother reading over it. He knew what it said. The whole spiel about the hospital not accepting responsibility if he dropped dead in the parking lot. Yeah, he got it. He scribbled his signature and thrust the clipboard back at the doctor.

He waited for Micah to head out, and he followed slowly behind, trying not to acknowledge the way the floor shifted and swayed underneath him. He felt like a goddamn sissy.

By the time Micah half dragged, half helped him to the lobby, Gray was sweating, and he was sure he had to be white as a sheet.

"Dude, I'm not so sure this was a good idea," Micah said. "You look like shit. Are you going to make it?"

"I have to find her," he said, allowing the desperation he felt to flow out in his voice. "Have you heard anything? What's going on?" And as they stepped out of the front entrance, sunlight blinded him. He blinked and then shook his head. "Where the fuck are we?"

"Houston," Micah said shortly. "Look, you stay here. Sit on that bench and don't move while I go get my truck. I'll be back in a second."

Gray slid onto the bench and tried to settle his rolling stomach. To be honest, he felt like he was going to fucking puke. He wiped his sweaty brow with the back of his hand and tried not to let panic overtake him.

Faith. God, what must she be thinking? Not only was she scared to death, but she thought he'd betrayed her. Used her. Fuck. He had, but not in the way she thought. He closed his eyes and tried to hold back the rage that consumed him.

A few minutes later, he felt a hand on his shoulder, and he looked up to see Micah standing over him. He groaned as Micah helped him up, and as much as it pissed him off to do so, he had to lean on Micah in order to make it to the truck.

"I'll dump your prescriptions off at the pharmacy down the block from the office, and I'll go back and get them when they're ready," Micah said as he slid into the driver's seat.

"Tell me what's going on," Gray said as they drove away. "What was that about Mick and a news story? And Faith. Have you been able to get any leads? Has the bastard contacted Pop?"

"Slow down, dude. One question at a time. I'm sorry about Mick, by the way."

Gray closed his eyes and leaned his head back against the seat. "I want this bastard, Micah. First Alex, then Mick and now he has Faith. I want him."

"I know, man. We all want to nail his ass. And we will. You have to believe that."

"What about the rest?" Gray asked tiredly.

"Mick was pissed that not enough was being done to catch Samuels. His words, not mine. So he took it upon himself to try and draw Samuels out. It was stupid and desperate. I don't know what the fuck he was thinking. He contacted a local news station and gave them the entire story. He wasn't thinking clearly. The interview was a mess. I can't even believe they ran it. He was obviously out of his mind. He put himself out there, and Samuels capitalized. I don't know much else. Neither do the cops. They're all waiting to talk to you. They're going to be pissed when they learn you left the hospital before they got a chance to question you."

"Too fucking bad," Gray muttered. "Goddamn it. What was Mick thinking? It's such a damn waste. How did Samuels get to him so quickly? And how the fuck did Mick know where I was?"

Micah grew silent, and Gray yanked his head to look at him. "Jesus, you don't think I used her as bait do you? I never told

Mick where Faith and I were. Nobody but you and the others knew."

"I don't think so," Micah said after a long pause. "But I can't guarantee you what Pop and the others think. This whole thing has gone straight into the shitter. We have no leads, thanks to your buddy."

Gray closed his eyes and pounded his fist on the seat, ignoring the sharp burst of pain that washed over him.

Micah pulled up at a drive-through pharmacy and handed the prescriptions through the window. He answered a few questions then asked Gray for his date of birth before he rolled his window back up and drove away.

They rode the rest of the way in silence, and a few minutes later, Micah parked outside Malone and Sons. Gray sat there a moment, steeling himself for the confrontation that was to come. He didn't blame Pop for being angry. Gray had let Faith down in a big way.

Micah opened the door. "Come on, buddy, I'll help you in. You look like you're about to fall over."

Gray slid out of the seat, wincing when his feet hit the ground. He felt the jolt all the way to his chest. Like an old man, he staggered to the entrance, and Micah went in ahead of him.

The office was in chaos. When Gray entered, Pop, Connor and Nathan all turned around to stare at him.

Pop started forward. "What the hell are you doing here? You should be laid up in the hospital."

Nathan quickly shoved a chair in Gray's direction, which was good, because he was about to fall over. He sank into the chair, grateful that the room quit spinning at least.

Connor, however, stayed back, arms crossed, a glare on his face.

"Any word?" he heard Micah ask.

"Bastard called a half hour ago," Pop said grimly.

Gray surged to his feet. The room spun at a dizzying angle, and if Micah hadn't caught him, he would have fallen on his face.

"Jesus, dude, cut that shit out. Sit your ass down," Micah said.

"Faith. Is she all right?" Gray demanded as he sucked in steadying breaths.

"He says she is, but he wouldn't let me talk to her," Pop said. "He wants a million tomorrow morning, or he says he's going to kill her."

The tears that he'd been trying to hold back flooded his eyes. Gray closed his eyes and tried like hell to get a grip on the anger and grief storming like a locomotive through his head.

When he opened them, he saw anger in Pop's eyes but no condemnation.

"I didn't sell her out," Gray croaked out around the knot in his throat. "I love her."

Pop sighed and put a hand on his shoulder. "I know. You shouldn't be here. You need to get back to the hospital or at least go home. Let us take care of this. We'll get her back."

Gray shook his head fiercely. "She's out there. Scared. Alone. She thinks I betrayed her. No way I'm going to bed until she's safe."

He looked beyond Pop to where Nathan and Connor stood. "That bastard killed my partner, and now he's killed Mick. I won't let him take Faith from me."

He saw grudging acceptance in Connor's eyes.

Micah touched him on the shoulder. "Man, there are two

Galveston cops here to talk to you. They want to question you about what went down at the beach house."

"I'd like to hear as well," Pop spoke up. "If I'm going to get my daughter back, I need to know everything I can about this asshole."

CHAPTER 37

*F*aith became aware of someone shaking her shoulder. She tried to open her eyes, but it hurt too much.

"Faith, Faith, baby, you have to wake up."

The harsh whisper, urgent, roused her, and she pried her eyes open. She blinked when she saw her mother staring down at her.

"Mama?"

"Shhh," Celia Martin said, placing a shaky finger over her lips. "He'll be back any time. You have to be quiet."

Faith tried to order her muddled thoughts, but she was having trouble focusing. When she tried to move her arms, she discovered she couldn't even feel them. Same with her legs.

"What happened?" she whispered.

"I need to get you untied. Don't move, okay?"

Faith nodded and winced as another excruciating bolt of pain seized her skull. As Celia fumbled with the knots at her wrists, Faith closed her eyes and tried to reassemble everything that had happened.

An ache grew in her chest, horrible and black as she remembered the gunshots. She saw Mick fall and then Gray. Betrayal. Grief. Confusion. Nothing made sense.

Hot tears leaked from her eyelids. Then the rope around her wrists loosened, and a thousand little needles attacked her as the blood started flowing again. She moaned in agony, and again Celia hurriedly shushed her.

A few minutes later, her legs were free, but she lay there, unable to move. Celia pulled at her arms and forced her into a sitting position.

"Listen to me, honey, you have to get out of here. He's crazy. He's going to kill you whether he gets the money or not."

The stark fear in her mother's voice roused her from her lethargy.

"Did you hear me, Faith? You've got to go now. He won't leave you here alone for long. I'll help you out the back way, and then you'll have to run for help. I'll stall him as long as I can."

"You can't stay here," Faith whispered. "You have to come with me."

Celia made a sound of impatience. "He won't kill me. He needs me. But you have to go. I don't have time to argue with you. Come on."

Her mother's urgency spurred Faith to action. She stood and wobbled as pain shot down her spine. Had he hit her? She had to think hard. The time after the beach house was one big blur. She remembered struggling, trying to escape. Then he'd struck her in the head with the butt of the gun.

She raised a hand to her head, and her fingers came away sticky with blood.

Celia pulled her out of the dark room. Where were they? It

resembled some kind of vacant warehouse. Her mother paused at the doorway then pulled Faith into the large open area. The rough concrete abraded her bare feet as she stumbled along behind her mother.

When they reached the back, Celia opened a battered door and shoved Faith into the night.

"The alleyway leads out to a street. You have to go. He'll be here any minute. I love you."

With that, she shut the door, leaving Faith alone and shivering in the humid alleyway.

She clutched her arms around her midsection and started toward a distant streetlight. Dizzy, disoriented and in pain, she started to run, the memory of her captor shooting Mick and Gray vivid in her memory. He would kill her. Of that she had no doubt.

Her feet pounded the broken cement of the narrow alleyway. Trash, rotten food and God knew what else squished beneath her toes. She tripped as she neared the end and went sprawling. She cried out despite her best effort not to, but pain knifed through her body as she went crashing to the pavement.

In desperation, she dragged herself up and started running again. When she reached the end, she ran onto the street and looked left and right. God, it was empty. No cars, no lights other than what lined the street. It was an older section of town, and what businesses might be located on the street had long since closed for the day.

She chose a direction and ran. Her breath tore from her throat in painful bursts. Her surroundings blurred and passed with dizzying sickness. It felt as though someone had shoved a knife right through the back of her head.

One block. Two. She continued on until she feared passing out. When she'd gone approximately three blocks, she tripped again and went down, her hands flying out to break her fall. She landed face-first on the hard, broken street.

Tears flooded her eyes as she gasped for breath. Pain rendered her immobile. She couldn't force herself back up. She struggled to her knees and looked down at her torn, bleeding palms.

As she glanced behind her, she was blinded by a bright light. She threw up her arm in a protective measure to shield her eyes as she tried to scramble up and flee.

"Ma'am, ma'am, are you okay?"

She strained to see who was talking to her. The light shifted, and she could see the outline of a man walking her way. She whimpered and threw herself the rest of the way up, prepared to run for her life.

"Houston Police. I'm here to offer assistance."

She froze then looked down, and for the first time saw what he was seeing. Her clothes were torn and bloodied. Her hair hung around her face in disarray.

As he approached, he shone the light down and farther away from her. His expression was guarded, but he viewed her with concern.

"Ma'am, are you hurt? Do you need an ambulance?"

His voice was soft and reassuring, like he was afraid she'd run. His hand touched her shoulder, and a shudder worked through her.

He turned the light toward her face again, and she flinched away from the glare. "Ma'am, are you Faith Malone?" There was excitement in his voice.

"Y-yes." Her voice cracked and she tried again. "Yes, I'm Faith Malone."

"We've been looking for you. God almighty, how did you escape?" His voice was all business now, and he picked up the mic to his radio.

She listened as he excitedly called in their location and requested an ambulance. Then he turned his attention back to her.

"Ma'am, can you tell me what happened? How did you come to be out here?"

"He's back there," she croaked.

The policeman whirled around, drawing his weapon.

"At a warehouse," she said. "We were at a warehouse. A few blocks back. My mother . . . she helped me escape. You have to go back for her. She's in danger. He's holding her too. She helped me."

As she finished, she started to sink with exhaustion. The policeman caught her before she landed back on the street.

"Easy," he murmured. "You're going to be okay now. An ambulance is on the way."

As he held her, he radioed for backup and relayed what Faith had told him about the warehouse and her mother. The rest was a dim blur. She was cognizant of his arms around her and the comforting words he murmured, but little else. She closed her eyes, wanting to escape her reality, even if for a little while. She heard the distant sound of sirens, and then she heard no more.

CHAPTER 38

$\mathcal{G}$ray fought against the effects of the painkillers he'd taken. They'd dulled the pain, but he was drowsy as hell. He stood up, ignoring the renewed agony the movement caused. He paced the small confines of the office, about to go out of his mind with worry.

When Pop's cell phone rang, they all jumped. Pop snatched it up and stuck it to his ear. Gray, Micah, Connor and Nathan all stopped and leaned forward in interest.

"Where?" he heard Pop ask. Then, "Thank God. We'll be right there."

Pop closed the phone and closed his eyes. His hands shook as he laid the phone down.

"They found her," he reported. "They're taking her to the hospital now."

Gray exploded forward. "Hospital? Is she hurt? Where did they find her? Was Samuels taken in?"

Pop held up his hand. "Slow down, son. I know you're worried.

We all are. I don't know much. That was dispatch. An on-duty cop found her down in the warehouse district. Apparently she was able to escape Samuels, and she was running. She's hurt. I don't know how bad. The dispatcher said the cop stayed with her until the ambulance arrived and that Faith supplied them information on Samuels's whereabouts. That's all I have."

"Let's go then," Gray said in a strained voice. "I need to see her."

Pop nodded. "I'll drive you."

Gray stood in the doorway of Faith's room, unable to tear his gaze from her. She was asleep in the hospital bed, her face so fragile looking. Her forehead was creased, even in her sleep, and he worried about what nightmares she faced in her dreams.

A large bandage adorned her head, and she wore smaller ones on her hands and knees. Even her feet were bandaged.

A comforting hand clasped his shoulder, and he looked behind him to see Pop standing there.

"What did the doctor say?" Gray asked in a weary voice.

"Bastard hit her on the head with the butt of a pistol. She has a concussion. But otherwise she was unharmed. The cuts and scrapes she suffered were from her escape. Doc says he wants to watch her overnight, and if she does well, she can go home tomorrow."

Gray closed his eyes as sweet relief poured over him. "Thank God," he whispered.

"Son, you need to get some rest. You're not doing anyone any good here. You can see her tomorrow."

Gray shook his head. "I won't leave her. I can't."

"You have two choices, son. You can get your ass home and get some rest on your own, or I'll have those boys cart you out of here forcibly." He gestured with his thumb over his shoulder to where Nathan, Connor and Micah stood in the hallway. "It's up to you."

Gray cursed long and hard under his breath.

"I doubt she'll even wake up," Pop said. "They gave her something for pain, and well, she's never been able to handle it. Hell, once she went to the dentist and he prescribed a mild painkiller. She was out cold for twelve hours straight."

Micah walked up to where Pop was standing. "Come on, Gray. I'll drive you home. We'll come back up in the morning so you can see her."

Gray sighed in defeat. "Give me a minute."

He turned and walked over to Faith's bed and stared down at her for a long moment. He reached out his free hand and brushed his fingers softly over her cheek.

"I'm so sorry," he whispered. "I love you." He bent and pressed his lips to hers, inhaling her sweet scent. "I'll be back tomorrow. I swear."

Reluctantly, he turned and trudged toward the door where Micah waited. He looked at Pop and Connor, who had moved inside the doorway. "Is someone staying with her? I don't want her to be alone."

Pop nodded. "We'll be here. You go get some rest. You'll do her a whole lot more good when you can hold your head up."

Gray looked him square in the eye. "I love your daughter. I want you to know that."

Pop's expression softened. "I know you do."

Gray turned and slowly, painfully made his way down the hall. Micah caught up to him. "You can crash at my place tonight. You shouldn't be alone with your injuries."

Gray nodded, too tired to argue. "I wasn't out there when the news came in. Did they catch Samuels?"

"Yeah, they got him," Micah said grimly.

"I want to kill the son of a bitch."

"Yeah, me too," Micah said.

"What about her mother?" Gray asked. "Pop said something about her helping Faith escape."

"Last I heard, they were questioning her. I don't know if they've decided what her involvement has been yet or not."

Gray nodded. "No matter what, it's only going to upset Faith in the end."

"Yeah, it sucks."

They walked out of the emergency room exit and headed toward Micah's truck. It was only a few hours until daylight, and he needed about twenty-four hours of sleep.

When he climbed into the cab, he leaned back against the seat and closed his eyes.

Micah got in and started the engine. He put it in reverse but didn't back up. Gray looked over to see him staring at him.

"What?"

Micah paused. "What are you going to do, man? I mean about your job? Are you going to go back now that it's all over?"

Gray tensed. Over. The man who had killed Alex, killed Mick and had hurt Faith was in custody. For all practical purposes, his time here was up. He had a while until his official leave was over. A month ago, he would have said he had no reason to stay. But now he had absolutely nothing left for him in Dallas.

"I can't go back," he said, the decision settling over him, the first thing that had made him feel good in two days.

Micah nodded. "I hoped you'd say that. Faith's a good woman. You fit in well here. We could use you on a permanent basis."

"I'm not so sure Pop will feel that way," Gray said. "But whether I work for him or do something else, I can't leave Faith."

"I hear you. It'll work out."

Gray hoped so. He still had to face Faith. He was just thankful she was alive and well, and he had the opportunity to make her see how much he loved her.

CHAPTER 39

$\mathscr{F}$aith woke feeling like she had a mouth full of cotton. She blinked, trying to remember where she was, but it was dark. She was really starting to hate the dark. A whimper worked its way out of her throat as she shifted, trying to get her bearings.

"Faith, are you okay?" Connor asked.

"Light," she rasped out. "Turn it on, please."

She heard him fumble around in the dark, and then soft light flooded the room. She winced and blinked, covering her eyes with her hand.

The bed dipped, and when she moved her hand, she saw Connor leaning over her, concern etched on his face. "How are you, honey?"

She licked her lips and pondered that question for a while. "I think I'm okay. Connor . . . is Gray . . . is he dead?" she asked fearfully.

"Oh God, no, honey. He's fine. We sent him home because he took a bullet in the shoulder, and he's been running around like mad. Left the hospital against medical advice and has been generally raising hell."

She sagged against the bed in relief. "I saw him go down. That man shot him. I thought he was dead." A tear slid down her cheek, and she closed her eyes to the horrible memory.

Connor laid a hand over her forehead. "Don't get yourself worked up, Faith. He's fine. I'm more worried about you."

So much had happened. Even without the head injury, her head would be spinning.

"What the hell is the light doing on?" Pop demanded from the doorway.

She looked up to see him holding two cups of coffee. He looked tired and haggard. Worry had carved deep lines on his face, and she felt terrible that she had been the cause of it.

It hit her like a ton of bricks. Everything that had happened had been because of her. She closed her eyes, and in that moment wished she could just go to sleep and wake up somewhere else.

Pop's rough hand curled around hers. She opened tear-filled eyes to see him standing by the bed.

"You scared ten years off me, girl," he said gruffly. "And I don't know what's currently going through that pretty head of yours, but I assure you I won't like or agree with it."

"Everything's such a mess," she whispered. "I just want to go home."

"And you will," Pop said gently as he rubbed her hand. "The doctor said if you're doing okay that you can go home today. I reckon he'll be around to see you in a bit."

"Can I get you anything?" Connor spoke up.

"Water," she croaked.

He hurried to pour her a cup of water and then held it to her lips so she could sip at it.

"Gray was here to see you last night, but I made him go home," Pop said. "That boy was hurting pretty bad. He should still be in the hospital."

Faith closed her eyes. "I don't want to talk about him right now."

"Faith, honey . . ."

"Please," she whispered.

"Pop, let it alone," Connor said firmly. "She needs to rest and get better."

Pop sighed and nodded.

A knock sounded at the door. When no one immediately came in, Pop frowned and walked to the door. He returned a moment later, a peculiar expression on his face.

"Who was it?" she asked.

He cleared his throat. "It's your mother, Faith. She's here to see you. She asked if you would mind her coming in for a minute."

Her heart seized, and dread filled her chest.

"You don't have to do anything you don't want," Pop said soothingly.

Tears filled her eyes again then slid down both cheeks. A sob caught in her throat. How bad was it when the mere mention of her mother reduced her to tears?

Connor picked up her hand and squeezed. "Don't let her upset you, Faith. If you want her to go away, I'll make it happen. You don't have to see her if you don't want."

"Let her come in," she said tiredly.

Connor squeezed her hand again. "I'll be right here, honey."

Pop walked back to the door and opened it. A few seconds later, Celia Martin walked hesitantly in. She paused several feet from the bed before finally approaching.

For the first time, Faith got a good look at the mother she hadn't seen in three years. Time hadn't been good to her. She looked tired, worn, *old*. Not at all the vibrant young woman Faith remembered from her childhood. She had the regrets of a life-time reflected in her dull eyes.

Faith waited, not knowing what to say. Thank you? For rescuing her from a situation Celia was responsible for? She swallowed against the rising anger and clenched her jaw until her teeth ached.

Connor stroked his fingers repeatedly over her hands, and she curled her fingers around his, holding on for dear life.

Celia looked up at Pop and Connor first. "I'll always be grate-ful to you for all you've done for Faith. I failed her. I'm just glad she had you to turn to."

Faith bit her lip to keep from crying more.

Celia moved closer to Faith and looked as though she too was battling to keep from crying. "I messed up, baby. But then that's nothing new. I just wanted to come by and tell you how sorry I am. And to thank you for what you said to the police. They aren't going to press charges against me as long as I testify against Eric."

"I'm glad," Faith whispered.

"I hoped . . . I hoped maybe we could get together sometime. Maybe when you're better."

Faith tensed, and again, Connor stroked his thumb over her hand in an effort to calm her.

"I'm s-sorry. I just can't do this right now," Faith said. The knot grew so big in her throat that it was hard to breathe around. More tears slipped down her cheeks, and she damned them. "I need you to go away." It was hard to keep the hurt from her voice. Her utter sense of betrayal. At the moment, she felt let down by everyone she'd ever loved.

She shut her eyes and turned her face into the pillow as the sobs mounted in her throat.

"That's enough," Pop said tersely. "She's had enough."

"Of course. I'm sorry," Celia said. "I'll go now."

"Shhh, honey, don't cry," Connor said as he tucked her hair behind her ear. "It'll only make your head hurt worse."

"I want to go home," she said in a muffled voice.

"I'll talk to the doctor and see what he says," Pop said soothingly.

As he walked away, she only cried harder. Thank God they weren't noisy, gulping sobs, because it would have split her head right open. Instead silent streams of tears ran down her cheeks. Faster and faster. Like a dam breaking.

Connor eased onto the bed beside her and gathered her in his arms. He didn't say anything, just held her while she cried and occasionally dropped a kiss on top of her head.

A few minutes later, Pop walked in, and close on his heels came the doctor. The doctor frowned when he got a good look at her.

"Your father tells me you're ready to be discharged, but I hesitate to send you home when you're visibly upset. Are you in any pain?"

She shook her head, nearly wincing with the effort. "I just want to go home," she whispered.

"She'll go home with us," Pop interjected. "And straight to bed. She won't so much as lift a finger. You have my personal guarantee."

"Well her CT scans all came back normal, and other than that bump on her noggin, her other injuries are negligible. I'll consent to discharging her, but if her condition worsens, if she feels nauseated or has vomiting or her level of consciousness decreases, I want her back here ASAP."

Pop nodded. "We'll watch her. You have my word."

"All right then. I'll give the nurse her discharge orders. Someone should be down in a little bit to send her home."

"Thank you, Doctor," Pop said.

After the doctor left, Pop walked to her side and patted her arm. "We'll get you home and taken care of. You'll be right as rain in no time."

She nodded, but a heavy feeling descended on her chest. She'd tried really hard not to focus on Gray, but now that the issue of her mother had been dealt with, he was all that was left. As cowardly as it sounded, she just didn't have the strength to face him right now.

CHAPTER 40

*G*ray awoke with a start. Sunshine blasted through the window, hitting him square in the eyes. Which told him he'd slept entirely too damn late.

He rolled over, and his body screamed in protest. When he hit his wounded shoulder, his breath left him in a staggered gasp.

Ignoring the protests of his body, he shoved himself out of bed and stumbled over to retrieve the watch he'd taken off the night before. Ten-fucking-thirty.

He left the room with a bang and nearly tripped over his shoes in the hallway. Bending, and nearly passing out with the effort, he scooped up his shoes and walked into the living room.

"So the dead has awakened," Micah said from where he was slouched on the sofa.

"You should have damn well woke me up hours ago," Gray snarled.

Micah lifted a brow. "You needed the sleep, and Faith wasn't going anywhere."

"Except I need to see her," Gray bit out. "I have a lot of explaining to do."

Micah shrugged. "As soon as you get your shoes on, we'll go."

Gray sat down and yanked his shoes on. Then he shoved himself upright again and looked expectantly at Micah.

"Okay, okay, man, I'm coming," Micah said as he got up from the couch. "You ought to have someone look at that shoulder while we're at the hospital. Make sure your arm isn't going to rot off or something."

Gray glared at him. "I'm taking the antibiotics. It'll be fine."

They walked out of the apartment and climbed into Micah's truck.

"Have you heard from Pop this morning?" Gray asked as they drove off. "Do you know how she's doing?"

"Nope. Nothing yet. She's probably still sleeping."

Gray sighed impatiently. Not seeing her, touching her, holding her was driving him nuts. He should have been there with her. Soothed her hurts. Comforted her when she was scared. It tore his damn guts out that some cop had found her out on the streets, scared half out of her mind and running for her life.

"Quit beating yourself up over there," Micah murmured. "It won't change anything."

Gray pressed his lips together and didn't say anything.

Twenty minutes later, Micah pulled into the hospital parking lot.

"I'll drop you off out front, and I'll go park. I'll meet you in Faith's room."

Gray nodded, and when Micah pulled up at the patient loading and unloading point, he pried himself out of the truck, trying to keep the pain at a minimum. He hadn't taken any painkillers this morning because he wanted to talk to Faith with a clear head.

The automatic doors swooshed open, and Gray walked inside. He stopped short when he saw Faith across the lobby getting out of a wheelchair pushed by a nurse.

Connor stepped to her side, wrapped an arm around her and tucked her against him as they started forward. Gray's heart raced. Fuck. She was being discharged, and he'd never even been to see her. He'd left her alone the entire goddamn night.

He hurried forward as fast as he was able without taking a nosedive. When he was a few feet away, Faith looked up and saw him. He stopped short when he saw the flood of pain fill her eyes. His chest nearly caved in.

"Faith," he began.

Her lips trembled and tears filled her beautiful eyes.

He closed the distance between them and reached for her hand. He flinched when she pulled it away and cupped it with her other one.

"Baby, are you okay? God, I'm sorry I wasn't here. I just woke up."

"It's okay," she said in a faltering voice. "Pop and Connor stayed with me." She looked away, but he saw a tear trail down her cheek.

"Faith, baby, look at me," he said. But she refused and closed her eyes.

"This isn't a good time," Connor said evenly. "She's had enough for today. She needs to get home and rest."

He started forward, but Gray couldn't let it go like this.

"Faith, I love you. That's all that damn well matters. Nothing else."

She turned her gaze on him, and all the breath was sucked right out of his chest at the raw pain he saw there. She opened her mouth but closed it just as rapidly. He could see her retreat, fold in on herself. Her shoulders sagged, and he could see the utter fatigue draped over her like a mantle.

Connor's arm tightened around her as though he feared she might crumble. But it was Gray who was crumbling. Connor pressed his lips together and ushered Faith past him. Gray turned and watched her walk slowly out of the hospital entrance where Pop had pulled his SUV around.

Micah strode up then, and he stopped in front of Faith. He bent down and kissed her cheek. "How are you, baby doll?"

Gray didn't hear her answer, but he saw Micah's reaction. Worry narrowed his eyes, and he reached out to touch her face.

"You go on home and get some rest. Let Pop and Connor take care of you for a while."

When Connor helped Faith into Pop's SUV, Micah approached Gray, a look of sympathy on his face.

"I fucked up," Gray said in a low voice. "I should have told her the truth. If I had, none of this would have happened. She'd be in my arms, in my bed, safe."

Micah shook his head. "You can't think like that, man. Give it a day or two. Let her come down from all the emotional turmoil."

"I can't let her go," Gray said simply. "Not when I've finally found her."

CHAPTER 41

*F*aith accepted Damon's hand as he helped her out of the car. She closed her eyes and allowed the ocean breeze to wash soothingly over her face. The sun beat down on her, warming her skin, but she still felt cold on the inside.

"I don't like leaving you here alone, Faith," Damon said, worry evident in his voice.

She sighed. Pop and Connor hadn't been thrilled with her wanting to leave so soon after her hospital stay either, but she desperately needed some time away from everything. She had to think. Collect her thoughts. Do something other than lie around while Pop and Connor fussed over her.

"I'll be fine, Damon. You're so sweet to do this for me."

He inserted the key into the front door lock then opened the door. "You know all you have to do is ask. If it's in my power, you can be sure I'll do it."

He walked in ahead of her and dropped her suitcase in the foyer. The beach house he owned was wrapped in police tape and would be cordoned off for the investigation for months to come. When Faith had called, in need of a getaway, he'd rented a similar beach house close to Galveston.

Part of her felt bad for taking advantage of his generosity, knowing full well she couldn't return his interest. But he'd offered her his friendship, and friendship was something she was currently in bad need of.

"I've hired someone to come look in on you twice a day," Damon said. He held up his hand when she would have protested. "Your meals will be delivered. I don't want you to overexert yourself. You need to rest and recover. If there is anything you need, anything at all, pick up the phone and call me."

"Thank you," she said softly.

He leaned forward and kissed her forehead. "I just want you to smile again."

She complied and gave him the best one she could muster. "I just need a few days to regroup. Sort some things out in my head. Pop told me everything that happened, but it's hard to process. I just wish everyone hadn't been so determined to keep me in the dark."

He cupped her cheek and rubbed his thumb in a soothing motion over her skin. "You can't blame them for wanting to protect you, Faith. I would have done the same."

She went into his arms and hugged him tight. "I wish . . ."

"Yeah, I know," he said as he pulled away. He smiled down at her and nudged her nose with his knuckle. "I'll get on out of here and leave you alone. Call me if you need anything."

She nodded and watched as he left through the front door.

When she was alone, she found the couch and sank gratefully

down onto the cushions. What she really wanted to do was pop a painkiller and zone out for about twelve hours. But that was cowardly, and it solved nothing.

A regular nap sounded damn good though. Not bothering to move from the couch, she curled into the soft cushions and closed her eyes.

A tear slid down her cheek, and she squeezed her eyes tighter shut.

Of everything that had happened, the part she was having the most trouble reconciling was her feelings for Gray. She loved him. Or what she thought was him. But how could she be sure?

The idea that she'd fallen in love with a fantasy filled her with despair. She'd never felt so alone in her entire life. She couldn't run from the situation forever. She knew that. But she needed time, needed to be less emotional when she eventually faced Gray and the truth of what was between them.

Gray swore as he caught yet another traffic light on Seawall Boulevard. His free hand curled tightly around the steering wheel as he waited impatiently for it to turn green again. His other hand rested on his lap. He'd torn the heavy bandages off his shoulder, freeing his arm, despite medical warnings not to. It was still tender as hell, and he kept a smaller bandage over the stitches, but enough was enough. He couldn't go around one-armed.

After spending a frustrating couple of days trying to see Faith, he was ready to put his fist through a wall. And then, when he'd gone back to Pop's with no intention of taking no for an answer, he'd been told that she was gone.

In the hours that ensued, he'd felt like peeling his skin off and turning himself inside out. The absolute helplessness he felt not being able to talk to her, to see for himself how she was—it was about to send him right over the edge. Not that he needed much at the moment.

When he'd discovered where she'd gone and how she'd gotten there, his hopes had plummeted. He knew damn well that Damon Roche was interested in Faith, and that if she gave him the slightest bit of encouragement, he'd be all over her.

The sun was sinking over the horizon when he pulled into the driveway of the beach house. He got out and walked as quickly as he could up the stairs to the front door. He debated for a moment about whether to knock, but he shrugged off the urge. It was door-or-die time. The worst she could do was tell him to fuck off.

He tried the knob and found it unlocked, so he opened the door and walked in. As he walked into the living room, his gaze fell on the couch where she was asleep.

His mouth went dry. His heart beat a little faster, and he clenched his hands into fists at his sides.

He moved quietly and dropped to his knees beside the couch as he drank in her appearance. She looked unbelievably fragile, like she required tender handling. He was almost afraid to touch her. Almost.

Unable to resist the softness of her cheek, he trailed a finger down her jawline to the corner of her mouth then eased it over her velvet lips.

A painful surge rushed through his chest when he saw the tearstains on her face. He leaned down and kissed each reddened spot.

She stirred beneath him, and her eyes fluttered open. "Gray?" she whispered.

"Yes, baby, it's me."

Shadows fell over her eyes, and he could sense her withdrawal. As though she was steeling herself against him.

It damn near broke his heart.

Not wanting her to withdraw even further, he reached for her and pulled her gently into his embrace. He held her close, absorbing the fact that she was safe and alive. She felt fragile and oh so very precious in his arms.

"I couldn't bear to lose you," he said, his voice catching with emotion. "These last few days have been hell, when all I've wanted to do is hold you, touch you, tell you how much I love you."

She went still against him. Then she pulled slightly away until their gazes met. "I needed some time to think," she said quietly.

He reached out to cup her face in his hand. "Faith, I didn't use you as bait. I didn't set up our time at the beach house to lure Samuels out. I would never do that to you."

She put a finger over his lips. "I know, Gray. Pop told me what happened. I understand. He told me that he asked you not to tell me about the potential danger I was in. He feels terrible."

His brows drew together in confusion. "Then why . . . I don't understand. If you know . . ." He stopped and started over again. "Why are you upset?" he finally spit out.

Deep sadness welled in her eyes. His heart dropped to his stomach. God, he'd do anything to take that sadness away.

She looked away as a tear slipped down her cheek. He reached up and thumbed it away. "Oh, baby, don't cry. Tell me what's wrong so I can fix it."

She looked back at him. "You can't." She took a deep, shuddering breath. "Gray, I understand why you did what you did. I'm not angry. I accept that you didn't come to the beach house in order to draw your partner's killer out. What I can't accept is the fact that nothing that happened was real. I can't live with the fact that you only gave me what you knew I wanted in order to get close to me, in order to get information and then ultimately to protect me. You were so sure I was playing games and only wanted a fantasy, but what were you doing if not providing a facade for me?"

"Faith, oh my God—"

She shook her head. "No, let me finish. I want you. God, I want you. But only if it's real. I can't live with the fact that I've found exactly what I want and need so badly if it's all an act. I don't want it if it's not *real*."

He framed her face in both hands, urgent, his need to make her hear him, his heart, all consuming. "Listen to me, Faith. And listen good. I love you. *You.* Not some idea of what I've always wanted. Not some fantasy that I think I need to give you. I. Love. You. *You.*

"God almighty, it was never a game. *Never.* It couldn't have been more real for me. I hated having to deceive you. I was determined to tell you the truth, even though Pop wanted me to remain silent. But when I got here, and you looked so vulnerable, all I could think about was protecting you. I didn't want you to hurt. Ever. And I paid for that. I paid dearly.

"I love you, baby. I love you so damn much it hurts. I ache.